THE IMPOSTER

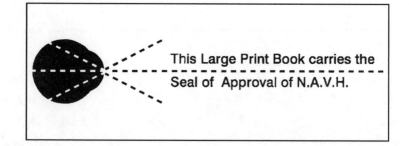

THE IMPOSTER

SUZANNE WOODS FISHER

THORNDIKE PRESS
A part of Gale, Cengage Learning

GALE
CENGAGE Learning·

Farmington Hills, Mich • San Francisco • New York • Waterville, Maine
Meriden, Conn • Mason, Ohio • Chicago

GALE
CENGAGE Learning®

LIBRARY OF CONGRESS CATALOGING-IN-PUBLICATION DATA

Fisher, Suzanne Woods.
  The imposter / Suzanne Woods Fisher.
    pages cm. — (The bishop's family ; 1) (Thorndike Press large print Christian fiction)
    ISBN 978-1-4104-8319-5 (hardback) — ISBN 1-4104-8319-3 (hardcover)
  1. Large type books. I. Title.
PS3606.I78I47 2015b
813'.6—dc23   2015030199

Published in 2015 by arrangement with Revell Books, a division of Baker Publishing Group

Printed in the United States of America
1 2 3 4 5 6 7 19 18 17 16 15

To those 2 a.m. pastors,
for all you do as Keepers of the Faith

CAST OF CHARACTERS

David Stoltzfus — in his early 40s, widowed minister, father to six children: Katrina, Jesse, Ruthie, Molly, Lydie, and Emily. Owner of the Bent N' Dent store in Stoney Ridge

Katrina Stoltzfus — 19 years old, oldest daughter in the family

Jesse Stoltzfus — 16 years old, oldest son

Ruthie Stoltzfus — 14 years old, in the eighth grade

Molly Stoltzfus — age 11

Lydie and Emily Stoltzfus — 8-year-old twins

Freeman Glick — in his 50s, bishop of Stoney Ridge

Levi Glick — late 40s, minister of Stoney Ridge

Birdy Glick — 31, only sister to Freeman Glick

Thelma Beiler — (touchy about her age), elderly widow to former bishop, Elmo

7

Stoltzfus; runs a farm called Moss Hill

Andy Miller — 20-something, farmhand for Thelma Beiler on Moss Hill

Hank Lapp — 60ish, uncle to Amos Lapp of Windmill Farm; runs a buggy repair shop; made his first appearance in *The Keeper*

Fern Lapp — 50ish, wife to Amos Lapp of Windmill Farm; arrived in Stoney Ridge in *The Keeper*

PROLOGUE

Surprises come in two shapes — good and bad. This one, though, felt indeterminate.

David Stoltzfus awoke in the middle of the night with a clear prompting in his heart: leave what was familiar and comfortable and go forth into the wilderness. He had developed a listening ear to God's promptings over the years and knew not to ignore them. God who had spoken, David believed with his whole heart, still speaks.

But where was this wilderness?

A week passed. David searched Scripture, prayed, spoke to a few trusted friends, and still the prompting remained. Grew stronger. A month passed. David's daily prayer was the same: *Where is the wilderness, Lord? Where will you send me?* Another month passed. Nothing.

And then David received a letter from a bishop — someone he had known over the years — in a little town in Lancaster County, inviting him to come alongside to serve the church. *Go,* came the prompting, loud and clear.

So David packed up his home, sold his bulk store business, and moved his family to the wilderness, which, for him, meant Stoney Ridge, Pennsylvania.

As the first few months passed, it seemed puzzling to David to think that God would consider Stoney Ridge as a wilderness, albeit metaphorically. The bishop, Elmo Beiler, had welcomed him in as an additional minister, had encouraged him to preach the word of God from his heart. It was a charming town and he had been warmly embraced. A wilderness? Hardly that. More like the Garden of Eden. When he casually remarked as much to Elmo, the old bishop gave him an unreadable look. "There is no such thing, David." Elmo didn't expand on the thought, and David chalked it up to a warning of pride.

No place was perfect, he knew that, but the new life of the Stoltzfus family was taking shape. His children were starting to settle in. They were a family still adapting to the loss of Anna, David's wife, but they weren't stuck, not like they had been. It was a fresh start, and everything was going about as well as David could expect.

Then, during a church service, Elmo suffered a major heart attack. In a dramatic fashion for a man who was not at all dramatic, Elmo grabbed David's shirt and whispered, "Beware, David. A snake is in the garden."

Later that evening, Elmo passed away.

Two weeks later, Freeman Glick, the other minister who had served alongside David, drew the lot to become the new bishop, his brother Levi drew the lot to replace him as minister, and in the space of one month, the little Amish church of Stoney Ridge was an altogether different place.

Almost overnight, David sensed the wilderness had arrived.

1

When Hank Lapp burst through the door of the Bent N' Dent in Stoney Ridge, Katrina Stoltzfus whirled around from stocking the shelves to see what was wrong. He'd lost his hat and his white hair was poking out in every direction, like a dandelion puff. His dog was right on his heels, barking like he was chasing a bear.

"What in the world, Hank?"

"Candidates! I've got candidates!" He waved a fistful of envelopes in the air. "From the letter I wrote in the *Budget.*"

"About . . ."

"Your father! Needing a bride! I think we've got some suitable options."

Katrina stared at him while the words sank in. "No!" The word came out sharper than she intended, so she softened it a bit. "Hank," she said, "what have you done?"

Bethany Schrock, her best friend and best employee, walked over from behind the front counter, a horrified look on her face.

"How many times have I been in this very store and heard you girls talk about how much David Stoltzfus needed a wife? So I got to thinking, 'Now, Hank, what was it you done to get Amos a wife?' I couldn't remember, not 'til I was halfway home. Then it hit me, like a brick from heaven dropped on my head! For Amos, I put a letter in the *Budget* and next thing you knew, Fern showed up at the door and married him."

"Please, please, please don't tell me you advertised for a wife for David in the *Budget,*" Bethany said in a slow, shocked voice.

"Not an advertisement, exactly. More like a gentle appeal." He pulled out the newspaper from the back of his coat and pointed to it.

CALLING ALL SINGLE LADIES EAGER TO LAND A MAN! THE MINISTER OF STONEY RIDGE IS IN DESPERATE NEED OF A WIFE AND A MOTHER TO HIS SIX REDHEADED CHILDREN. PLUS, HE'S A REAL NICE GUY. SEND A LIST OF YOUR QUALIFICATIONS TO HANK LAPP.

He jabbed his finger at the quote that wrapped up his scribe letter. "Look at that.

'From an old maid you get a faithful wife.' I thought that was an especially fine touch. Just to be sure I got the point across."

Katrina felt sick to her stomach, an uneasiness she couldn't place. "Oh, Hank. Dad is not going to be happy about this."

"Well, neither was Amos. But Fern was the best thing that ever happened to him. She tells him so every morning."

A heavy, awkward silence covered the room. Hank looked from Katrina to Bethany. "You both said he needed a wife. Just a few weeks ago, I heard you both say so, standing right in this very spot. Birdy was here too, and she agreed wholeheartedly. Now, what's so wrong about doing something about it?"

Bethany put her hands on her hips. "It seems like David should do the choosing of a wife."

"He can do all the choosing he wants to do!" Hank said, hurt. "Plenty to choose from. All I did was let the ladies know that he was interested."

And that was the problem, right there, Katrina thought. Her father wasn't interested in getting remarried. She watched Hank try to jam the letters into his coat pocket, only to miss his pocket so that the bundle of letters scattered on the ground.

She felt a twinge of guilt as she watched his happiness evaporate. The more he picked up, the more fell out of his coat. He had become a clumsy bundle of anxiety.

And that made her think of her father, the number one anxiety in her life at the moment — no, scratch that. Definitely the number two anxiety in her life, if she allowed herself to think of her boyfriend, John, which she tried not to do but couldn't help herself.

John. The thought of his name sent a sharp pain through her ribs, an invisible dagger into her heart. She refused to believe it was truly over between her and John. Surely he would come to his senses soon. They were supposed to be forever.

Her father strongly — strongly! — disapproved of John, for all kinds of reasons that Katrina thought were unfair and biased. After the accident that took the life of her mother and nearly took hers too, her father had become ridiculously overprotective. Katrina had worried him to pieces in the hospital.

She knew her behavior lately was spiking his concern that she was still suffering effects from the accident. She'd been quieter than usual and kept to herself as much as she could. He suggested, more than once, that she see a doctor. But what could a doctor do to mend a broken heart? And fix dreams that had turned to dust?

Hank cleared his throat, pulling her back to the matter at hand. Katrina placed her fingers on her temples — a headache was threatening. "*What* were you thinking? When I said that I hoped my father would find someone, I didn't mean to imply that it was our business to do something about it."

That wasn't entirely true. Katrina was doing something on her own — she had made a list of every eligible female over the age of forty in Stoney Ridge who bore some resemblance to her mother, either in some physical attribute or in personality. And she was systematically inviting each woman over to dinner. Two, so far. Two disastrous dinners in which her father never even showed up — though, to be fair, his untimely absence was through no fault of his own. His work as a minister meant he was often called away from home at unusual hours. When all was said and done, Katrina decided it was not such a bad thing to have a test to weed out those women who might not have the patience or endurance to be a minister's wife. After all, interruptions were part and parcel of the calling.

The only sound in the store was the

17

crackle of the letters as Hank stuffed them into his coat pocket. "That's the trouble with the world today. All talk, no action." Insulted, Hank spun around, muttering about women and their lack of understanding.

Katrina hadn't meant to hurt his tender pride. "Wait! Wait, Hank. I'm sorry. You just surprised me, that's all." When he slowed to turn around, she tried to feign interest and ignore the queasy feeling that rose up in her stomach again. "Did you read the letters? Any possibilities?"

Hank patted his pockets. "Fourteen women, all sensing a divine calling to move to Stoney Ridge, all eager to meet the widowed minister David Stoltzfus."

Honestly, that is exactly what Katrina hoped might happen. Her father needed to find someone. He hovered over her like a worried hen, objecting to any activity that might bring risk with it. He was getting worse too. Lately, he insisted on dropping Katrina off at the Bent N' Dent as if she were nine and not nineteen. She was starting to suffocate under her father's watchful concern. "Maybe . . . we should take a look at some of those letters."

Hank lit up. "Now you're talking!" He grabbed the letters from his coat and plunked them on the counter. "I like most of them. But skip that one." He pointed to a pink envelope rimmed with flowers. "That's from a lady who loves cats. Has over twenty of them."

"Katrina," Bethany frowned at her.

Katrina set the pink envelope aside, but picked up a blue one. "Look at the bright side, Bethany. One of those women might be the right wife for my father."

"The bright side isn't always the right side."

"Don't sound so sour on true love, Bethany," Hank said. "You might give Jimmy Fisher another chance."

The on-again, off-again romance of Bethany Schrock and Jimmy Fisher was a source of great interest to everyone in Stoney Ridge. Katrina's brother, Jesse, held bets on who would be the first to break up. Bethany and Jimmy would teeter toward matrimony, only to have one or the other pull back as if getting too close to a fire.

"Ha!" Bethany rolled her eyes. "You know how unreliable he is."

"That I do," Hank said happily.

At that moment, Jimmy Fisher materialized out of nowhere. "Who's unreliable?" he said, holding the door open.

"You," Bethany said. "You've never had a

19

plan that lasts longer than five minutes."

"Not true!" Jimmy turned to Hank. "Want to go fishing this afternoon?"

Katrina and Bethany exchanged amazed glances.

"Where've you been, Jimmy Fisher?" Bethany asked, scowling. "I haven't seen you in over a week."

Jimmy grinned and closed the door behind him. "She can't do with me and she can't do without me."

"Oh, I can do without you just fine," Bethany said. Lately, she was the one full of doubts about Jimmy as suitable husband material. "I'm going to the storeroom to unpack some boxes."

Jimmy watched her go, then leaned his elbows onto the countertop. "She can simmer up faster than a teapot on a hot stove." He gave Katrina his most charming grin. "But I have learned to weather it."

Katrina lowered her voice. "She thinks you're suffering from a temporary case of permanent immaturity."

"Katrina!" came her voice from the storeroom. "I told you that information in private."

Katrina shrugged. "But she tells that to everyone. She says so all the time." She pulled out a box of ground cumin–filled containers and weighed them to mark their price. The strong smell of the cumin made her stomach twist. Was cumin always this strong? Or was this a particularly pungent batch? "I wish people would say what they mean and mean what they say." John, for example. *There I go, thinking of him again!* She put the cumin container back in the box. That overly aromatic chore could wait until tomorrow.

"Which reminds me," Jimmy said. "Katrina, your dad said to ask Bethany to close up so you could leave early. Your brother just got home."

"Jesse?" Katrina said. "My brother is . . . home?"

"I gave him a ride from town in my own buggy," Jimmy said. "Dropped him off a few minutes ago. That's why I'm here. Your dad sent me to tell you. The prodigal has returned!"

"I need to get home." Her thoughts jumbled together like tangled yarn in a basket. Jesse was home! Finally, she could stop being her father's favorite child and let Jesse have a turn at it. "Would you mind asking Bethany to lock up? I need to get home."

"What about these letters?" Hank roared.

Katrina reached out both hands and

21

scooped up the letters from the countertop, all but the pink envelope from the cat lady. She hurried to the door. Over her shoulder she shouted, "I'll handle it from here, Hank."

Being the most favorite child of David Stoltzfus had been both a gift and a burden to bear for Jesse. It was hard enough to be the only son among five daughters, but added to that was his father's constant attention and concern and worry . . . well, it meant quite a lot of attention was focused on him. Happily, he loved being the center of attention.

Most of the time. He thought back to the stricken look on Katrina's face last night when he told her the news that her ex-boyfriend, John, was getting married. His dad had been right about John, all along. He wasn't a keeper, his dad had said.

"Is that really true?" Katrina's voice was thin and wobbly, but she kept her gaze fixed on him. "You're not just making that up so I'll stop pining for him?"

"It's true," Jesse had said. It pained him to be the bearer of that news, dreaded his sister's reaction, but he was impressed with how stoically she was handling the shock. Maybe she wasn't as head over heels in love with John as she had seemed for the last year.

Later that night, Jesse stopped by Katrina's door and heard her sobbing as if her heart had shattered. It actually hurt to hear her cry.

Unrequited love. It was a predicament he hoped he would never face.

This morning, as soon as Jesse heard the kitchen door slam shut behind his twin sisters, and he knew his father had left to take the girls to school, he jumped out of bed to take a shower. He borrowed Katrina's best lavender soap and hoped she wouldn't mind. He had never smelled better, never looked more handsome, as he sauntered across the street to pay a call on a special someone at the Inn at Eagle Hill.

He knocked tentatively on the door to the farmhouse, hoping that the bad-tempered grandmother of Eagle Hill wasn't hovering nearby.

The kitchen door opened and there she was, Miriam Schrock, his special someone, almost as if she were expecting him. He looked, and looked again. Why, she had changed over the summer, filled out in certain places, gone from girl to woman. Her dress, snugly fitting her compact form, was rose-colored with a hint of blush. Even

23

her complexion had a new glow. Her gray eyes met his in mutual appraisal. She pushed a rather fetching raven wisp of hair off her forehead and studied him as if he was an oddity.

"Miriam," he began with a lift of his hat, "I have returned, as promised."

"You also promised to write to me," she said, cool as custard. "And you never did. Not once." The door began to shut in his face.

"Let me start again," he amended rapidly. "I was kept extraordinarily busy by my hardworking relatives. You know there's always more than enough work to do on a farm."

She kept the door open a crack and peeped around the doorframe to consider his words.

"There wasn't time in the day to even pick up a pen and share with you all that was in my heart."

"You could have called."

"Ah, yes. That, too, would have required a surfeit of spare time, of which I had none."

"I heard you had plenty of free time on Sunday nights to drive Sicily Bender home from singings."

Sicily Bender? How in the world had she ever heard that he had been going out with

24

Sicily Bender? Who would have told her? Unless . . . news had trickled to Ruthie from one of those Ohio cousins. The traitors.

He felt the collar around his neck tighten up. "It's a long story," he said, as if that explained everything.

"Then it will have to wait until I have time to hear it." And with that, the door shut tight.

So much for a storybook *Welcome back!* to Stoney Ridge.

Wide awake at four thirty in the morning, David Stoltzfus gave up on sleep and decided to go downstairs to work on Sunday's sermon before the household started to stir. He paused at each bedroom door in the hallway, as he did every morning, to thank God for the gift of his children. All six, each one his favorite.

He went through the motions of scooping tablespoons of coffee grounds into the filter, filling the coffeepot with water, waiting for the pleasant percolating sound to begin, but his mind was far away.

Jesse was home — a wonderful surprise. But . . . why? And so suddenly. When he asked his son, Jesse answered with a shrug, as if . . . why not? David would have to call his sister for the real story.

Also troubling was Jesse's news about Katrina's boyfriend. Truth be told, David was relieved to hear that John was engaged to someone else, but he ached for his daughter's pain. His heart felt pierced as he watched her absorb the information: First, complete shock. Then she flinched, as if she'd been struck.

But as distracted as David felt by his children, it was the condition of the church that weighed most heavily on him. He poured a cup of coffee and sat at the kitchen table, books spread out, right under the light of the hissing kerosene lamp, and bowed his head, asking God for guidance and wisdom as he prepared for Sunday.

"Sunday," he said again, this time aloud.

His thoughts immediately traveled to the Sunday before last, when he had told the young people in the baptism class, "If you're going to choose to be Amish, be Amish with your whole heart. Don't be half-Amish. Don't live your life with one foot out the door." Bishop Freeman Glick glared at him and cornered him right afterward to give him an earful of criticism.

That week, six young men dropped out of baptism class. Parents were frantic, Freeman was livid. He was first at David's door to tell him *I told you so.*

But David stood by his words. He believed them, believed them with his whole heart.

Freeman said David didn't understand young people. "That kind of talk is going to make being Amish obsolete. The youth will leave in droves. They can't think for themselves. We need to do the thinking for them. Coax them in and lead them down the path."

If a young person didn't know what he was bending at the knee for, what was the point of being Amish? What was the point of all those who had gone before to ensure that baptism was an adult decision? And what would the church look like if it were filled with confused, lukewarm, halfhearted members? *That,* David felt, would make the church obsolete.

He rubbed his forehead, tense with the image of a scowling Freeman Glick. His private opinion of the bishop, inconstant in the best of times, varied almost hourly. Every single discussion ended up in a stalemate. Sometimes David thought Freeman exercised certain neck veins just for discussions with him.

These were the moments when David most sorely missed his wife, Anna. She was such a good sounding board. She listened at all the right times, gave him advice when he asked. She would know what to do, where to turn. Leave it in God's hands, she would say.

David looked up to the ceiling and lifted his palms. *Leave it in God's hands.*

A tapping sound on the window made him jerk in his chair. Birdy Glick, the only sister to the Glick brothers, stood at the kitchen window in the cold and murky light of dawn, waving timidly. He jumped up from the kitchen table to open the back door for her.

"David!" she exclaimed. Her face was bright, as if with happiness. "I hope you don't mind such an early visit. I'm on my way to Windmill Farm to watch the peregrine falcon hunt for breakfast and happened to notice your light was on."

She took a step and tripped over the door's threshold, sailing straight into David. He braced himself to catch her and ended up knocking bonnets and hats and coats to the floor.

"I'm terribly sorry! I'll get them."

But David was already picking them up, fearing the worst. A visit from Birdy was like inviting a kind and gentle bull into a china shop. David was tall but not as tall as Birdy: she was six foot two inches, taller than most men.

As her gaze settled fully on him, her eyebrows drew together in a slight frown. "What's the matter?"

"What makes you think something's wrong?"

"I stood knocking at the door for five minutes before I finally yoo-hooed at the window."

David felt his cheeks grow warm. "Sorry, Birdy. I didn't hear the knock. My thoughts were elsewhere." He lifted his palm in the direction of the kitchen table. Books and notes were piled helter-skelter.

"Miles away, I'd say."

Not quite that far. More like down the road at the Glick farm. Intentionally redirecting his thoughts, he smiled at Birdy. "Are you looking for Katrina? She's still asleep."

"Actually, no. I stopped by to let you know that Thelma Beiler hired a farmhand. She said it was your idea."

"What?" David's smile faded. "I told her I'd help her interview a few possibilities, to narrow it down. I even gave her some suggestions."

"She thought you were too busy to be bothered, so she posted an ad on the bulletin board down at the Hay & Grain and hired the first fellow who called. She liked

29

the sound of his voice on the phone. He started a few days ago." Birdy stepped up to the window, then turned back to face David. "I also learned that Thelma has taken a fall and hurt her shoulder. Nothing broken," she hastened to add at the look of alarm on David's face. "Her arm is in a sling while it heals. I thought, perhaps, it might be wise if someone were to stay with her for a while. After all, Thelma's alone up on that hilltop."

Thelma Beiler, Elmo's widow, was in her late seventies but acted like she was in her twenties, insisting she didn't need anyone fussing over her.

"Though, of course, it would be best if it were presented in a different light to Thelma. Perhaps, as someone who wants to apprentice the moss business."

David nodded. "This farmhand, he's Amish, isn't he?"

"Of course!" Then her brows gathered into a frown. "He spoke to Thelma and me in Penn Dutch. I think . . . he's one of us."

Something didn't sound quite right. "Birdy, would you be willing to stay with her?"

Birdy frowned. "Oh, I would if I could. I really would. I'm very fond of Thelma." She lifted her head with a deep breath. "But apparently I'm going to be teaching school this term."

David tried to hide his surprise. Surprise and annoyance. Yet *another* decision made by Freeman and Levi that excluded him. Big decisions, starting with allowing cell phones for business use. Then Freeman added computers.

David couldn't ignore the fact that quite a few church members welcomed Freeman's soft attitude toward modernizing. The farmers of Stoney Ridge were struggling to make ends meet; many were abandoning farming altogether to try their hand at business ventures. Computers, they believed, could help aid a small business's success. Cell phones would help a business owner be readily available to their customers.

All true.

But these decisions weren't without repercussions. They were choices about principles. Yes, a computer might make keeping accounts more efficient, but its access to the internet ushered in a host of new complexities. Discovering Jimmy Fisher had a Facebook account, for one thing.

And a cell phone might make life more convenient than an answering machine in a cold shanty in the middle of winter, but it also brought in all kinds of options. His mind trailed off to last week's wedding, when he spotted Luke Schrock slyly taking cell phone pictures of the bride and groom.

More to the point, since when was ease or convenience the goal of the Plain life? He believed the purpose of the Amish was to love God and others well.

Birdy cleared her throat and David snapped back to the present, to the news that she was now going to teach at the new school. He had nothing against Birdy. He didn't know much about her other than a few obvious facts: she lived in a small cottage on her brothers' property, she led bird-watching tours for tourists. And she was quite tall.

"I think there's one person Thelma wouldn't object to," Birdy said. "Your Katrina. It's a perfect solution, you see, in that it was Katrina's idea in the first place for Thelma to start selling all that moss she's got up there."

"I suppose you're right about that." It came from a casual comment Katrina had made at last June's school program. A few of the eighth-grade boys had doubled back for another year or two, easy to spot by the rim of fuzz on their upper lips. Katrina had said it looked as if they were starting to grow moss from all their years in the schoolroom. Thelma had laughed so hard at her remark that she had tears running down her cheeks.

A few weeks after her husband Elmo's passing, Thelma called David to her home and said one word: "Moss!" She'd been searching for some kind of business venture, but her property was a shady, steep, rocky hillside. Moss was the only thing that grew in abundance. David researched the topic and discovered that several states and national forests had banned harvesting wild moss; there was, indeed, a need for a commercial moss market.

"It seemed, well, I thought, perhaps Katrina might benefit from spending time with Thelma . . ." Birdy paused and regrouped, searching for the right words. "Sometimes, people never get over losing somebody."

David's eyes strayed to his wife Anna's knitting basket, gathering dust in a corner of the room, but he didn't let his gaze linger there. An all-too-familiar stirring of worry started to swirl in his chest. He hated to admit it, considering the source came from a Glick, but there was a lot of sense in that suggestion. Katrina seemed so wounded and bruised. The poor girl looked tired. Worse than tired — exhausted. She was too slim and too pale, with dark circles under her eyes.

Birdy took David's brief silence to mean he was thinking it over. "It's a bit like hitting two birds with one stone, don't you think?"

It couldn't hurt. "I'll suggest it to Katrina this morning."

"Excellent. Wonderful. I think it's a splendid solution," Birdy said cheerfully.

The conversation grew suddenly silent. The distant clip-clopping sound of a buggy horse sifted through the awkward silence.

Then Birdy spun around to leave and, in doing so, swept two books off the table with her elbow. They both bent down to pick up the books at the same time and knocked heads. A sharp pain creased David's forehead and he put his hand over it.

"Oh, I'm so sorry. Terribly sorry," she said, scrambling to collect the books.

David stepped back to avoid another collision. Katrina said Birdy's clumsiness was David's fault, that Birdy said he made her "frightfully nervous." But what could he do about that? He didn't know any cure for just being himself.

The early morning sun started to stream into the kitchen windows. The day had begun. "I'll walk you down the driveway. I forgot to pick up yesterday's mail." About halfway down the path, his attention was caught by the Glick buggy turning into the Inn at Eagle Hill. He saw Freeman and Levi climb out of the buggy and walk toward the house.

"The brothers are making the rounds to speak to each family."

"About . . . ?"

Birdy lowered her eyes and said in a hushed voice, "Finances. They plan to review each family's finances."

David's fists clenched. It was a fairly common practice for a church to nominate trustees to make an assessment of each family's finances, every five years or so, to support the teacher's salary and maintain the schoolhouse. But the trustees were chosen, not self-appointed, and the church leaders were never nominated as trustees. Elmo would've never done such a thing.

"I'd better go." She took a few steps, then turned around to face him, a face that was kind and open and sincere. "Don't let my brothers wear you down. The church, Stoney Ridge . . . ," Birdy dropped her eyes, "we need . . ." She kept her eyes locked on her shoes.

They were rather substantial shoes, David noted. As large as her brothers'. But unlike her brothers, she had the nature of a gentle, artless young woman, surprisingly diffident and shy. Well, it was a good thing she had such stature — she would need everything she could muster to manage the boys in that schoolhouse.

The next came out as if she were talking to herself, "David, just don't give up."

2

Katrina sliced through the long grass of the meadow, getting the hem of her dress soaking wet. She still felt an aching sadness over the news her brother brought from Ohio. John was engaged to be married. He had moved on.

What was this craziness with John, anyway? It was as if her heart were a teacup that fell to the floor and shattered. Why was she hanging on? It didn't make any sense. It was making her miserable. She had to find a way to get over it.

But how do you stop loving someone? Obviously, John found a way. It wasn't easy for Katrina to turn off her emotions. She'd been so sure he would come to his senses and seek her out, begging her to take him back. And she would!

The first time she'd seen him, well over a year ago, he was waiting outside her father's store in Ohio. He had just moved to town and was looking for work. She was recovering from the accident and her mother's death, and was trying to work a few hours a day at the store.

John sat on a bench, carving a piece of wood as he waited for someone to arrive. He worked cleanly, quickly, and he was whistling to himself, unaware that she was watching him. His hands were works of art, long and powerful and impeccably clean, the fingernails perfect ovals. The skin was tanned, and his wrists were covered with golden hair.

Finally, he looked up at her and gave her a quizzical expression. "Where do I know you from?"

It was as if she'd known him forever, as if she only had to remember his name. Her heartbeat actually sped up, filled with a sensation like a warm ray of sunlight. She felt a spark of happiness rise up within her. It was the first glimmer of happiness she had felt since the terrible accident. He explained that he was waiting for the store to open because he wanted to post an advertisement for border collie pups on the bulletin board. He was a breeder, he said, new to the area, and was trying to get established.

He gazed at her for a long time, looking at

her eyes and mouth, and a giddiness danced through her. She fell in love just that fast, at first sight.

Which it was. It was fast and real and true, their beginning.

John loved her with an ardor, as passionate, as consuming as it was possible for a man to love a woman. That was one of the things she treasured most about him — his fervor, his intensity, his undeniable, romantic, jealous love. "I saw the way all the boys fluttered around you like moths," John told her once after church, "and I made up my mind to beat them all to the flame."

He hated when other boys flirted with her, always feared one would catch her eye. He worried that he was too old for her, twenty-six to her seventeen when they met. When her father decided to move the family to Stoney Ridge, he worried obsessively that she would drift away.

As often as she could save up the money for the fare, she took a long bus ride to Ohio to see him. Her last visit was eight weeks ago. They'd had a wonderful, romantic weekend together — a picnic at the lake on Saturday, a rainy, lazy off-Sunday morning at her aunt Nancy's house.

Then, as John put her on the bus that last

Sunday afternoon, he took both of her hands in his and solemnly announced that he wanted to break up. She stared at him, mystified, absolutely shell-shocked. She had given him everything, absolutely everything she had to give, confident of their future together. It made no sense. She'd had no clue whatsoever.

She'd been completely blindsided.

The only explanation he gave was that he had stopped loving her. She knew, just *knew,* that wasn't true. But it was also true that he didn't love her enough.

For the last eight weeks, she had kept checking for phone messages, hoping in some bizarre way that there would be something from John to explain all this, something that would say, "Hey Kat, I don't know what I was thinking. I'm coming for you."

Would he ever come for her? Or had he completely disappeared from her life forever? She simply had to believe that somehow, some way . . .

What? That he'd send a message to her? What would it even say? *Sorry, sweetheart, there's been a big misunderstanding.* And she would forgive him and everything would go back to the way it was.

But, so far, there was no phone message

40

from him.

What would she do without him? It frightened her to even think of a future without John. It was more than love she felt for him. She needed him, needed him in her life, and it was a need so consuming, it was like needing air to breathe. What would she do without him? The question was so enormous that she shoved it away.

A crow cawed overhead and another answered back, snapping Katrina back to the present. She stopped in front of a new big wooden sign with MOSS HILL painted in purple and green. Beneath the name were the words NO SUNDAY SALES. Near the top of the hill sat Thelma Beiler's modest little house. Chickens wandered around the grass yard, clucking in a busybody sort of way.

Before Katrina reached the steps that led up to the house, the front door opened and a man stepped onto the porch. She knew exactly who he was — Thelma Beiler's new farmhand. She shielded her eyes from the early morning sun and realized that Birdy had described him perfectly: reserved, aloof, and much too good-looking.

He stepped farther out onto the porch, until he was standing almost on top of her. His hair was thick, dark brown and curly, too long, and yet it fell perfectly around an

41

extravagant face — shaped into angles by high cheekbones and a hard jaw. He had a dramatic cleft in his chin and piercing blue eyes over which his brows slanted upward like the slopes of a hill. A lock of hair, dark as coal, tossed on his forehead. His body was shaped by years of hard physical labor. Not her type at all, but definitely beautiful.

"Hey," he said in a low voice, his eyes locked on her.

Oh no. She could tell, from the approving look in his eyes, that he found her attractive. No, no, no, no. Not what she wanted or needed right now. She met his gaze with challenge. "So you must be the new farmhand."

"Andy Miller is the name." A slight grin creased his face. "And you must be the one they sent to keep an eye on Thelma. To make sure I'm not a crazy serial murderer."

Katrina cocked her head. "Are you?"

A hint of amusement lit his eyes. "Maybe a little crazy, but definitely not a serial murderer."

He was older than she was, somewhere in his twenties, and had a certain world weariness about him. "I'm Katrina Stoltzfus. I'm going to stay with Thelma and learn all about her moss business." *Or until Thelma's shoulder mends.*

"She's resting right now. We just got back from the doctor."

This stranger seemed territorial of Thelma. Why was that? She would have thought he'd be glad to have someone else tend to the needs of an elderly woman. Most men would be delighted to pass off the tasks. "Don't let me stop you from what you were going to do."

"I'm heading out to gather moss."

"I've never seen all this moss that Thelma's talked about."

He tipped his hat to leave, then hesitated. "Well, come on then, it's a sight to behold." Abruptly, he took her small suitcase and set it on the porch. "Follow me."

"Um . . . okay."

He took long strides toward a well-beaten path that led up a steep hill, then stopped, as if it occurred to him he should wait for her to catch up to him. "What do you know about moss?"

"Well, I know it's green."

He gave her a single glance, not quite rolling his eyes. His mouth twitched. Amusement? Annoyance? "And you're going to learn all about her business?"

She gave him a rueful smile. "I'm a quick study."

"So, I guess there's no chance that I'd be

boring you."

Boring her? Not likely, Katrina thought, then caught herself before she said it out loud. Don't encourage him, she told herself. Keep things strictly businesslike.

They passed a large vegetable garden in its last burst of summer growth, a small barn, a battered-looking greenhouse with cracked windows, then climbed to the top of a small rocky hill. They passed some trees with branches and trunks covered with moss.

"Is this it?" she asked.

"Hardly. You'll know when you see it."

At the crest of the hill, he stepped sideways, out of the way, and gestured with his hand, casting a large half-circle. "Here it is."

"Oh!" she gasped. "Oh, my." In front of her was the moss, spread out like giant green pincushions over the rocks that hugged the hillside. A breeze swept over them and made the green hillside shimmer slightly like waves, like water. Moving her gaze downhill, she studied the landscape, enveloped by the grassy smell of the moss wafting over them, the bees buzzing, the sunlight tumbling down over the moss-covered rocks. Reflexively, Katrina put her hands to her face. "Oh, wow."

"Told you it was a sight to see," he said, hands on his hips.

"It's . . . stunning." And it was. She was in awe. But then she realized that Andy was watching her. "Is it always like this?"

"Like what?"

"The aroma . . . why, it's intoxicating! Like . . . fresh-cut grass. But . . . better."

Amused, Andy gazed over the rocky hillside. "Probably more aromatic because it's such a warm, sunny day today."

"I know this reveals my ignorance, but why would anybody buy . . . moss?" It was such an odd product to her, almost laughable.

"Gardeners. Florists. Decorators. Landscapers. It's an alternative to growing grass. Parks use it for walkways."

She bent down to rub her hand along the top of the smooth surface. "I'm enchanted." She looked up at him and he smiled. The grin started slowly, but when it reached his eyes, it became dazzling. She felt a little disoriented, snared by those China-blue eyes.

"Take your time," he said at last. "I'll tell Thelma you're here. I've got some work to do. I'm trying to get a lead on a reputable breeder of border collies."

Katrina did not move. She barely

45

breathed. "I know someone who breeds border collies. Trains them too."

His dark eyebrows lifted in interest.

"People come from all over to get one of his dogs."

"Come to my office in the barn when you're done and leave his info on my desk. I'll look into it."

"Oh, perhaps I should contact him for you," she said quickly. "He's got a waiting list . . . but I might be able to help expedite your name to the top of the list."

"Okay, sure. Ideally, I'd like a male pup. Neutered. If it's trained, all the better. But not older than a year." He gave her a satisfied nod and turned to leave.

She watched Andy Miller stride back down the hill toward the barn. And she was suddenly, overwhelmingly, filled with happiness. A little spark of hope, fizzy as a bee, suggested that this might be the way back to John.

As Birdy walked toward the schoolhouse, she sorted out the twist her brother Freeman had thrown her this week and tried to focus her thoughts. Teach school? She didn't know the first thing about teaching school to a roomful of children. And Freeman must have thought so too, because his own four children as well as Levi's three children would remain in the old schoolhouse under Danny Riehl's tutelage, though where they lived, the Big House, was much closer to the new school.

Birdy never had any desire to teach school but that mattered not to Freeman. And if it didn't matter to Freeman, it wouldn't matter to Levi. Freeman was the sort to leap headfirst into a raging river without a care for whether it was deep enough. And where Freeman leaped, Levi followed.

Birdy loved her brothers, but she also feared them and knew not to cross them, especially now. Since Freeman had become a bishop, he had started to make sweeping changes in the little church of Stoney Ridge, and she knew he had many more plans in the works. David Stoltzfus was the fly in his ointment. He didn't go along with Freeman's ideas the way Deacon Abraham, a peacemaker at heart, did. David questioned her brother, pushed back, tried to slow down his pace of change. He was a constant aggravation to Freeman.

To many in the church, perhaps most, Freeman Glick was only facing reality and helping to preserve the church for a new century. That's certainly how it appeared, and she hoped he was setting the right path for the church. She doubted it, but she hoped so. But the one thing she knew for certain was that David Stoltzfus must not give up.

David.

A year ago, after hearing David Stoltzfus's very first sermon, she knew she was a goner. He preached in a way she had never heard anyone preach. His words stirred something inside her, something she couldn't explain. She only knew he made her want to lean closer to God. And she knew David Stoltzfus had a grip on her heart like a balled fist.

Each church Sunday, Birdy tried to sit on the far side of the bench so she could look at David from the side. Actually, she liked looking at him from any angle. Although heaven help her if he ever knew, if anyone ever knew, what was in her heart. Loving David Stoltzfus was something she kept carefully guarded.

How handsome he was! David was lean, not even a hint of paunch hung over his pants. His skin was tanned but not bronze, leathery but in a good way, the complexion of a man who spent time outdoors. His hair, like his beard, was ginger, a color that made his warm brown eyes look even warmer.

This was the man she had been longing for her entire life, despite the fact that thirteen years separated them, or that she wasn't exactly the type of woman for whom men swooned. She was taller than nearly all of them.

Birdy was thirty-one years old. She had no prospects of marriage, nor any hope of such on the horizon. And she had accepted that. What was it Freeman always said about her? "Liked by all but loved by none."

Her mother, gone ten years now, had tried to encourage her only daughter to be more graceful, more feminine. To improve her posture by walking around the house with a book on her head, to move with more poise, to practice her conversational skills. Birdy had tried so hard to please her mother, but to no avail. Years passed by without any suitors and she saw her mother's mouth and eyes etch with shame and disappointment.

No, Birdy had no grand illusions that David would ever think twice about her.

Sooner or later, some lucky woman would capture David's heart. He was everything: kind, intelligent, wise, attractive, a wonderful father. However, until such a woman appeared on the scene and stole his heart, Birdy was content with the interaction she and David did have, however awkward those encounters always seemed to be. And they were. On her best days, she was clumsy.

Around David, she was thoroughly uncoordinated. He flustered her.

As she turned down the road that led to the schoolhouse, she pondered how to make this teaching situation a win-win. That was always her aim in every circumstance — to find the bright side of every situation. Such an attitude annoyed her brothers, but Birdy was used to people reacting that way to her. Levi was embarrassed by her relentless good spirits. He would say with a silencing sneer, "Where water is deepest, it is stillest." But there were things you couldn't help. She had been born cheerful.

She'd gone a full two blocks before a wonderful thought occurred to her. As teacher, she would be involved in the lives of David's younger children — Ruthie, Molly, and the twins, Emily and Lydie. As their teacher, she might have extra opportunities to see and interact with David. It might be as close as she could ever get to him.

An iridescent bubble of happiness engulfed her, and she nearly laughed aloud.

David got home later from a hospital visitation than he'd planned. The horse had picked up a stone in her shoe. He was able to dig it out, but the horse kept favoring one leg and so he decided to come home on foot, leading her by the reins, though rain had begun. He removed her harness, washed her down, curried her, fed her, and checked her leg again to make sure it wasn't swelling.

He'd barely made it home before the full force of the storm hit. Rain pounded on the barn roof, noisy and furious. He pushed the buggy into an upright position against the barn wall, his mind still on Ephraim Yoder in the hospital.

A week ago, Ephraim had been stacking fresh hay in his haymow, slipped, and fallen headfirst onto the concrete floor of the barn. His son, Noah, had found him, lying unconscious, his neck broken, and ran over a mile to get help.

In the emergency room of the hospital, Ephraim was placed on a ventilator with a machine doing the breathing for him. But his mind was clear and he could now communicate short words at a time. He was just hanging on, one day at a time right now, but the future, David knew, and Ephraim knew, was bleak.

Ephraim's wife, Sadie, wanted David to read Scripture to him, so he did, staying much longer than he intended. After

Ephraim dozed off, he stared at the broken man.

When David's wife, Anna, had died, it had been quick. One moment she was driving the buggy home after picking up Katrina, and the next moment a pickup truck had rear-ended the buggy. He was told she'd died before the ambulance had arrived. He prayed it was so, that Anna never suffered agony or even knew what was happening.

Ephraim knew exactly what had happened to him, and the resignation in his eyes made David want to weep. Ephraim and Sadie had a son to raise who was about the same age as his Ruthie, a boy on the cusp of leaving childhood. It wasn't fair. But it was.

God's ways are not our ways.

He knew that. He believed that. But it was hard, so hard, to understand the ways of God.

He slid open the barn door and peered out into a storm that flung lightning bolts like arrows. The warm yellow light from the house beckoned, but he paused to stare at the dark sky.

How Anna would love to see this thunderstorm. She had relished thunder and lightning storms. A quick clutch of emotion seized his throat, and he looked away, overcome by a wild sense of loss.

No, he thought. Anna had left him, but she'd gone to God. His wife knew a better life now, the eternal life, warm and safe in God's kingdom and the glory of heaven. It was selfish of him to miss her so much. And to be perfectly honest, he felt a little envious of her. There were moments, like tonight, as he sat by Ephraim's bedside, that he felt tired of trying to navigate through life. More toils, more troubles. The words of King Solomon echoed in his head: "I have seen all the things that are done under the sun; all of them are meaningless, a chasing after the wind." Sometimes, going to God seemed far more appealing than the trouble that this world had to offer.

But who was he to question the mysterious will of God? Anna was gone but he was here. If only for the sake of their children, he had to find the courage to keeping moving forward in life.

The emptiness was there, but he would fill it. With mornings full of the flurry of breakfast and lunch making and seeing his daughters off to school. With days spent at the store, where he would cross paths with nearly everyone in the church. And nights when he'd sit at the kitchen table and spread his Bible and books out to prepare for Sunday church.

David pushed away from the barn door and ran to the house. He yanked off his slicker and tossed it on the porch bench, then made himself smile as he stepped into the warmth of the kitchen. Jesse looked up from the table. "Hey, Dad. There's some dinner left for you in the oven. Molly cooked tonight. Not sure what it was, but I ate an hour ago and so far I'm not stricken with food poisoning."

"Thanks. That's a solid recommendation." As he passed by his son, he gently ruffled Jesse's hair. Sixteen years old. Where had the years gone? "Are the girls asleep? School starts tomorrow."

"Yup. They're excited. They want you to take them. They're worried about the new teacher."

"Birdy? But they know her."

"Not as a teacher. They were crazy about Teacher Danny."

David scooped a large amount of casserole on a plate and sat down next to Jesse. He bowed his head for a long moment, thanking God for the gift of this day, for so many things to be grateful for — Katrina agreeing so readily to stay with Thelma. In fact, almost surprisingly eager to leave home. When he suggested that she give it a little thought, she said firmly, "Dad, I'm not a

little girl anymore. I'm a grown woman."
He knew that all too well. He reined in his
thoughts, circling back to giving thanks for
this day. For Jesse's homecoming. For the
timing of the start of school tomorrow —
so that his four daughters would have a
place to be while he devoted more time to
the running of the store.

Jesse was waiting for him to lift his head.
"Just so you know — the girls are going to
try to talk you into going to the old school."

"So they can stay with Danny Riehl."

Jesse winked. "Excellent deduction."

"We've needed a new school for a long
time."

"Even if everyone under the age of
eighteen is running off for greener
pastures?"

David's fork stopped in midair. "Where
did you hear that?"

"From Aunt Nancy. Sounds like your
sermon convinced cousin Peter to leave the
straight and narrow life."

He grimaced. "That wasn't the point of
the sermon."

"Aunt Nancy saw it differently, especially
after Peter wrote that he was leaving for
Colorado to try his hand as a cowboy."

David's nephew Peter had been living with
his family for the last six months to help

manage the store — happily, David thought, up until that Sunday morning sermon. At breakfast the next morning, Peter announced it was time for him to move on. And what could David say to stop him? Peter was twenty-one, nearly grown. David leaned back in his chair. "Jesse, is that why you've come home? Did Nancy ask you to leave?"

Jesse seemed suddenly very interested in a stain on the tablecloth. "She didn't call you?"

"No. But I haven't checked messages in a few days."

Jesse brightened with relief. "Let's just say that I might have worn out my welcome."

What did that mean? David wasn't sure he wanted to know more . . . at least, not tonight. Changing the subject, he said, "Well, you've come home at just the right time. I need you to take over Katrina's hours at the store while she's helping Thelma. With both Peter and Katrina gone, the store's a little shorthanded."

Jesse made a scrunched up face. "Well, Dad, you see, I have discovered that I'm not the indoor type. I need to be outside, allowing fresh air to fill my cranium."

"You want to farm?" David's property was only five acres and not tillable, nearly vertical. But Amos Lapp had a large farm and was always looking for an extra hand.

"Oh no! No, no, no. Not farming. I ruled that out this summer at Aunt Nancy's. Hopefully, I have mucked out my last pigsty."

"I see." David tried not to let his face show his exasperation. He had been hoping that the time in Ohio this summer would have given Jesse some much needed focus. "So what *would* you like to do?"

"Spare yourself that worry, Dad." Jesse stretched his arms over his head. "I will figure it out soon enough. For starters, Jimmy Fisher and I are going fishing tomorrow morning. Early."

David pushed himself upright, the front legs of the chair hitting the floor with a soft thud. "I have a better idea. I'm going to talk to Hank Lapp about taking you on as a buggy repairman."

Jesse's jaw dropped wide open. "Buggies?" His voice rose an octave. "Me?"

"Why not? Stoney Ridge needs another buggy repairman. Hank means well, but he's as slow as molasses in the middle of January."

"That's because he's too busy helping you find a wife." Jesse jammed a finger at a letter in the *Budget,* sitting in the middle of the table.

"What are you talking about?" David reached for the paper and nearly spilled his glass of water. He read through Hank's scribe letter. Hank was begging — begging! — for a wife for David.

How *dare* Hank do such a thing! Why, David must be the laughingstock of Stoney Ridge. He jammed his fist down on the paper and felt the pressures of the day overwhelm him. He tossed the paper into the rubbish bin. And that was when he realized Jesse had slipped away, unnoticed.

3

Everyone thought that because Katrina Stoltzfus was the oldest in the family, she was a plucky girl, but in truth, she wasn't as confident as everyone assumed. In fact, she had the temperament of a turtle. Whatever dread, fright, or bump appeared in her path, she wanted nothing more than to drop in her tracks and hide. That's what she was doing now, at Thelma's. Hiding. Under the guise of helping Thelma.

Thelma's shoulder *was* in a sling, and it was unfortunate that it was her right arm, but the woman had more energy than men half her age.

Take now, for example.

Thelma was walking the perimeter of her property — over a mile long — something she did every morning, rain or shine. She strode along the barn, the greenhouse, and the henhouse, checking the hens to make sure the pen hadn't been raided overnight.

She eyed the fences and rounded the beehives, then headed back along the vegetable garden. "Keeps me healthy and vibrant," she told Katrina, and offered her a standing invitation to come along.

"Maybe tomorrow," Katrina had said, but she doubted it. She was profoundly exhausted, as if she'd had the stomach flu for a week or hauled hay for three days straight. Like she could sleep for two solid days. She wondered if she should go see the doctor and have her anemia tested, like her father had been encouraging her to do. She felt just like she did after the accident when she had lost so much blood. It took weeks before she felt as if she had some get-up-and-go again.

No, it took John's arrival into her life to bring her energy back. And now he was gone and so was her get-up-and-go. She knew she was depressed. Not sad, not blue or wistful, not filled with regrets or the fury of a scorned woman, but truly down-and-out depressed.

A breeze came through the window, fluttering a faded curtain so threadbare that it was hardly cloth anymore. Katrina watched it sail up, up, up and fall back, the light pouring through it, tiny holes showing along the hem. The movement made her dizzy, and she closed her eyes.

What must it be like for Thelma to walk the same mile path, day in and day out? At some point, wouldn't she stop seeing it? She could guess Thelma's response, knowing her as she did. Thelma would say that God had made her a steward of this particular patch of land, and it was her privilege to care for it well until the day the Lord had in mind for her to toddle off this mossy earth.

Moss. What a strange "crop." Yet in a way, Katrina thought it was pretty resourceful of Thelma to think of it. She and Elmo had lived on this hilltop all their married life. They'd had one son, who had died before he was twenty. Elmo had a harness repair business that ended when he passed unexpectedly. Thelma didn't want to move — she loved this hill and its beautiful views — and had to figure out some kind of livelihood. So . . . moss gathering, growing, and selling it was.

In a way, a good way, Katrina envied Thelma. She was a woman who faced facts: She was a widow left without resources, she needed to find a way to earn a living or go live with her nephew, and she loved her land. She knew who she was and what she wanted out of life. Katrina envied her faith too. Rock solid. So unlike her own faith that seemed as wispy and insubstantial as that threadbare curtain on the window.

Katrina knew she had always been considered to be a little restless. Scatterbrained. Her mother used to call her capricious, which sounded a little better. Countless half-done projects at home bore witness to that. A half-finished quilt, an almost finished crocheted afghan, a pile of barely begun knitted scarfs. She started things with great enthusiasm, which quickly wore off. She dabbled at different jobs but nothing held her interest for long. Usually, she ended up back at work in her father's store.

She wondered why her father had seemed concerned about Thelma's new farmhand. There wasn't anything particularly threatening about Andy Miller, at least nothing she could put her finger on, and she was looking for a reason, *something,* to dislike about him. So far, she found nothing. If anything, he was very mother-hen-ish toward Thelma. At supper last night, he encouraged her to eat more, rest more, to let him worry about the moss fields. And that it was high time, he thought, to get a good dog to do the fence checking and keep the moss free of marauding raccoons.

Dogs. *Dogs!* She sat up in bed. Yesterday,

Katrina had left a telephone message for John, boldly and quickly, asking if he happened to have any border collies available — she knew he did, he always did — because someone in her church needed one right away. She felt proud of the way her voice sounded on the machine. Short and to the point.

Surely John must have gotten her phone message by now. Maybe he'd already answered back! Maybe his voice was just waiting for her on that machine in the shanty. "Yes, Katrina," she could hear him say in his beautiful baritone voice. "I've got a dog waiting for you. My heart is waiting for you too."

She jumped out of bed, dressed in a flash, and dashed down to the phone shanty.

The morning wind brought the mulchy odor of wet earth into the kitchen to mix with the smells of hot starch and steam. Ruthie's eyebrows were knit together in a frown as she ironed her prayer covering, the iron hissing as it glided over the dampened cambric cap. She had added so much starch that David thought he could hear it crackle.

So many times over the years he had watched Ruthie like this, from afar. He wondered what thoughts were running through her fourteen-year-old mind to make her look so serious. Such a somber child. Of all his daughters, Ruthie was the one who most resembled his wife, Anna. It was more than the same strawberry blonde hair and green eyes with the thick dark lashes and the high cheekbones. Her laugh, especially, was the sound of her mother's. But when had he last heard her laugh?

Because Ruthie had Anna's fair and delicate looks, people always assumed on meeting her that that she would have a mild, amiable way about her, but they were wrong. She had always been a girl who guarded her thoughts, who didn't reveal herself much, but when she did, it was worth the wait. Anna used to say that getting Ruthie to talk took an investment of time.

Once, Ruthie was silent for an entire buggy ride to and from town, and as they pulled into the driveway, she asked Anna, "Mom, have you ever had something happen . . . done some small thing and it ended up changing your life?"

Anna had reported the conversation to David, stunned by the question from a then-twelve-year-old child. She said she didn't even know how to respond. What could Ruthie be referring to? The twins ran out to meet them at the buggy and the moment passed. Anna told David that she was going to try to find out what Ruthie meant, if it took her all summer and dozens of buggy rides . . . but the next week, it was too late. A small, everyday thing had occurred — Anna had gone to pick up a daughter in the rain — and the buggy was rear-ended by a truck. Anna was gone, and their lives were changed.

But that was then, and this was now. And today was the first day of school.

David walked his daughters down the road to the new schoolhouse. Ruthie had her nose in a book, eleven-year-old Molly was eating an apple, twins Lydie and Emily were about to explode with nervous excitement. He was in a hurry to drop the girls off at school so that he could get over to see Hank Lapp before the day got away from him, like Jesse had. The boy left to go fishing with Jimmy Fisher before David rose from bed.

Birdy was waiting on the schoolhouse steps, eager and anxious, watering flowerpots with a clay pitcher. "Good morning, girls. You're the first to arrive. The first to see the brand-new schoolhouse. So you can be the first to choose your cubby and hook."

Wise woman, David thought. Even Ruthie

showed a spark of interest with that kind of welcome. She strode toward the schoolhouse door and her three sisters followed behind her, like a duck and her ducklings.

David felt apprehensive over the whole notion of Birdy being tapped to teach. For one thing, she had never taught school a day in her life. For another, it would take only one awkward mishap to make a laughingstock of her among the big boys, with Luke Schrock as the ringleader. He was their neighbor at the Inn at Eagle Hill, and David had enough interactions with Luke to know he was tough enough to drive a nail through a butterfly. If he could find a way to brand Birdy as ridiculous, it would be a long year ahead with Luke leading the clump of older boys.

But . . . whatever his concerns, it was too late now.

"Hello, David. A day like this is so *good,* don't you find it so?"

David took in the view of the hills in the distance, the diffuse light of the cloudy day. "Yes. I suppose you're right. I was so busy getting the girls ready for school that I hadn't noticed."

Birdy sent him a sympathetic look . . . or was it pity? She had probably read Hank's letter too. Did everyone pity him? Good grief, did his life look that pitiable?

"Well, you obviously did a fine job. You're the first to arrive and your lovely daughters look fresh as daisies."

How did a person stay so cheerful all the time? David realized he had never seen Birdy without a smile on her face, a ready laugh. What a happy thing she was, all that shine to her. It was almost as if she sensed he was thinking about her, because her cheeks reddened and she abruptly returned to watering the plants but ended up knocking over a pot of marigolds on the first step. The little yellow flowers tumbled out on the ground. "Oh, clumsy me. So sorry!"

He started to help clean up but remembered knocking heads recently with her at the house and thought better of it. "Birdy, before I go, I wanted to give you a tip about how to know which twin is which. Emily has —"

"Oh, but I know," she said, scooping up soil to repot the marigold. "A little scar near her eyebrow. Lydie's front two teeth are missing and she speaks with a whistle."

"Yes," David said, surprised and impressed. "Yes, that's it exactly." A sound of children's shouts approaching from different directions made him look around.

"Sounds of the thundering herd, soon to arrive. I'll be off, then." He stepped off the porch and watched as running children converged on the schoolhouse. "You'll have your hands full with this mob."

"Dad! Wait!"

David jerked his head around to see Molly standing at the open door of the schoolhouse, a look of sheer panic on her face. "You forgot to make our lunches!"

After a quick return trip home to pack and then deliver four lunches back to the schoolhouse, David hurried over to Windmill Farms to find Hank waiting at the end of the driveway with a fishing pole in his hand. "Any chance you're headed to Blue Lake Pond to meet up with Jimmy and Jesse?"

"I am!"

"I think they've already gone."

"Dadgummit! Did they go without me? They were supposed to come get me at seven."

"They might've, and kept on going. It's half past eight."

Hank took out his pocket watch and shook it, then peered at the watch face. "Blast. Musta broke again."

"Hank, there's something I need to talk to you about."

Hank went still. "If it's about the *Budget* letter, I only put it in there because the girls at the store, they've been talking about how much you need a woman."

Good grief! How mortifying. David lifted a hand to stop his defense. The least said about that *Budget* letter, the better. "That's not why I've come to see you. I need a favor."

"But that's exactly what I was trying to do for you! A favor." Hank's eyes looked hurt. At least, the good eye did.

"I know your intentions were good, Hank, but the next time you feel an inclination to try your hand at matchmaking, please stop yourself." He leaned his back on the fence and folded his arms across his chest. "My son Jesse returned from Ohio a few days ago. He's a bright boy. Probably too smart for his own good. Gets bored very quickly. He needs a challenge and farm work causes his mind to yawn and sneak off elsewhere."

David wouldn't tell Jesse that, but he empathized. The drip-by-drip sameness of farming never appealed to him, either. He preferred running a store to plowing a field, but that was because he wanted to be around people. Now Jesse, he didn't have that same inclination. He was just as bored stocking shelves as he was milking a cow.

"It seems to me that buggy repairs might challenge Jesse. You know, fixing things. I was hoping you might be willing to take him on, as an apprentice. Like I said, he's very bright, an astute learner. And it seems like you have more than enough work to keep you busy."

It was well known that any buggy repair would take twice as long as Hank predicted, but some of that had to do with his fondness for fishing. David was watching Hank as he spoke, trying to gauge his reaction, but the old man had his head bowed, spinning his worn straw hat in his hands. David knew what the risks were for himself and for his son — Hank wasn't given much respect in the church and David would be criticized for letting his son be an apprentice to wild-eyed Hank, but that was the very thing that made him a good choice for Jesse. Hank might be the only person in Stoney Ridge who understood the need to give Jesse a margin of grace. That is, if his son didn't thoroughly exasperate him first.

"You have the patience Jesse needs in a teacher, Hank, and the good humor. I'll be candid with you. Jesse tends to wear people out. Always has. He can talk his way out of anything and make you think it was your idea. I can't blame his character flaws on

Anna's passing — he's been a handful since the day he was born. Raising him has been like trying to rein in a runaway horse. He's got a slippery work ethic and can find a shortcut out of any hard labor. Oozes away like a barn cat. He lacks . . . purpose. But he can be good help if you can keep his mind on it. And he's got a good heart. He's at the stage where he's less than a man but starting to be something more than a boy. It pains me to say so, Hank, but I don't seem to be able to help him become the man he's meant to be. But you . . . I think you might have what it takes."

David ran out of things to say and still, there was no visible reaction from Hank. Maybe this was a terrible idea. He waited, dreading the prospect of trying to find another solution for Jesse.

Finally, Hank looked at David with tears rimming his eyes. He bobbed his head in almost schoolboyish fashion, evidently not trusting his voice. Clearing his throat, he said, "I'll teach your boy everything I know."

4

Birdy had no scientific proof that fresh air made any difference, but it did with birds and plants so, she reasoned, why not keep the children outside for as long as possible? Sooner or later, she was going to have to actually gather them into the schoolhouse and teach them something. She rang the bell and two dozen children dropped their games to pour into the schoolhouse and scramble to find a desk.

"Good morning, young scholars."

Four dozen eyes peered back at their new teacher. She cleared her throat and fingered a piece of chalk. "First things first. I want to learn all of your names." She whirled to the blackboard but forgot there was a step up and tripped, falling to her knees onto the raised platform. "Not to worry," she said, recovering quickly, jumping to her feet. She made it to the blackboard in one large stride and started to write *Teacher Birdy* in her most excellent penmanship, but pressed so hard that the chalk snapped in two. Two boys in the back of the room guffawed and her confidence, never robust, started leaking away. "Well, then, never mind." She turned back to the wide-eyed children. "So. I'm Teacher Birdy. If you will please stand one by one and tell me your name, then I'll be sure to remember." She glanced down at the first graders, little birds in a row. "Let's start with this fine young man at the end of the front row."

Shy with this unexpected honor, little Peter Keim barely managed to find the floor with his feet and blurt his name. Then the rest of the first graders, the largest group according to Birdy's roster, wobbled up one after the other, five in all.

Birdy noticed a murmur from the back of the room grow bolder and bolder. She knew it belonged to Luke Schrock, adding his own commentary to each child. She knew Luke well. Everyone in Stoney Ridge did. If there was trouble to be had in the town, its source could be pinpointed to Jesse Stoltzfus or Luke Schrock. Often, both. You had to watch your step around those two.

"Tharah Thook," said a second grader.

Birdy's forefinger traced down the roster. "Tara, I'm sorry but I don't seem to have you on the roll."

"Tharah," she said again.

"Hannah?" Birdy tried again.

A snort came from the back of the room. Birdy spied the source — Ethan Troyer. "Perhaps you can help me identify this child?"

Caught off-guard, Ethan gulped out, "Sarah. Sarah Zook." Then he glanced nervously in Luke's direction.

"Of course!" Birdy said to Sarah. "You're Gideon and Sadie's daughter."

The next few grades proceeded without fanfare. Then Ethan Troyer stood up. "Teacher Birdy, my name is pronounced Eee-thon."

"You want me to call you Eee-thon?"

In the back of the room, Luke yelled out, "Yup! That's what we call him. Eee-thon." All the boys in the back row nodded their heads enthusiastically.

"I'll make a note. Next student, please."

Molly Stoltzfus raised her hand as high as it would go, then sprang up and identified herself. "My name is Margaret Stoltzfus. You can call me Margaret but everyone calls me Molly."

"Actually, everyone calls her the class hippo," Luke piped up, a foxy grin spreading over his face.

Molly dropped her head, her cheeks flaming red, and slipped back into her desk.

In the hush, all the children turned to watch Birdy intently as she deliberated. These were the moments she had dreaded, the moments she knew she would need the wisdom of Solomon.

Suddenly, Luke yelped loud enough to raise the hair of the dead. "I've been shot!" He clutched his neck with both hands. The entire class swiveled in their seats to see the severity of Luke's injury. Several sets of feet drummed on the floor excitedly. Heads turned back and forth between Luke and Birdy; everyone seemed interested in how the new teacher would fare with this crisis.

Breathing a little hard, Birdy walked to the back of the room and slid down onto one knee in front of Luke. She could see a red welt forming on his neck. "It does look like you've been stung by a bee. There's a clean rag on my desk and a glass of water you can dip it into. That might help the swelling." Quietly, she whispered, "And then sit up front on the bench next to my desk."

Luke took his time about getting onto his feet and made a face at the whole process, dramatically unfolding himself from a desk that was too small for him. He waited for a moment, a sneer on his face with one hand on his injury, standing tall above Birdy, who was still kneeling.

She tried to appear unperturbed. Slowly, she rose to a standing position, towering over Luke, until he had to lift his chin to face her. By the time she reached her full height, he looked uneasy. And then his shoulders slumped and he trudged up to the front bench, glaring at each student as he went.

Catching a second wind, Birdy marched to the front of the class to resume roll call. She hoped that sitting on the front bench might cure Luke's cheekiness for the rest of the day, though she did keep hearing snickers. The rest of the class reeled off names without further event until the last student of all. Nathan Kropf, a boy who was making another stab at eighth grade. He was a sweet boy, an earnest one, and his mind moved as slowly as his large body. "Teacher Birdy, I just thought you should know someone stuck a sign on your backside."

Birdy gasped and reached behind her to feel a piece of paper. She grabbed it: "The Jolly Green Giant." She looked down. Her dress. It was her favorite, a sea green that had a shimmer to it, a color she particularly loved because it always gave her a boost of confidence. No longer.

She could see she had her work cut out for her.

High, thin clouds kept the sun dim, and David hardly saw a shadow as he walked down the road. Tired from brooding — tired *of* brooding — David turned his thoughts to his blessings: his six children, each one so unique, so dear to him. The work God had given him as a minister, to look after the spiritual needs of those entrusted to his care.

And the store.

For David it was always the best moment of the day when he arrived at the Bent N' Dent to start the morning. To his way of thinking, an Amish store was the heart of a community. Nearly every church member, old to young, flowed through that front door in the course of a week, giving him a chance to see how each one was faring. He thought back to two days ago, when the five elderly sisters from the Sisters' House came in for their weekly groceries. They had lived together for so many years that they had grown to resemble each other, wizened and bent as apostrophes and nearly telegraphic in their talk. He had great affection for them and was saddened to see how rapidly Emma's dementia was advancing. She could no longer recall her four sisters' names, though last Sunday, he had noticed that she could remember the verses of every hymn sung at church.

Strange, how the mind held some information and dispensed with other.

David smiled to himself as he poured tablespoon after tablespoon of fresh coffee grounds into the coffeemaker. Yes, he loved being a storekeeper and all this store represented.

The door flung open. Freeman Glick filled the doorway, as commanding a figure as Moses, and bellowed, "David," as if identifying David to himself. Freeman's brother Levi peered over his shoulder as he pronounced, "I'm here on church business."

"Strictly business," Levi echoed.

Freeman Glick always looked freshly ironed, with a touch of starch. Not his clothing; Freeman himself. His shaggy brown eyebrows knitted, contemplating David in either bewilderment or extreme irritation, it was always hard to tell which. A hard look came into those dark eyes.

"Would you like some coffee, first?"

"I don't drink coffee," Freeman announced.

"He don't," Levi added.

Freeman stepped forward with a frown etching his forehead. "Two more boys dropped out of baptism class."

"We've got a real crisis on our hands," Levi said, nodding solemnly.

And it started with your sermon, was what they were thinking. David could practically hear them spit out the words.

"We've got to keep the young people here," Freeman said. "They're our future."

"And how do you propose to do that? You can't force someone into getting baptized."

"We can make it more appealing."

"More appealing?"

"It's time to adjust baptism classes."

"Adjust?"

"Shorten. Condense. It's the only answer."

With difficulty David held his tongue from asking, "To what question?"

"You've done it before. You did it last spring with Tobe Schrock."

"I didn't *condense* the 18 Articles of the Confessions of Dordrecht." Normally, while everyone sang hymns, the ministers met with those who planned to be baptized and taught two Articles at a time. David had met with Tobe Schrock midweek to go through the Articles and help him catch up with the class. But he *never* abbreviated the lessons.

"David, times are changing," Freeman said. "Young people don't have the attention span they used to. We can talk these boys into staying if we promise to make a few adjustments."

"Like . . . shortcutting over the Articles."

"Shortening," Freeman said crisply. "Condensing." He took a step closer to David with a look on his face like the business end of an ax. "Must you resist everything?" He was used to having his instructions obeyed.

"How are you going to encourage these boys to get baptized? Through pressuring their parents about finances?"

Freeman waved his hand as if brushing away a pesky fly.

"You never discussed meeting families to discuss finances with either Abraham or me."

"There's no need for four of us to meet with families. Besides, doing an annual financial review is something many church districts do."

"Trustees are *chosen* by the church members. When the bishop and the minister self-appoint themselves as trustees and burst into people's homes and ask them to take an inventory of everything they own — it becomes intimidation."

Freeman and Levi exchanged a glance. "We do nothing of the sort. We want to make sure everyone is using their resources wisely and properly." Freeman took a step closer to David, hands on his hips, long beard jutting. "And you might be surprised to learn that three families are in serious debt. Last year's heavy autumn rains took a toll on the harvest and this year is looking just as bad. The price of feed is still rising. Meanwhile, milk prices are low and going lower. We'll be lucky to break even. We need a good year just to keep our heads above water." He crossed his arms over his large chest. "And then there's the unexpected expenses. Ephraim Yoder, for example. His hospital bills are already sky-high and going higher."

"Exorbitant," Levi added. "Outrageous."

"We'll host a fundraiser," David said, "like we always do, to help pay those bills. Ephraim and Sadie won't be alone in this."

A loud snort punctuated the air. This came from Levi. "A fundraiser? That's like squeezing blood from a turnip."

Freeman nodded in agreement. "I keep telling you that our church is facing some serious difficulties. Plenty of families are talking about cashing out and moving elsewhere. I don't know that this church is going to be around much longer."

"Freeman, I run a store," David said

slowly, not quite able to conceal his impatience with this subject. "I know how many people aren't settling their accounts. I'm not blind to the kind of troubles that people are facing. Our church has problems, of course — what church doesn't? But we have to keep in mind we are primarily ministers. We are not dealing with people as problems. We're calling them to worship God. Our responsibility is not to fix people. It's to lead people in the worship of God and to lead them in living a holy life."

"Our responsibility is to make sure this church survives for our children and their children."

No, David thought. *That is not our responsibility.* "The church does not belong to us. It belongs to God."

Freeman narrowed his eyes. "I don't need a reminder."

"He's the bishop," Levi said.

David caught sight of someone walking toward the store. "Is there anything else? I need to get my workday started." He couldn't resist adding, "You know, to stay afloat."

Freeman and Levi were not amused. "No one is forcing you to stay in Stoney Ridge, David."

There. Freeman had landed his punch.

"In the meantime, you're to condense the baptism classes. End of discussion."

"It's not right."

"You heard me."

"You heard him," Levi said.

"I won't do it."

Freeman tipped his head toward his brother. "Well, then, Levi will take on your teaching responsibility."

And *that,* he realized, was what he'd been after all along. David eyed him steadily and spoke two words. "I see." And he did too. In that moment, he saw Freeman quite well.

A customer came in and Freeman and Levi left. David made small talk with the customer, an English tourist who wanted to stock up on spices while she was sightseeing. After she left, he refilled his coffee cup and held the warm mug between his hands, ruminating on the Glick brothers' newest idea.

Condense the Articles? What kind of future did the church have when no one would even know what it meant to be a church member? Without any appreciation for what their ancestors had done to preserve the faith?

If Freeman and Levi were so quick to dispense with honoring tradition in obvious ways, what might they be dispensing with in less obvious ways?

The day passed slowly with bursts of customers, then long gaps of quiet. A typical day at a store.

Around noon, Bethany Schrock arrived for her shift, Katrina at her side with her arm around her as if she needed shoring and bolstering, and David quickly realized why. Bethany looked sad and sorrowful, her eyes red and swollen.

"Bethany, are you all right?" David asked. She looked *awful,* truly dreadful. Her hair hadn't been combed, her prayer cap was slightly cockeyed, her dress was wrinkled. The sight alarmed him; Bethany was a young woman who took great care in her appearance.

She burst into tears and buried her head in her hands.

He'd seen her only yesterday. What in the world had happened? Flustered, David looked to Katrina for an explanation of what was distressing Bethany. She was a girl with a wide range of emotions, including an explosive temper, but he'd never seen her full of woe. Not like this. "Did someone die? Not her grandmother? Did Vera pass?" As long as David had known Vera Schrock, she constantly warned everyone of her imminent demise.

"Jimmy Fisher is leaving town," Katrina said. "Peter talked him into joining him out in Colorado."

"Peter? Our Peter?" David's nephew?

"They think they're cowboys out in the Wild West," Bethany said, her voice full of tearful scorn. "After all we've been through, Jimmy just ups and leaves."

Oh no. Jimmy Fisher had been attending baptism class, urged on by Bethany. Everyone thought he was finally growing up. Finally getting close to making commitments that lasted longer than the end of the week.

Another one, gone. David had to admit, his sermon was having a cascading effect. He cringed, thinking of the reproach he could expect from Freeman.

David's stomach tightened. How did Jimmy Fisher get his mother's blessing to leave? Edith Fisher had relied on his help with her chicken and egg business, especially after Tobe and Naomi Schrock moved to Kentucky to start their own chicken and egg business. He couldn't imagine that Edith would let Jimmy leave without protest. She was a woman who didn't like the wind to blow unless she told it which way to go.

Things started to piece together in David's mind. Maybe those chickens were why he left. Jimmy hated chickens.

A fresh round of tears started up in Bethany and he quickly found a box of tissues to hand to her. "Maybe he'll be back soon." He hoped both boys would find what they were looking for — adventure, no doubt — get it out of their system, and come home to Stoney Ridge.

"And maybe he'll love it there and never come back. Maybe he'll meet someone else and marry her and raise a passel of Colorado children." She grabbed a tissue, gasping between sobs.

Katrina nodded deeply, confirming that Bethany's prediction was entirely justified. "Jimmy gave his horse to Galen King."

"Lodestar? He gave Lodestar away?" David felt the vise around his stomach tighten another turn. Jimmy Fisher loved that horse of his. He had big plans to use him as a stud and start a horse-breeding business. Plans that never seemed to get off the ground.

"He's never coming back!" Bethany wailed. "There's no men left in Stoney Ridge! Only toothless old men and bald babies."

David let that implied criticism pass. When Katrina said she had to get back to Thelma's, he encouraged Bethany to go with her, but she insisted she wanted to stay and work, to keep busy. He went to his desk in the storeroom to finish up some orders. Out in the shop front, there alternated long jags of crying and long stretches of silence. Mixed in between were big, sad sighs.

This workday was a lost cause.

It took some doing, but David finally convinced Bethany to go home, that it was a slow day and there weren't enough customers to keep the store open — which was partially true. A little before three o'clock, he couldn't take it anymore. He closed the store, and walked to school to meet his daughters. He wanted to hear about the first day of school while it was fresh on their minds. Nearly halfway there, he regretted that he hadn't driven the buggy today. The strong north wind that had come in to blow away lingering clouds from last night was now surrounding him at every turn, slamming against him. He barely snatched his hat before it went sailing, and he walked the rest of the way with one hand firmly on its brim.

A metaphor, he realized, for this was how he felt as a minister in Stoney Ridge — pushing against a strong but invisible force. Maybe he *should* consider returning to Ohio. Certainly, he wasn't doing much good here. Maybe his children had enough time away to heal by now. Maybe the fact that Katrina's ex-boyfriend was getting married was a sign — it was time to go home.

As he turned onto the road that led to the schoolhouse, he saw that the playground had already emptied out. Only Birdy was left, standing on the porch in nearly the same spot she had been this morning, her eyes fixed on the sky.

"Isn't it amazing?" she said, pointing to a hawk riding the wind. "That majestic creature is playing. The wind is his friend."

David laughed. "After trying to walk straight into the wind to get here, it's no friend of mine." He looked to the hawk flying low on the horizon. The hawk aimed his head toward the sun and thrust his body upward. When he reached an invisible peak, he adjusted his angle, succumbed to the force of the wind, and gently glided left, then right, down, and up again.

"It's such a vivid picture of the Christian life."

"The same thought had just occurred to me," David said, more to himself than to Birdy. "The wind is constantly pushing us backwards, making life more difficult."

Eyes on the bird, Birdy shook her head slowly. "I meant, the hawk. About not fighting the wind, but embracing it. Recognizing it as God's presence, engulfing us."

David turned toward her, surprised at the parallel she had drawn. Surprised by the depth of her thoughts. When she realized he was staring at her, she became awkward and ill at ease, backing up toward the schoolhouse door until she bumped into it. "I have a few things to finish up before I go home."

"Birdy, hold on."

She spun around and looked at him. She had brown eyes. Warm like coffee. Funny, he'd never really noticed those eyes before. They were the same dark color as Freeman's, David realized, having just seen him earlier today, yet Birdy's eyes were soft and sweet. Frankly, despite her substantial height, everything about her was soft and sweet. It was hard to believe she was related to Freeman and Levi. "How did the day go?"

Birdy thought for a moment, then grinned. "Let's just say there's room for improvement."

On the way back to the store, David realized how tense he had felt as he'd walked to the schoolhouse, how tightly he had been clenching his muscles. Fighting the wind. He deliberately tried to loosen his body by moving his neck and arms about.

Instead of perceiving the force of the rushing wind as an enemy, he began to imagine it as the presence of the Holy Spirit enveloping him. And if that were true, then it was a reminder that God was with him, in this and around this. He had been fighting so hard, ready to give up, exhausted by the fight, because he assumed he was alone. He wasn't. And he wouldn't give up on this little church. Not now. Not yet.

Something incredible happened. He suddenly became relaxed. His soul settled, as if it had found its still point. He found peace.

A great spiritual lesson about submission, he realized, had been given to him today, through two unlikely sources: Birdy Glick and a bird.

For the third day in a row, Jesse had missed breakfast. The household was well into its day as he opened cupboard doors, trying to remember which one held cereal boxes. His father came down the stairs two at a time and went straight toward the door. Catching sight of him, his father backtracked and stuck his head in the kitchen. "Morning, son," he said pleasantly, "what's left of it."

Jesse lifted the cereal box. "Care to join me?"

"No, I need to get to the store. A delivery is due in by ten. And you don't have time for a leisurely breakfast, either. Hank Lapp is expecting you."

What? So his father had been serious about this buggy repairman notion?

His father studied him in a way he knew all too well. "It's time to put that head and body of yours to work."

"I see." He wished he did. "Dad, I've been thinking it over. I don't think I'm really suited for buggy work."

"Son, you seem to think you're not suited for most employment."

That was a fair statement, one that Jesse agreed with. The problem was that boredom set in so quickly in a routine job, and his mind left for greener pastures. "It doesn't seem fair to Hank Lapp to have an apprentice who doesn't want to learn how to repair buggies."

His father waved away that concern as he opened the door. "Just remember . . . inspiration follows perspiration." He stuck his head back around the kitchen doorframe. "Hank was expecting you at Windmill Farm two hours ago."

Hank Lapp. Jesse wasn't quite sure about that wild-eyed fellow, who always seemed slightly off-kilter.

For now, another bowl of cereal would definitely lift his spirits and mask the fact that he had a very real problem to face. Employment.

Jesse peered into the open door of the buggy shop, though there was no sign of life. It was a glut and bedlam of a place, utter chaos. Tools lay scattered on every horizontal surface, crinkled brown bags filled with tacks and grommets and nails lined the floor, spare buggy parts sat heaped in piles, fishing rods angled against a wall. Spectacles lay atop a worn ledger — had Hank Lapp forgotten them? Jesse poked around in the dimly lit room, wondering how anyone could ever find a tool in this mess. His heart sank. This apprenticeship was a terrible idea. Then a sliver of hope grew in his heart. If Hank Lapp were nowhere to be found, it seemed entirely reasonable for Jesse to return home. What good was an apprentice without a tutor?

Jesse was of medium height — still growing, he fervently hoped — but when he turned around, he was staring straight into a shock of wild white hair. Hank Lapp stood before him, wearing work coveralls that showed no evidence of work. One eye peered right at Jesse, the other eye wandered to the open door.

"Why, Jesse Stoltzfus," Hank said, his voice as gravelly as a gizzard. "You've gone and gotten tall!"

Jesse swept his hat off his head and bent over at the waist in an exaggerated bow. "Your humble apprentice is at your service, O wise one."

Hank held out a knobby hand for a shake and grinned at Jesse like an elf. Although he was only somewhere in his late sixties, he did not look strong: he was a slight man, with a willowy look, as if the powerful gusts of wind that swept through Stoney Ridge yesterday could've easily lifted him up and carried him off. In his mind's eye, Jesse saw Hank in his overalls and shirt, arms flailing, being picked up by the wind and cartwheeled through the sky, off toward Philadelphia somewhere, and dropped down suddenly on the ground, confused, in a bustling city.

"What's so funny?" Hank asked, frowning.

Jesse corrected himself quickly. "I'm sorry," he said. "I was thinking of something else. Funny things come to mind."

"Well, don't keep them to yourself. This world is in serious shortage of laughing matters."

"Hardly." A tall, thin, stern-faced woman stood at the open door, fixing a look on Jesse as if she had shrewdly caught him at something.

"FERN! Here's my new apprentice, Jesse. He's going to take over the buggy shop when I retire."

A small smirk lifted Fern's stern countenance. "I thought you'd already retired."

"Nope! Just the tired part." Amused at his own joke, Hank slapped his knee in delight. "Jesse, best part of the job is taking the noon meal in Fern's kitchen."

Jesse had hoped the wages might be the best part of the job.

Fern looked Jesse up and down. "I can tell from here, your belly button is hitting your backbone. Wash up, the pair of you, and come on up to the house."

The table was laid for three when Jesse followed Hank up to the house. Fern popped out of the kitchen with a pan of hot-from-the-oven cornbread and nodded to where he was to sit, saying, "Amos won't be joining us."

Tucking in his napkin, Hank dropped his head to signal a silent prayer. Then Fern speared a broccoli crown and passed the dish to Jesse. "You must have hit Hank when he was hard up for help."

"I was as taken by surprise as you appear to be," Jesse said honestly.

"Do you have experience with buggy repairs?"

"Not really."

"He doesn't hire just anybody."

Hire! There was a word that appealed to Jesse's sensibilities. He felt a glimmer of hope rise within. "We hadn't quite finished that conversation when you called us in." He looked expectantly down the length of the table at Hank.

Sadly, the hint fell flat on Hank's ears. He was preoccupied with buttering his cornbread, lavishly and thoroughly. "Where's Amos?" He lifted his empty coffee cup.

Fern poured coffee into Hank's cup, then filled her own.

"Sugar there behind you," Hank grunted. Jesse reached over to the counter and handed him a sugar bowl. Hank stirred in the sugar, added cream, took a sip, added more sugar, took another sip, let out a loud "Ahhhhh," apparently satisfied.

"Freeman Glick is making his rounds to assess everyone's finances, and Amos had to go down to the bank to get a copy of the most recent statement."

Hank looked like he had bit down on a

sour pickle. "Freeman's poking his nose into everybody's business."

Between bites, Jesse asked, "He's the minister, isn't he?"

"Bishop," Fern said. "Elmo Beiler passed on a month or so ago and Freeman Glick drew the lot."

Hank lifted a fork in her direction. "I blame myself. I shouldn't have slept in that morning. Mighta changed everything." He shook his head. "Freeman Glick is the type who takes pleasure in kicking puppies." He glared at Jesse with his one good eye. "If you find yourself around him, you better watch your sweet —"

"Hank! Don't blaspheme."

"— step, is all I was gonna say, Fern."

"He's our bishop," Fern said, in a tone to put an end to Hank's tirade.

"That man is tougher than —" sawing strenuously at the piece of pork chop on his plate, Hank glanced in Fern's direction and hedged off — "leather."

"Hank, rules," Fern said. "Use a knife, not a fork."

"So Hank, I hoped you could enlighten me about the parameters of this gainful opportunity."

"Righto," Hank confirmed, spooning more sugar into his coffee.

"The kinds of hours you keep, for example. And then there's sala—"

"NOW YOU'RE TALKING!" Hank slapped the table resoundingly. "Come early, stay late!" A rooster belted out a loud crow, and Hank paled, then "Chickens!" came from his lips in a hoarse whisper. He thumped his chair down on all four legs and bolted to his feet. "Blast it all! I forgot to feed Edith's chickens. She'll skin me alive." And suddenly he bolted for the door.

Jesse popped the last crumb of cornbread into his mouth. "Edith?"

"Edith Fisher. Jimmy's leaving left her in a pinch with all those chickens to feed and clean up after. Hank's trying to help her out."

Fern Lapp and Jesse considered each other. An awkward silence filled the room — awkward, at least, for Jesse.

He finished swallowing his last bite of pork chop and bowed his head, then quietly rose to his feet. "I thank you, Fern Lapp, for the splendiferous and robust meal."

"Save your charm for the girls," she said. "You don't need all that embroidery with me."

Jesse blinked innocently back. "Why, I meant it!"

She nodded. "I'm sure you always do."

97

"I'll be off, then."

"Just where do you think you're going? You're on the clock." Her arched eyebrows expressed all that was needed.

Jesse wondered if it would make a difference if he pointed out that there really was no clock because there really was no work to do because there was no boss. Upon deeper consideration, he chose not to debate that point. Fern Lapp did not seem to be a woman who invited questions. "Regrettably, I am not seer enough to know what Hank's intentions are." He smiled, then swallowed it when she frowned at him. He tried again. "Unfortunately, in his haste to depart, Hank failed to give me instructions about what to do in his absence so that I could be of better assistance. Therefore I will wait until —"

Fern leaned over the table. "Boy, you have a brain. Make yourself useful." Her eyes swept downward toward the buggy shop. She swept a few dishes off the table and whisked them to the sink. "Freeman wants an inventory of everything on this farm. Every cow, every sheep, every tool. He said he wants it down to the number of nails in a brown paper bag. You get started on the buggy shop. And while you're making the inventory, do a little cleaning. We're hosting church in a week's time. Everything in that shop needs to be spick-and-span. I'll be down within the hour to check on your progress."

And that was definitely that.

Caught by surprise, Jesse had an odd feeling that the supervision of his apprenticeship had just changed hands and he was now reporting to Fern Lapp.

5

A blast of wind slammed into the windows, and upstairs something rattled.

Katrina stretched out under her covers, gobsmacked by the exhaustion that had plagued her for the last few days. She'd had indigestion all last night, so badly that she had to get up for Tums six or seven times, and it still bothered her now. Eating eased it a little, though the coleslaw she'd had for supper hadn't helped.

Neither had the fact that John had yet to return her phone call.

She had tossed and turned every night since making that call, dozing off and on, reviewing their relationship, flashing on memories she'd struggled to stop thinking of. It amazed her to think that leaving a simple phone message for John would cause her to lose sleep. How many times would she and John sit together and talk for hours about everything and nothing? Just ordinary things, all of it.

Gone.

She wondered if Bethany was feeling the same way after Jimmy Fisher's abrupt departure yesterday. Why did love have to be so difficult, so filled with peaks and valleys? More valleys than peaks, it seemed.

She finally gave up on sleep and got out of bed. She checked on Thelma, listened for a moment to her whiffling snore, and decided to take a walk before breakfast. A soft morning light was gently, slowly filling the sky. Chickens clucked and flapped when they saw her, expecting breakfast. Her ladies, Thelma called them. "You'll have to wait a little longer, ladies," she said as she passed the henhouse. She took a deep breath of sweet morning air and found that it eased her anxiety a little. Just a little, but it helped.

She climbed the path that led to the moss hill. The sight of the morning sun hitting the bright green giant pincushions caught her right in the throat and she halted, almost aching. The rocks were almost glowing, nearly iridescent, in the slant of the morning sun.

She sat down on a rock and took a deep breath, in and out. The pain she'd been carrying let go, as if she'd dropped a heavy backpack to the ground.

This. This was what she needed. Time alone, time without responsibilities. Time to think. To heal.

She turned around and saw Andy cresting the hill. She lifted a hand in a wave.

"You're up early," Andy said. He'd come up the path, carrying a shovel in one gloved hand and a heavy burlap bag in the other. He pushed the brim of his straw hat back with one hand, and she could see that he'd been working hard. Sweat rolled down the sides of his face.

"I couldn't sleep."

He hesitated, then set down his shovel and sack and sat down on the rock next to hers. He was staring at the trees that lined the base of the hill, and this gave Katrina a chance to study him. He was quite a fine-looking man. Different than John, but definitely attractive in his own way. She wondered what Bethany Schrock might think of Andy Miller, now that Jimmy Fisher had abandoned her for Colorado.

He turned toward her so suddenly that he caught her staring at him and his blue eyes crinkled with amusement. Probably used to women admiring him, she thought.

"I've never given much thought to moss before I came to stay with Thelma."

Andy brushed a hand over the cushion top of a rock. "Moss is an all-purpose sponge. It stores water, releases nutrients, houses tiny critters. Pretty amazing stuff, actually. But it has to be harvested carefully."

"How do you harvest it? By stripping the rocks?"

"Yes, but you never gather it all," he said. "Not if you want it to grow back again. Always leave clumps behind to help the plant regenerate. It's spore-driven. To thrive, it needs moisture, cool temperatures, and shade. And plenty of runoff, because moss can't tolerate saturation." He spread his palm in a wide half circle. "Just what this hillside has to offer." He rose to his full height, towering over her.

"How long will it take to grow back?"

"All depends — if it's taken properly, it survives and grows back. Sheet moss is the most common moss that's harvested illegally. That's why I'm trying to harvest it properly, here." He tilted his head. "Come with me. I'll show you where I've been harvesting this morning." He led her through a wooded area on the north side of Thelma's hill and pointed to a section on the hillside that had been harvested. She had never noticed moss before, and suddenly, it was everywhere. On the trees, on the ground, on the rocks.

"So that's what's in the sack you were carrying? You're taking a sack of clumps to the greenhouse to transplant?"

"Yes. I place those clumps of moss on a similar substrate. It's critical to keep them moist until they reestablish rhizoids."

He had launched into that overexplaining thing, a characteristic of most every male she knew, but she also realized this was as much as Andy had ever spoken to her — he didn't have much to say at meals, only to answer Thelma's questions — and, curious, she tossed out another question. "Where did you learn so much about moss?"

"My grandmother." His face softened and Katrina could see that he had special feelings for her. "She loved plants, all kinds. Taught me everything I know. She died when I was thirteen. Thelma reminds me of her."

Oh! So that's why he was so protective of Thelma. Frankly, she couldn't imagine anyone better suited to help Thelma get her moss business up and running. To think he was the first one who called about the job! A fortuitous event. "Amazing to think that she found you, or you found her."

His mouth tightened, and something

flashed over him, a memory of his grandmother, she thought, sensing there was a story there, one she'd like to hear. She found herself intrigued by Andy. She couldn't quite figure him out. At times he seemed so kind and tender, other times, aloof and a little mysterious.

Then he gave her one of those dazzling smiles. "Pretty fortunate for both of us."

"So, this work. You really like it, then?" She wondered if he had plans to stay, or if he was a tumbleweed, like she was.

He gave a quick nod. "Picking moss is hard work on a hot day. Sweaty. Dirty. But I like the solitude and independence of it." He grinned. He reached down and picked up his sack. "I'd rather harvest moss than deal with most people," he said, hefting the heavy sack over his shoulder. "Did you know the color green is supposed to reduce stress?"

She could believe that. As she stroked the soft carpet she felt less stress. Peaceful, even. She felt the first glimmer of optimism, a sliver of hope that everything was going to be all right.

David stood in the small cemetery where so many of Stoney Ridge's earliest worshipers were buried. It was a pretty spot, this hill, shaded by trees. He was driving past it this afternoon and stopped by, just on impulse. He knelt in the grass by Elmo's new grave and brushed some leaves away from the plain marker. This afternoon the sun shone warm and bright in the sky, but on the day they'd buried Elmo, it had been raining. He heard the clip-clop of a horse trotting along the road as it slowed to a stop. He looked over to see Amos Lapp climb out of his buggy and make his way through the graveyard.

"You've saved me an errand," Amos said with a grin. "I was heading over to your house and saw your horse." He dipped down at the grave of his first wife, Maggie Zook Lapp, to brush away a spider's web. "David, I thought you should know there's rumor brewing that Freeman wants to split the church."

David wasn't surprised by that news. Disappointed, but not surprised. He looked down at Elmo's grave. "I didn't know Elmo well, but I did know that he was passionate about keeping the community intact."

"That he was. Stoney Ridge was one of the first Amish communities in America."

David turned slowly in a full circle, his mind thinking about each family that filled the land he gazed on. Mattie and Sol Riehl, whose son Danny was one of the brightest boys he'd ever met. He sensed a mantle on Danny's future, that God had an unusual plan for him. Another half turn and he was looking at Carrie and Abel's farm. How many children did they have now? Over eight, at last count. If they moved away, like he'd heard they were considering, they would take a substantial part of Stoney Ridge's future with them.

Another slight shift to the right and he saw the rose fields of Rose Hill Farm. Jonah and Lainey Riehl had moved to Florida over a year ago, leaving Bess and Billy Lapp to manage the roses. They wouldn't leave, would they? He'd heard such stories of Bertha Riehl's passion for her old-fashioned roses. Would Bess be able to leave her grandmother's roses?

Another turn and David could spot the tops of the pine trees that belonged to the Inn at Eagle Hill. Certainly, Rose and Galen King wouldn't leave after all the work they'd done to make the inn profitable. But he knew that Galen's uncle had asked him to move to Kentucky to take over his horse breeding farm, and if there was one thing that could make Galen leave Stoney Ridge . . . it would be the lure of horses.

Even Abraham, the deacon, and his wife,

Esther, were considering a move to live closer to family in Iowa.

"Amos, am I wrong in wanting Freeman to slow down? To think of the long-term consequences of his decisions?"

Amos swept his hat off his head and ruffled his hair. "Maybe it would help if you tried to see things from Freeman's point of view."

"I do understand his concerns. I do. Farmland in Lancaster County has become exorbitant."

"It's not just the price of a farm. Taxes are increasing. Folks can cash out their farms and live on half as much in another state. Jonah Riehl told his daughter Bess that he lives all year in Florida on just the taxes he paid in Pennsylvania."

"So you think Freeman is on the right path?"

Amos took a long time answering. "He's our bishop."

For a moment their gazes met, then David averted his face to hide his thoughts. *Yes, Freeman is our bishop. That means his word is final. That means the entire community depends on his leadership.* But he also knew that settlements failed when leadership failed.

Squinting, Amos put his hat back on and

looked out over the sun-seared graves. "The Lord chose Freeman to receive the bishop's lot. Maybe it's better not to think too much about his ways. To just try and accept his will." He adjusted his hat on his head. "Well, I'll be off. I just wanted to be sure you had a heads up about the church split."

As Amos walked back to his buggy, David pondered his remarks. God's ways were indeed mysterious. But this conflict with Freeman didn't feel like something to file under that subject.

David had a strange sense of things being out of kilter. It felt as if he had to keep his guard up, alert to whatever was coming. But what was coming?

It happened two more times that week. Luke Schrock was stung or bitten by some insect, right during class. If Birdy hadn't seen the welts swell up on his neck right before her eyes, she would've thought he was just trying to get attention. Luke would do anything to get noticed. But he was starting to look like he had some kind of hideous disease or an unusual case of hives.

Today, Friday afternoon, it happened during the spelling bee, a favorite event for the children. No sooner had Birdy announced that it was time for the bee than she was nearly swept aside by the students' stampede to line up along two sides of the room. She paired first graders with eighth graders, second and seventh, third and sixth, fourth and fifth. Each child had a fair chance at winning, and the students were getting a taste of teamwork. No one was excluded.

A one-room schoolhouse, Birdy was quickly discovering, had a way of acting like a giant sponge: younger children soaked up the lessons given to the older children.

On this warm September afternoon, the students were rattling off letters in no time at all, knocking each other out one by one, and the normally quiet schoolhouse was filled with exhortations of encouragement or despair, depending on the team's spelling ability. Birdy added her own noise: "Well done!" or "Excellent!" or a more subdued "Better study up a bit for next time."

Lyle Smucker went down on *gnat,* neglecting the *g* and adding a surplus *t.* After a frenzied whispered conference with her teammates, Sarah Zook went down on it, too. Ethan Troyer spelled it correctly, then slipped up *asthma,* spelling it *asma.* Ruthie flounced down in defeat on *receipt,* forgetting the *p.* Luke Schrock haughtily spelled it correctly, and Birdy decided he needed to be taken down a peg. She tossed him *clique,* a small group of people who do not readily allow others to join them, hoping the double meaning might not be lost on Luke. He controlled a tight clique of his own choosing.

"C-l-i-c-k," he said.

"You have to be careful about words," Birdy said, waving him out of the round. "Words can be sneaky."

Luke traipsed back to his seat with a flaming red face.

A few more rounds reduced the teams to two students left standing at the blackboard. Molly Stoltzfus, an earnest fifth grader, and Noah Yoder, a tall and skinny seventh grader who was definitely not included in Luke's clique.

Molly was up next to spell the word *hoard.* "How's it pronounced again?" she asked Birdy.

"Ho-ar-d," Birdy sounded out the word crisply.

Molly barely got the first few letters out — "W-h-o-r" — as Luke Schrock quickly realized the direction where she was going. He howled with laughter, slapping his desk with his hands, which set the other big boys off in gales of raucous hoots and hollers, though Birdy doubted they had any idea

111

what was so funny.

And suddenly, in mid-guffaw, Luke stopped laughing. His eyes went wide, a look as if he'd been stricken. "I've been shot!"

The big boys leaped up to examine the extent of his injury. Ethan contributed a panicky, "I think he's dying!" The rest of the class scrambled out of their chairs to see Luke writhing on the floor, grasping his neck with his hands.

Sensing a riot, Birdy leapt in. "Everyone! Take your seats!" She helped Luke outside to put a rag of cold water on the red welt forming on his neck. How curious! Inside, she looked carefully at the ceiling, studying corners, nooks, and crannies for signs of a wasp's nest. There was *nothing.* The building was so newly constructed there wasn't time yet for a spider to spin her web.

This was a frightfully distressing situation to Birdy, especially because it kept recurring at the most inopportune times. Luke's neck was starting to look like a battlefield.

Katrina was supposed to be taking care of Thelma and yet it was the other way around. She came into the house with a basket full of sun-dried laundry and found Thelma in the tiny kitchen, mixing breadcrumbs and eggs and ground pork and ground beef in a big glass bowl, one-handed.

"What are you doing?" Katrina said, putting the basket on a chair by the door. "Making meat loaf?"

"Seemed like a good day for it, with the look of those clouds. Andy won't be able to get much done this afternoon." She pointed to the coffeepot. "There's coffee fresh brewed."

The thought of acidic coffee on her turbulent tummy made Katrina feel woozy. "Thanks, but no. I think I'll just fold this laundry here."

"How are you feeling, Katrina?" Thelma said. "You seem a little under the weather."

"I'm fine. I'm . . . preoccupied." She reached for a brightness she didn't feel and redirected the conversation, a skill she'd finely honed in recent weeks. "Trying to absorb all that I can about moss from Andy. It's really quite interesting. Funny how you can see moss and walk on it and never think a thing about it."

Thelma slipped the meat loaf into the oven and turned toward Katrina, a delighted look on her face. "You're catching my vision! And here it's been, all these years, waiting to be noticed." She refilled her cup of coffee — one-handed — and stopped to take a sip. "When I tell others that I've gone into the moss business, they look at me as if I might be getting a little dotty. But this is the way I can hold on to my home."

"Did you ever consider selling your property?"

Thelma's eyes narrowed. "Don't tell me Freeman's gotten to you too."

"No! No. It just seems like a lot of work at your age. At any age," she quickly added when she saw the huffy look Thelma got at the mention of age. She could be touchy about some things. "Why would Freeman want you to sell?"

"Freeman is my nephew. He says a widow of my age should be living with family to be looked after, but I'm not moving into the Big House and have Freeman and Levi's wives fuss over me." She leaned toward Katrina and cupped half her mouth with one hand, conspiratorially. "He also knows that this property could be sold for a tidy bundle."

"You aren't even a little, tiny bit tempted to sell?"

"Not for a moment," she said, pushing her lower lip out. "Certainly not to developers. They'll ruin it, every bit of it."

It was common knowledge that Thelma and Elmo's land was worth quite a bit of money, but not as farmland. Developers wanted to turn it into a spot for outlet malls. It was close to the highway, but not too close. Katrina remembered the developers had plans drawn up to present to Thelma at a meeting Freeman had arranged, but she didn't show up for it. Freeman was outraged.

Thelma shook her head. "No, I'm not budging. And besides, I love this new adventure. It's . . . like starting a new book and not knowing how it will end. It's . . . invigorating!"

Thelma eagerly explained some ideas she had to build the business — convert a shed into a gift shop, add another greenhouse. Katrina wasn't really listening but wondering about Thelma, and why she felt so comfortable and happy in her company. How could someone be so full of joy? At her age, even after her husband's death?

The impact Thelma made upon her — upon most people, she realized — was all out of proportion to her words or her appearance. She wasn't imposing or commanding in any way. She wasn't a very big woman. She wasn't even particularly brainy. But something radiated from Thelma and, ponder as Katrina might, she couldn't understand it.

The buzzer went off and Thelma hurried to the oven. She tugged the oven door open with her cane. She pulled out the meat loaf with her good hand in a big oven mitt, frowning at it.

"Thelma, how do you do it?"

"Do what?"

"How do you manage to have such an optimistic view of the future . . . even after you've had some pretty hard blows in life?"

"Life can certainly take some unexpected turns. We can only put ourselves in God's hands." She squirted ketchup on top of the meat loaf, then pushed the rack back into the oven and kneed the door to a close. "One thing I've learned, my dear, is that life is to be lived as it comes."

At supper, Andy asked if Katrina had heard anything back from her breeder friend. "I'd like to get a dog as soon as possible. This time of year, the raccoons are digging everything up to look for grubs. One section looks like it's been used by very bad golfers."

"I . . . haven't heard back yet," Katrina said, pouring water into glasses. "Probably, he's just busy." *But probably not.* By this point, it seemed John had no intention of returning her call.

Andy sat in the chair and spread his

116

napkin over his lap. "Maybe I should just go ahead and look for another dog."

"Let's give it just a few more days," she said quickly. She picked at her food, drawing a look of concern from Thelma.

"You're not eating. Aren't you feeling well, dear?"

Down the table, Andy's dark eyebrows squinched together in similar regard of her. Pushing away her plate, she said, "A touch of stomach disorder is all. Nothing a good night's sleep can't fix, I'm sure."

Later that night, flat on her back atop the coverlet while she stared at the ceiling, Katrina never felt less sure of anything.

One thing Jesse couldn't deny: Hank Lapp's lightning mood changes kept a person alert. His style of management was as curious as it was unpredictable. One day, he could be in high spirits, offering up corny jokes, talking a blue streak for hours on end. Then the next day, without warning, he would barge into the shop wearing the mournful expression of a hound dog on a cold trail, silent and sullen. It didn't take long for Jesse to realize that Hank's moods had nothing to do with the buggy repair business and everything to do with Edith Fisher's pleasure or displeasure with him.

Jesse had yet to touch a broken buggy — Hank was very territorial about those buggies, he had discovered — but he didn't have much interest in learning about buggies, anyway. The only thing Jesse did care about was to get some kind of recompense for his tireless apprentice work.

It was a mystery how the buggy shop managed to operate before he was there to catch all the tasks delegated from Hank, via Fern, to Jesse. Fern Lapp kept him hopping from chore to chore. If Jesse ever slowed down, even for a minute, *barely* a moment, she appeared out of nowhere, peering at him in that way she had — inspecting him as if she had missed some major facial feature — and instantly thought up something else for him to do. She was relentless, running him ragged.

Jesse looked around at the nooks and crannies of the buggy shop: Tools hung neatly on pegboards, cupboards and drawers were labeled and organized, the concrete floor was now visible, swept and clean. The only part of the shop Jesse didn't dare touch was Hank's desk — it was covered with stacks of paperwork, piled helter-skelter. Judging by the way Hank avoided his desk, Jesse knew there was something on it that he did not want to face.

If you were going to do a thing, Jesse believed, there was no point wasting time. He waited until he saw Fern had finished hanging white sheets on the clothesline and walked back to the house. Then he sauntered over to the buggy that Hank was working on and sat down, leaning his back against the wheel.

Without looking at him, Hank asked, "What's on your mind besides your hat?"

"What I need to know is the scope of my job."

"Scope of the job?" Rubbing his chin, Hank sat up and gazed into the shop, directly at his cluttered desk, as if some task for Jesse might be hiding behind one of the piles.

"Hank, we've never discussed the fiscal arrangements of this apprenticeship."

"Huh?"

"The monetary agreement."

Hank turned to him in exasperation. "Speak English."

Jesse sighed and held one hand in the air, rubbing his fingertips together. "Money, Hank. A wage. A salary."

At the mention of money Hank's long face grew longer. Slowly, he rose to his feet and lumbered into the buggy shop in search of a tool.

"Hank, you seem perturbed," Jesse said diplomatically.

Hank turned to him in exasperation. "I can't find anything since you got here." He started opening and shutting drawers. "WHERE'S MY FAVORITE WRENCH?"

Those unexpected bellows of Hank offended Jesse's sensibilities, as well as his eardrums. "Right in front of you. Hanging on the wall. It would bite your nose if you were any closer." Jesse pointed to the tidy row of tools, something he was rather proud of, though it had not received any mention by Hank or Fern. Not a word of thanks. "I put the wrenches in graduating sizes, left to right. Any apprentice worth his weight in gold would do the same."

Hank growled and grabbed a wrench off the pegboard. Straightening himself to new heights of white cowlick, he frowned fiercely down at him. "No shortage of opinions, I see."

"A man has to make a living, you know."

"I DO KNOW." He scratched his head as if digging out a thought. "The problem is, my income and my outgo run past each other in baffling ways." As he walked past his desk, overflowing with paper, he made an abrupt halt. Turning from the desk to face Jesse, he shook his head. "Jesse" —

there was a dip of doubt in his tone as he spoke it — "how are you at 'rithmetic?"

"My greatest strength. Sums come to me," he snapped his fingers, "like that." Sums of money left him with similar speed.

Hank dropped into his desk chair, visibly brightening. "So you've had experience with money?"

He tapped his head. "I'm faster than Dad's calculator at the store." Usually.

Hank yanked open drawers in his desk and pulled out handfuls of scraps and bits of papers. He dropped them all in an empty nail box and handed it to Jesse. "Here. They all got to be sorted out."

"I think I can manage that task." How hard could it be?

Hank settled into his chair. "I'm a little short of funds to put you on the payroll right now, seeing as how I'm a tad behind with my collections. If you can figure out my system —" he fixed his good eye on Jesse — "well then, whatever you collect, you can keep five percent."

"Fifteen."

"Ten."

"You drive a hard bargain." Jesse smiled, satisfied. "Hank Lapp, it's a deal."

He tapped on the box and smiled. "They're all yours now, Jesse."

And with that, Hank Lapp departed and Jesse was left with the onerous task of bill collecting.

6

The days fell into a pattern very quickly. Thelma and Katrina walked to the top of the hill and back each morning, regardless of foul weather. Some days, Thelma walked more slowly than others, some days she relied more heavily on her cane for balance than on other days. But she rarely missed that morning walk.

As they walked the dirt path that wound up the hill, Thelma would share stories of her life, and usually add a thought-provoking insight or two, something Katrina started to think of as coming across a blooming flower in the midst of a cornfield. "No one grows old by living, only by losing interest in living," or "Keep the past in the past."

She couldn't imagine Thelma Beiler ever being hearty and young the way, of course, she once had. The thought made her very sad. When she died, all this valuable knowledge would be lost.

In the mornings, Katrina worked in the vegetable garden, or cleaned house for Thelma, and also helped Andy out when he brought sacks of moss from the hillside down to the greenhouse. He taught her how to lay the moss on a moist substrate, so that it had all the conditions it wanted to spread. Once she got the hang of it, he would just hand off a sack to her. It allowed him to spend more time on the hill.

Each day, she tried to spend some time on the administrative side of Moss Hill — returning telephone messages, completing orders, coordinating deliveries. To her surprise, she enjoyed the work. Who would have thought? The most thought she'd ever given to moss was that it was soft to walk on in her bare feet.

Today was a sunny morning promising to be hot later in the day, an Indian summer, as Katrina walked through Thelma's vegetable garden, watching the bees gather pollen and nectar from the last tomato blossoms of the season. Bees were so certain of their place and purpose. Katrina envied them, then felt foolish for feeling envy for a bee.

She stopped by the phone shanty, just to double-check and see if John might — *might*

— have left a message. Lo and behold . . . there was a message waiting and it was from John! She listened to John's message, then replayed it again and again, stunned.

"Katrina, it's John. Look, I'm sorry, but I can't sell my dogs to you. It just wouldn't be fair to Susie. She thinks you're trying to finagle a way for us to get back together. I told her that you weren't that kind of girl, and assured her that it's completely over between us, but she's still freaking out. I shouldn't even be calling you. Look, I gotta go. Sorry about not being able to get you a dog. I'm sure you'll find one."

Katrina hunched her shoulders, using an arm to cover her ribs. A hurricane of conflicting emotions sucked the air from her lungs. As she stood there, she couldn't stop the tears from starting, then streaming down her face. Not noisy. Not dramatic. Just open faucets, pouring over her cheeks, dripping off her chin. She felt tears streaming, streaming, streaming down her face, and it suddenly made her furious. What had she done that was so wrong? Why had John stopped loving her?

Aware that Thelma would be wondering what had happened to her, she hurried up the hill to the house. She slipped in the door as quietly as she could and went straight to

125

the bathroom where she washed her face with cold water — very, very cold water — to ease the red around her eyes and mouth. She looked at herself in the mirror. "What is *wrong* with you?"

Her sad eyes looked back at her. *They've deserted you.*

John. Your mother.

God.

She squeezed her eyes tight. It all felt like death. It was all a tangle of loss.

She blew out a puff of breath, squared her shoulders, and pulled open the door. Dishes. The sink was still full of breakfast dishes. Glad for the task to do while Thelma was reading, she cleaned up the kitchen. Then she went to find Andy.

She practically bumped into him as he came out of the greenhouse. "I'm sorry, but the breeder doesn't have any dogs to sell right now. Puppies or trained or anything in between."

Andy stood with his arms crossed against his narrow waist. His forearms corded with powerful muscle, and his hair gleamed in the sun. She didn't know what to make of someone like him. And she was having a hard time meeting his eyes, the way he stared at her. She felt he was looking straight through her, that he could see everything, knew everything.

"Then let's go find one," he said, in a matter of fact tone. "Is there a shelter in town?"

She tilted her head. "In fact, there is. A new one."

Twenty minutes later, they were heading toward town in Thelma's buggy. Andy glanced at her. "So, care to tell me why you run to the phone shanty ten times a day?"

She cringed. Was she that obvious? "I'd rather not, if you don't mind."

"Tell me something else, then, why don't you?" he said, and bumped her arm with his. "I'd like to know a little more about you."

"Well," she started, "I . . ." She stopped. What was there to say? And where to even start? The last year of her life had been horrific, filled with pain and loss. It had brought love too, or so she had thought, but that ended up bringing even more confusion and sorrow.

He could see she was struggling. "Okay, let me make this a little easier. Do you like to ice skate?"

She laughed. "Yes. Do you?"

"Nope. I broke my arm in two places when I was ten. Haven't put on skates since. You ever break any bones?"

"My nose. My brother Jesse threw a

127

baseball that hit me in the face when I was eight."

"Oooh. Let me see." He peered down at her, touched her chin to move her face side to side. "Can't tell at all. That's a very nice little nose you've got."

She gave him a wry smile. He was flirting with her, but she found she didn't mind. Not so much.

Katrina directed Andy to the Wild Bird Rescue and Animal Shelter on Main Street, across the street from the Sweet Tooth bakery. Will Stoltz, a vet, had started the Wild Bird Rescue Center a year or so ago. When he married, he and his wife, who was also a vet, expanded the center to include a no-kill animal shelter. Andy and Katrina wandered through the aisle of the animal shelter, holding their hands out to the different dogs. First was a terrier that barked incessantly, then a Shih Tzu, but Andy thought that would be too close to having a cat.

"So what kind of dog do you need?" Katrina asked.

"Wrong question," Andy said, looking at each kennel. "We're looking for a dog who needs us."

And it turned out to be a large yellow mutt with white spreading around its muzzle. It had the kind of sadness in its eyes that Katrina recognized clear to the bottom of her heart. "Andy, look at this one."

Andy knelt and the dog just looked at him, sighed and hung its head showing that it'd given up all hope.

"He's a good dog," Will Stoltz said, opening the kennel latch to let them in.

"We found him waiting patiently on the doorstep one morning. Left behind."

Katrina's heart stopped. Left behind? Just like that. Over. Goodbye. Sometimes, she thought, the world seemed so harsh.

"Left behind," Andy repeated, rubbing the dog's big head. "Any idea what breed he is?"

"One part Labrador Retriever, lots of parts of something else."

Andy moved his hands on the dog in the way that told you he was somebody who knew and loved dogs. "Any idea if he has a good bark? Does he have a prey instinct?"

Will grinned. "Excellent bark. As for the prey instinct, he does chase after balls."

"How old is he, do you know?" He half grinned as the dog stretched his neck up so that he could scratch under the dog's chin.

"He's only nine," Will said, and hurried to add, "but he doesn't have anything wrong with him."

"Aside from being abandoned," Katrina said. Her voice came out a little louder than she meant it to.

Will looked at her in surprise. "I guess that's true enough."

Andy sat down and faced the dog. "I think you need us, and we need you." He glanced up at Katrina and smiled, and she felt her cheeks grow warm. He looked back at the dog and, leaning closer, scratched him behind the ears. "Okay with you?"

The dog looked at him a long time, considering, his brown eyes searching Andy's face. Andy scratched him under the chin and the dog lifted his head, then put a paw on his forearm. He smiled up at Katrina. "All right, then. He says yes. Let's go home."

After they filled out the paperwork, they headed to the buggy with their new old dog. Andy lifted the dog into the buggy. "What do you want to call him?"

"Me?" Katrina said. "You're the one who should name him. You're the one who needed a dog."

"But you're the one who spotted him. The dog that needed us."

"How about . . . Keeper?"

"I like that." He laughed, a soft laugh that turned into a cough. And then he looked surprised, as if he didn't really laugh all that often. It surprised her, as well, to hear him laugh, so that she blushed and looked away. As he turned onto the road that led to Moss Hill, he said, "Are you feeling better?"

The kindness, the way he looked at her with concern, made her eyes prickle. She ducked her head. "I guess." She shrugged, tucking some stray hairs behind her ear. "The reason I run to the phone shanty ten times a day is because of someone named John. We've been broken up for two months. You'd think I'd be over it by now."

"Or not," he said. "It takes as long as it takes."

She looked down at her hands folded in her lap. "I think this particular situation is going to take a long, long time."

Rain had left the village of Stoney Ridge rinsed and clean, scented with freshly mown hay. The sky was bright, creamed with thin, swirling clouds. Jesse felt exultant, a song in his heart, until he realized he was late for work. Hank wouldn't notice but Fern certainly would.

Jesse found his working relationship with Hank to be ideal. Hank left him entirely alone and never followed up on anything. This particular morning had started as usual, with Hank drawling, "You know what needs doing, or at least should," and disappearing off to somewhere undisclosed — most likely Edith Fisher's — while Jesse faced tabulating the chaos of his unpaid accounts, which were numerous.

Jesse's apprenticeship was now concentrated on learning the ins and outs of the buggy shop's finances. Trying to untangle Hank's curious methods, if you could call anything methodical about Hank Lapp. His style of bookkeeping had been what one might call casual, if in a generous mood. If not, sloppy and careless.

In many ways, this sort of apprenticeship fit Jesse from head to toe. Each afternoon, when he knew farmers would be in the field and their wives near the house — a safer situation for the loathsome task of bill collecting — Jesse hit the road with his scooter and made his collection calls. So far, he had collected six outstanding bills without fuss or fanfare. Women were far more sensitive to the need to keep straight accounts than their husbands, he had quickly discovered.

And Jesse had some spare coinage jingling in his pockets. The bill collection division of the buggy repair shop was turning a tidy profit. True to his word, Hank gave him a percentage of what he brought in, but the wage, while steady enough, did not seem to be a swift path to riches. The buggy shop ledger was always going to be tipped in Hank's favor, not Jesse's. Besides, money did not stick to Jesse, which was why a more substantial supply seemed such a good idea. How he would get that large supply continued to elude him. A plan. He needed to make a plan.

Three mornings later, while in town, he rounded the corner and a boy, running at full speed, nearly slammed into him but swerved around him at the last second and bounded away.

Temptation knew how to find him, Jesse had to admit. The gambling spirit took another leap in him. As he watched the swiftest boy he'd ever seen, the buggy business looked a little less appealing.

David made a point to get to Windmill Farm extra early on Sunday, hoping he might snag time alone with Hank Lapp to hear firsthand how Jesse's apprenticeship was going. His son was not forthcoming with information. Unfortunately, Hank was nowhere in sight. David looked around the buggy shop, impressed. It was spotless, clean, and organized.

Not much later, David was delighted to

see Jesse drive the buggy up the hill and went out to meet him. The buggy dipped and rocked as his daughters scrambled out of it, one by one. He noticed that they all looked exceedingly tidy, almost . . . starched. The credit, no doubt, went to Ruthie. As she climbed out of the buggy, he high-fived her. "Great job getting your sisters ready for church, Ruthie."

Jesse handed the reins of the buggy to his father. "Dad, Ruthie is turning into an absolute tyrant." He smiled his naughty-boy smile. "I'd never admit it to her, but she does a much better job at bossing the family around than Katrina did."

And it was true. Ever since Katrina moved to Thelma's, it seemed as if Ruthie had found the space to become . . . her best self. Home life ran remarkably smoothly after she stepped into Katrina's role. She had created schedules for everyone to take turns with chores, and for the first time in a year, David could actually count on a freshly cleaned and pressed shirt in his closet on Sunday morning.

He drove the buggy out to the field where the horse could graze during the service, unhooked the horse from the large harness, and pulled it forward, out of the traces, leading it through the fence and into the field. He patted the mare on her rump and turned to close the fence behind him. As he walked toward the house, he passed right by Birdy Glick. She was shielding her eyes from the bright morning sunshine to stare at something in the sky. It was a peregrine falcon diving down into the field, then swooping up again, whirring off to the top of the precipice at the far side of the stream. He watched the flight in some admiration. The nesting falcon, an endangered species, was a well-known fixture on Windmill Farm. For a moment they stood, an island of silence in the midst of a busy, bustling farm.

"The first great book," she said softly to herself.

"The falcon?"

Birdy startled. "David! I didn't know you were here." Her cheeks reddened. "I meant . . . the book of nature. I always like to start Sunday worship by noticing something about creation around me. God's first great book."

Intentionally preparing one's heart for worship was something David tried to practice at home. He did all he could on Saturday to make Sunday morning an easy, stress-free time. The buggy was washed and cleaned, clothes were laid out on beds, breakfast was simple, dirty dishes would wait. But he knew there was more to be mined in preparing one's heart for worship than merely checking off chores. He watched the falcon soar high in the sky, then dip down to catch an unfortunate field mouse, then up again and off to its nest.

"Listen now," Birdy said in a hushed voice. "As soon as the falcon is gone, the other birds will start to sing." The chorus began with one bird, igniting the morning chirping. Little by little, an entire choir of birds joined in. "They know it's safe now, to sing with all their hearts. Declaring that the world is bathed in the joy and love of God." She steepled her hands together, as if in a prayer. "Evidence of God is everywhere if only we take the time to find it."

David listened, and heard more sounds that shouted of God's goodness. The distant stream that ran along the road of Windmill Farm, flowing day and night, never taking a holiday. It echoed of God's faithfulness.

He saw the rock ledge where the falcon had made her nest, and he remembered how steadfast and solid God is. He watched the trees dance in the breeze, and thought of how flexible and adaptive God's Spirit could be, adjusting to the needs of every generation while still remaining unchanged. He studied the plants, grass, and trees scattered in a chaotic fashion and remembered that in the chaos of life, God remained in the business of making beautiful landscapes out of our messes. His eyes lifted to the sky, the blue, blue sky, and he took a deep breath of crisp morning air, a symbol that every day is a new chance to begin again.

Then he noticed how many faithful church members were heading toward the farmhouse, heads bowed low with worn hope and fresh wounds from the week.

Birdy is right! he wanted to shout to them. *All around you, God's great book of creation is being preached. Lift your heads! See what God has given you on this beautiful September morning. Signs of his glory, his wonder, his ability to make something beautiful out of your life. Lift your heads! You're not alone in this journey.*

David smiled at Birdy, perhaps a beat too long, because her cheeks started to flame with a bright red streak and she spun around, straight into the path of an approaching horse and buggy. The horse shied and reared, throwing his tail, starting a chain of spooked buggy horses, which invited distressed whinnying among the horses in the field, wondering what the excitement was all about. Birdy apologized profusely to the first horse and buggy's owner and scurried off to join a knot of women, gathered by the porch.

But for David, the worship that had filled his heart remained with him all morning.

The church rustled, bowing their heads. Birdy sat on the hard backless bench next to her identical sisters-in-law and let the quiet roll over her. In this time of waiting, of silence, with her family and friends close around her, she felt safe. She felt loved. She felt hopeful. And she thought of David.

Birdy thought of him so much. When she woke up in the morning he was on her mind, and her first thought was whether she would see him that day. Church Sundays were her happiest days of all. She could sit and watch David all morning, to her heart's content, and listen to his honeyed baritone voice as he preached. No one had a clue of all that was running through her mind. She did her best to keep her mind on the contents of the sermon — she knew it was a terrible sin to allow her thoughts to wander off in the direction they tended to go whenever David Stoltzfus was near.

Oh, she was so sure they'd had a "moment" this morning. David had looked at her as if he was seeing her for the very first time and Birdy wondered if there might be something blooming between them. But not much after that, she crossed the yard to head toward the barn and nearly walked right into David. He looked at her and smiled, and Birdy didn't turn away. For once, she didn't knock anything over or trip over her own big feet. A sense of anticipation had skittered over the top of her skin, brushing the back of her neck, her elbows.

Yes, she had thought, this was something possible. The thought made her feel giddy with joy.

Not two seconds later, Katrina had appeared at her father's elbow. "Dad, there's someone here I'd like you to meet." A beautiful woman stood behind her. "This is Mary Mast. She lives in the next town over. It's an off-Sunday so she came to worship with us today."

As David turned to say hello to Mary Mast, Katrina sidled to Birdy's side and whispered, "She was the most promising candidate of all the *Budget* letters. She's a widow with no children. Cross your fingers. I think she could be the one."

Mary Mast beamed at David. Positively beamed. Birdy didn't want her to be so pretty and charming. She was green with envy — another terrible sin.

And Birdy's delight over the brief moment

she had shared with David had disappeared. *Poof.* Gone.

Mary Mast had come as a complete surprise to Katrina. She'd forgotten all about Hank Lapp's infamous *Budget* letter, but Mary Mast hadn't forgotten. She had tracked Hank Lapp down and called him. Hank invited her to church on Sunday, then drove over to Moss Hill to tell Katrina what he had done, and to hand off the task to her. "You said you'd handle it from here," Hank had said. "In the store, that was the last thing you told me." He brushed his hands together. "I've done all I can to help get your father married off. The rest is up to you."

Katrina dug out Mary Mast's letter, read it to look for signs of oddity or mental derangement but was cautiously optimistic about its mild content. Then, after meeting Mary, she felt the first glimmer of encouragement. Mary Mast was a widow who lived in a town nearby, had no children — a *big* plus, because Katrina's own siblings were complicated enough, especially Jesse, though Ruthie could be sneaky — and seemed almost too good to be true.

As she watched her father and Mary Mast chat before church started, she thought they

140

made a striking couple. Looks weren't important, or so everybody said, but her father was a handsome man, and Mary Mast was quite attractive. In fact, if Katrina squinted her eyes and pretended Mary's hair was red, she even resembled her mother. A tiny bit. Her father had smiled at something Mary Mast said — a good sign. They had seemed to be enjoying each other.

All in all, Katrina was rather pleased with herself about this unexpected turn of events and spun around to say so to Birdy, but she'd gone.

Andy spanked the reins against the horse's rump, and the buggy harness jingled. The wheels creaked into motion, squelching through the mud in the yard at Windmill Farm. As the buggy rattled over the corduroy bridge that spanned the creek, Katrina looked back to see Thelma lift her hand in a wave. She had decided to stay and visit with Fern, so Andy told her he'd return to pick her up later because it looked like it was going to rain soon. Katrina turned her back to the farm, settling down on the seat. Andy seemed quieter than usual as he flicked the reins. "Anything on your mind?"

Andy's gaze lifted from the back of the

horse to her face and she saw something in his eyes, a sort of wary pride. "Your dad's sermon. I haven't heard a sermon like that before."

Katrina thought back to her father's sermon, trying to remember if he had said anything significant. In truth, she hadn't listened. Her mind had been occupied with how to get Mary Mast over for dinner this week on a night her father would definitely, absolutely, positively be home. "What were sermons like where you grew up?"

"A lot of stories about Anabaptist martyrs, with a few Scripture verses thrown in at random. Rules and regulations to keep everybody out of moral potholes. Pretty thin soup." He glanced at her. "Must've been different for you, to have grown up with your father's way of thinking. You're pretty lucky — to have grown up with a father like that. He's the real deal, your dad."

Katrina looked at the windshield, partly because raindrops had started to fall, but mostly to avoid responding. She had never paid much attention to her father's preaching. Or to any other preaching, for that matter. "What struck you as memorable?"

"I'd always heard the Bible described as a manual. Do this, don't do that. Your father talked about it . . . like . . . it was a story. A story to enter into, not a blueprint of rules to follow. And then when he said that we are part of that story today . . ." His voice trailed off.

Oh *that.* She had heard her father talk about the Bible in that way. "My dad is always telling people to read their Bibles."

"And then that part about the Bible being a conversation, between a Creator and the ones he created, that it should be a conversation someone has firsthand, not filtered through the hearsay of others." He tilted his head amazed. "That's not the kind of sermon that would've been preached in my church."

"How so?"

"The bishop didn't want people to read their Bible much, or even to pray much. He said that hearing it once a week in church was plenty. When I was a teenager, he caught me reading my Bible." A sneer came over his face. "He told me that I must be thinking of myself as godlike, to be so proud as to interpret Scripture for myself."

"Sounds pretty proud himself, that bishop."

"Oh yeah, he was tough, all right." He kept his eyes facing forward. "He was my grandfather. He'd made himself a bundle of money, but he didn't want anybody to know. We didn't even have indoor plumbing, though most everyone else did in our church. My grandfather would boast to his friends that he didn't need it because he already had running water. I can hear him like it was yesterday: 'Andy runs down to the lake with a bucket and runs back up the hill with the water.' He thought that was hilarious." He was quiet for a minute. "Funny how we rise and fall to the assumptions of others."

"What do you mean?"

"We become what others expect us to be."

She waited to see if he would say more. She thought he probably hadn't meant to reveal even that much about himself. "Did you grow up on a farm?" She had a funny feeling the past years hadn't been filled with happy moments for him.

"Yes. And hated it. So when I was eighteen, I ran off and I joined the army."

He gave her a look as if he dared her to say something, to look shocked, to hop out of the buggy in fear or disgust. Both, maybe. But she wasn't shocked or disgusted. She might be only nineteen, but she'd had enough experience to know that life takes a turn here and there, and you could find yourself mired in circumstances you'd never believed you could get yourself into. "Did you find what you were looking for in the army?"

"Not hardly. Three tours of duty — two in Afghanistan, one in Iraq." He glanced at her. "One thing I learned in the army — you can't undo a thing once it's done." He glanced in the rearview mirror. "Much as I'd like to."

Katrina nodded. "I do know that." She felt a nervous quiver in her belly and she unconsciously smoothed her apron. "So now you're back on a farm. A moss farm."

"It's better to grow things than to destroy them."

Something about the slant of his jaw, the set of his shoulders, told her there was much more there than that. She used a trick she'd learned long ago with her sisters — especially effective with Ruthie, who could be tight-lipped — of simply being quiet to let someone talk. After a few more blocks of silence, and as he turned up the hilly driveway that led to Moss Hill, she realized he might be the first who could outquiet her. "I'm a good listener," she finally said.

"I don't talk about it that much."

She gave him a sideways grin. "Still, I *am* a good listener."

He glanced at her, then had to focus on the road. "Yeah? Why is that?"

She shifted, wiggled a foot, crossed her arms. "Everyone has a story to tell. Everyone."

Andy pulled the horse to a stop at the hitching post by the barn. He turned to face Katrina and said, "You know what I can't stop thinking about? What really got to me was that last thing your dad said: 'Awake my soul. That wakefulness is the first thing.' He was looking right at me when he said that, like he meant it just for me." He tilted his head. "What do you think he meant by that?"

"I guess . . . I don't know."

He propped his elbow on the window ledge and started talking then, telling her about his tours of duty, how he was given specialized training to find deposits of natural gas and petroleum and how, once, he barely escaped death in a flaring accident.

She told him about the accident that took her mother's life, and very nearly hers. Rain kept falling and they kept talking. When she talked, Andy's attention was quiet, his face turned toward hers as he listened. It was almost an hour later that Katrina spied the time on the little battery-operated buggy clock. The poor horse! Standing in the rain all that time. "Oh, wow. You'd better get back to Windmill Farm to fetch Thelma before she wonders what happened to you. And I'd better get supper started."

"Would you let Keeper out to relieve? He's in my room, curled up on the bed, no doubt."

She nodded as she closed the buggy door and hurried away, though she couldn't resist looking over her shoulder as she ran toward the barn to let poor Keeper out. Andy waved, watching her.

She waved back.

Resting an elbow on the dresser top in his daughters' room that night, David smiled softly, listening to the twins' rationale about why they needed to keep a light on throughout the night. Lydie said that she needed it on to find the bathroom. Emily said she needed it on in case she woke up and needed to read.

"What's the real reason?"

Lydie and Emily looked at each other and said, in unison as if they had rehearsed it, "We're afraid of the dark."

"Ah, I see." He decided to leave the light on for now. "Don't forget that God made the night as well as the day. There is no dark so deep that you can't still see God, if you try."

He went downstairs to the living room to read. Ruthie was curled up by the fireplace, her nose in a book. Loving books was one of the things they had in common, and he gave her permission to go to the library as often as she liked. Unlike Anna had done, he never censored anything she read. Ruthie, he'd observed, had enough sense of her own to know what was worth filling her mind with and what wasn't.

The kitchen door squeaked open, fell shut. Jesse was home from the youth gathering. He popped his head around the corner to say hello and good night, then went straight up to his room. The rain that had let up during supper began again, softly against the roof at first, and then a steady drumming. When the grandfather clock in the hallway struck nine, David put his book away and locked the house. Upstairs, he paused to check on the twins and noticed that the light was still on. He went in to turn it off.

In these moments his love for his children swelled. Emily's skin was warm and damp; she stirred and opened her eyes, then settled back into her dreams. "Sweet girl," David whispered, and covered her.

"Dad?" Lydie whispered from across the room. "I tried to see God in the dark but it didn't work."

He knelt down beside her bed and looked into her big hazel eyes. "You don't have to see a visible face. You can feel God's presence, a feeling that everything is going to be all right." He stroked Lydie's hair until her eyes closed and he knew she had drifted off to sleep. He went across the hallway to check on Molly and found her sound asleep with her flashlight still on. He turned it off and set it on her night table. In the hallway, he closed Molly's door gently.

"Whatcha doing?" Ruthie asked, wandering upstairs from the living room. She had her finger in a book and that sleepy look that came from reading.

"Just listening to the rain."

Ruthie padded down the hallway to her room and shut the door behind her. David stood for a minute in the rain-echoing hallway, moved by the great responsibility he felt for his children. He searched for a way to express the fullness in his heart but couldn't find the words for the overwhelming love he felt for these six blessings. Surely for the ten thousandth time, he silently thanked God for the gift of fatherhood.

And on the heels of that prayer came the yearning for things David missed — sharing a moment like this with a partner. A wife.

The spring was gone in Hank Lapp's step. He hunched over to where Jesse was working on a buggy — the first time Hank had actually stuck around long enough at the buggy shop to teach Jesse something about buggies, but he was distracted and irritable and moody. More than usual. "What's got you so discombobulated?"

"What's that supposed to mean?" Hank said, his wide forehead crinkling in confusion.

"Agitated. Disquieted. In a dither."

Hank nodded, but he still looked confused. "The weather. Thought it was going to rain." He peered at the gray clouds in the sky. "Always promising, never delivering. That's what I keep telling Edith." He spun around to frown at Jesse. "She doesn't want to get married."

"To you?" Jesse was incredulous.

"YES. Me."

"Did she give her reasons as to why she's refusing you?" Jesse could think of dozens. Hundreds.

Hank tugged his ear thoughtfully. "She says things are just fine the way they are. And if I keep pestering her about it, she says she'll have to break things off with me. She's done it before." He shook his head mournfully. "I might've poked a hornet's nest." He whistled softly, as he sometimes did in moments of crisis. "This is very bad, very bad." He frowned. "I must seem like a crazy old codger."

"Nonsense! You had perfectly sound sense to hire me."

"So what am I going to do?"

"Hank, I have had considerable experience in matters of the heart." Jesse leaned forward. "Ignore Edith. Give her the cold shoulder. Drives women crazy. It works every time."

Fern snorted and Jesse jumped. That woman had a terrifying habit of materializing out of nowhere. "As if you should be the one giving advice to the lovelorn. Mim Schrock won't give you the time of day."

How insulting! And what could Fern Lapp possibly know of Jesse's temporary setback with Miriam Schrock? Were a man's private affairs of the heart not sacred in this town?

151

Mindful of his manners, Jesse stifled his outrage and politely asked her what she might recommend.

"Yes, what *do* you suggest, Fern?" Hank asked. "I'm listening."

She had her answer ready, along with a slight smile. "Women like kindness. Sweet gestures."

The two watched her trail away, considering her words. Hank looked at Jesse. "Could be a trick."

Freeman, Levi, Deacon Abraham, and David met together at the store on Monday morning, after Sunday's church service at Windmill Farm. They had about an hour before the store opened. David made fresh-brewed coffee and poured himself and Abraham a cup, waiting to hear why Freeman felt such an urgency for a meeting today.

"David, you've complained that you're not involved in decisions, so I wanted to get you up to speed on something."

Abraham and David exchanged a glance of words: Brace yourself.

"Two more families are leaving Stoney Ridge for greener pastures: the Hochstetlers and the Nisleys." He announced the names with a long look at David. *This is your fault,* it said.

David knew the Hochstetlers, a family of nine, had scouted out land in Montana last summer. But the Nisleys? That was news to him. "Where are the Nisleys going?"

"With the Hochstetlers. They can sell their land here and buy three times as much out west. They've got four sons, you know." Freeman stroked his long white beard. "Something must be done."

"Must be done soon," Levi echoed.

"The church of Stoney Ridge will soon dwindle down to fifty baptized adults."

"Fifty faithful," David pointed out.

Freeman ignored that. It was a perilously small number, because the chance of the trend reversing itself was remote.

"I have found a solution that works for everyone," Freeman said. "Even you, David, won't find something to object to." He leaned back in his chair and settled more deeply, one heel resting on one knee. "Tractors."

"Tractors?"

"Yes. I spoke to my cousin in Somerset. The oldest Amish settlement. They allow tractors in the field. It'll double farmers' yields. Maybe more."

A shortcut. Another path toward a quick

turnover. Always, always about money. "Freeman, have you given any thought to the long-term effects of a tractor?"

"Of course I have! And the benefits outweigh the negatives."

"What about soil compaction?"

"That can be fixed with a better plow." He stomped his feet down and leaned forward in his chair. "It's done. I've bought a tractor with church funds and am allowing any farmers who want to use it to do so."

"Church funds? You used church funds for a tractor? Without discussing it with anyone? Without getting a vote from the church?"

"He discussed it with me," Levi said. "And I think it's a grand idea. Positively inspired."

"What about those who object to tractor use?" Abraham said, the words so soft they sounded as if they came out of his short collar rather than his mouth.

Freeman waved a hand in the air. "If there are some who prefer a horse and plow, then they have that choice. But with all the rain we've been getting lately, a tractor will help farmers bring in the hay in half the time."

"Maybe a quarter of the time," Levi said.

"You've used church funds," David

repeated. "While Ephraim Yoder lies in a hospital bed, you used church funds to buy a tractor." He was amazed. "Freeman, this is the kind of thing that causes a church to split in two. Once you do something like this, you can't undo it. You can't take it back."

"I have no intention to take it back. Thunderation, David. Sometimes you make me sound like someone who flagrantly disregards all that we hold dear. Do you think I haven't laid awake for nights, wondering if accepting some new ways might be the best way to ensure our church's survival?"

How could David make them understand what was at stake? "There's a story of a woodsman who, at eighty-five years of age, was still using the same ax. Sometimes the blade would wear out and he would replace it. Sometimes the helve would wear out and he would replace that. But it was always the same ax."

"That's it exactly!" Freeman said. "Think of it as the blade wearing out, and it's time to replace it."

David shook his head. "You're missing the whole point of the story."

Freeman gave him a probing look, one he couldn't read. "Maybe you're the one missing the point."

155

Levi snickered.

David ignored Levi. He usually did. "The church will survive, and its survival has nothing to do with us."

"It has *something* to do with us," Freeman insisted.

"Well, if anyone asks me," David said, "I will discourage them from using a tractor."

Later that night, after the girls were tucked in bed, David went outside and sat on the porch stairs. He didn't know what to do, and whenever he felt that way, he liked to gaze at the stars, pinned to the evening sky. At times, it worked better than a prayer.

Sometimes, it *is* a prayer.

Rain had started this afternoon, right after Fern Lapp had picked Thelma up in her buggy to head to the hospital to visit Ephraim Yoder. Katrina peered through the windows at the rain obscuring everything with a blurry gray.

Restless and bored, she thought about going down to the greenhouse to see if she could find something to do, but then she saw Andy head into it and changed her mind. After the long talk they'd had in the buggy on Sunday, she had tried to avoid being alone with him. She could tell he was drawn to her, and she had to admit that she found him quite appealing. His thoughts made her think more deeply than she was used to. In fact, she couldn't remember ever having such a meaningful discussion with a man, other than her father. Far more meaningful conversations than she'd ever had with John. Still, her life could not handle another complication.

She decided to start dinner while the house was quiet and settled on chicken pot pie — one recipe she knew by heart and never failed. On the counter, she lined up her ingredients: onions and garlic, a bunch of flat leaf parsley culled from the garden, carrots and celery, a good boxed chicken broth since time was too short to make her own. She decided to poach the chicken rather than roast it, though roasting, bone-in, made a big difference in the depth of flavor. She smashed garlic cloves and minced them, slid the wrapper from an onion and set it aside.

If Katrina had her way, she would tear out a wall in Thelma's tiny kitchen to expand the space. It was so small that only one person could move around comfortably. She didn't know how Thelma and Elmo and their son had managed, but she supposed that those two males rarely ventured into it. In that way, her dad was different than most

Amish men. He was a pretty good cook and didn't mind doing dishes. He could make a grilled cheese sandwich exactly right, with the bread turned just barely crisp, light golden brown.

She wondered how her family was doing without her. Since her mother had died, she'd been the one who'd made school lunches, pinned hair for her sisters, kept the laundry rotation moving from washing machine to clothesline to closet. Did they miss her? She hoped so, but to her surprise, she didn't miss them. Maybe a little twinge, now and then, but mostly she was relishing the time she had to herself. The quiet. The peace. The freedom to not be responsible for everyone. Always, always, there were obligations.

For the first time in a long time, she had time to think. And feel.

That was a good and a not-so-good thing. But she knew it was an essential thing.

She heard a bark, then an urgent knocking at the door. "It's me, Katrina," Andy called. "It's raining out here, you know?"

She yanked open the door. "Sorry! I'm in the middle of cooking."

Andy leaped up the steps, bringing the storm with him. Rain slicked him from head to toe, the damp ends of his hair curling at his shirt collar. She gave him a dish towel as Keeper scooted behind him and shook, sending water all over them both.

Katrina shrieked and covered her face. "Oh no! Stop him, stop!"

Andy bent down and swiped the wet floor with the dish towel. Satisfied, Keeper curled up by the woodstove, pleased with himself.

"It's raining so hard that I can't get any work done. That old greenhouse is leaking like a sieve. Does it always rain like this?"

"Seems like we're getting more than our usual share this fall. Very bad news for the farmers who are trying to bring in hay."

"Very good news for moss on a hillside, where the water drains quickly," Andy said with a grin. "It's cold out there." He glanced at the teakettle whistling on the stove top. "Thought I could come up for a cup of tea."

Katrina put a tea bag into a mug and poured in the water. "This will take the chill away, and then you can go back to the barn."

He ignored her hint and lifted his chin at the chopping board with onions, carrots, and celery lined up in a row. "You're cooking? How about if I help?

She handed him the hot mug. "There's not a lot of room in here."

He grinned and she noticed that his teeth

were not quite perfect but they were very white, and his tanned skin glistened with the rainwater. "You mean you want to be alone to mope."

She frowned. "More like think things over."

"And is all that thinking making you feel better?"

She sucked her top lip into her mouth, let it go. "Not exactly."

He picked up the knife she had left on the counter and started to slice the onion into two halves, then diced each half, making sure each piece was the same size as the next.

"There really isn't room for two," she repeated.

"I'm pretty accustomed to small spaces." He scraped the diced onion into a bowl and picked up a celery stalk. "How much celery?"

"Two stalks. Thinly sliced." She poured olive oil into the pot with the diced onion and stirred. The heat was not high. She added the minced garlic, stirred again, sprinkled in a little bit of salt, then took a carrot and began to peel it.

"Next?"

Next? He needed to go, to leave her be. "The rain has stopped."

"But I want to help."

"You're in the way." She turned the heat up on the poaching chicken.

"I'll make myself useful." He grabbed the carrots she had peeled. "These need slicing, right?"

She tried to ignore him as she adjusted the heat under the sautéing onions. "Fine," she snapped. "Slice the carrots."

"Wow, that's a pretty intense scowl," he said. "Any chance you've been avoiding me lately?"

Yes! Of course she'd been avoiding him. She had already been down that particular road and she did not want to travel that way again. *So yes, I'm avoiding you,* she thought, *and you just don't seem to get the hint.* He was like Keeper that way. She glanced back at him, trying to look stern, but a corner of her mouth quirked. "You know —" her grin spread — "you are not exactly what I expected." She turned back to the stove to stir the onions.

"Hmm . . ." His voice rumbled up through his chest. "Such as?"

"Such as, I had you figured as the silent type," she said. "You're very talkative, actually."

"Not with everybody."

"It's just that, I usually have a sense about

people." Maybe that — along with her confidence, her sense of well-being, her happiness — had abandoned her.

After a long moment he asked, "So what do you sense about me? Something bad?"

"No," she said, trying to capture the feeling she got when she was around him. "More like . . . sad . . . I guess. Like you have to get something off your chest."

"Funny . . . ," he said.

She heard him move, felt him take a step toward her.

And then he was behind her, standing closer than he had any business being. "That's the same feeling I get around you."

She let the spoon rest on the skillet's edge, then turned and looked up at him, and he reached down to curl one of her prayer cap strings around his finger and give it a little tug. She knew she ought to pull away, that she ought not to encourage him, that she needed to keep their interaction business-like. A soft glow filled the air as they stood there, inches apart from each other. A stillness came over them. Andy's gaze took in her face, then slowly dropped to her mouth, and for a minute she thought he might kiss her. She thought she might want him to . . . and that awareness shocked her.

For the first time in a long time, she

thought about what it might be like to be kissed by someone other than John. She could feel the color building up in her cheeks. The silence in the room took on a prickly tension.

Suddenly a wet black nose came between them, Keeper's nose, and they both startled, jerking away from each other.

Grateful for the timely interruption, Katrina turned back to the onions and gave them a stir, added the carrots, and picked up a potato to dice.

A new relationship wasn't the answer. She wasn't over the old one.

Andy was a bit too close again and she had to scoot around him to get to the cutting board. He gave her a slow sideways glance. "So, how are you at giving haircuts?"

A laugh burst out of her. "Have you seen my brother Jesse's hair?"

"I don't think I've met him yet."

"You'd know it if you'd met him. He's one of a kind. Wait until you meet him, then you can decide if you still want me to cut your hair."

"His haircut is that bad?"

"No, no, it's that good. For a girl, anyway. He's got gorgeous, thick, wavy red hair. The best hair in the family. We five sisters are very envious of that hair of his, but he insists it's nothing but a bother to him."

Andy's gaze searched her face, resting on her prayer covering. "I can't imagine anyone having prettier hair than yours."

She did have nice hair, though she knew it was vain to think so. Not as nice as Jesse's, not as red, but it was thick and long, curling down to her hips, strawberry blonde in color. She gave him her best schoolmarm look, the one she used on her little sisters to get them to behave in church. "Andy Miller, are you flirting with me?"

He grinned. "Would I do a thing like that?"

"You might be trying to cheer me up."

"Maybe." He brushed her elbow with his own. "Is it working?"

Again, he made her laugh. "Yes."

Jesse was passing the schoolhouse one afternoon as the door opened and children poured out, happy to be set free. His attention was caught by a curious sight: that same skinny boy running for his life as three big boys — Luke Schrock in the lead — were hot on his trail after him. Jesse had never seen anyone run so fast. One by one, the big boys gave up and dropped to their knees, puffing and panting and gasping for air.

But Jesse, fortunately, had a scooter. He pumped the scooter with one leg and started to gain on the boy. "Wait! Hold on. I'm not going to hurt you. I just want to talk to you." The boy only sped up and dashed away on his storky legs, one arm flailing and the other holding down his hat, running for his life as if he were being chased by a swarm of yellow jackets.

When the boy made a fast turn off into the woods, Jesse gave up and turned his scooter around to ride back and talk to Luke Schrock. He and Luke had a cautious friendship — Luke was a few years younger than Jesse and had a reputation for meanness, all points against him, and Jesse didn't like bullies. Yet Luke had a swagger that was admirable. And, there was always the fact that he was Miriam's younger brother. Jesse hadn't seen Luke since last spring and was surprised at the change in his appearance. He must've grown six inches this summer, with the beginning of fuzz on his upper lip. Luke would be, according to Jesse's sisters' assessment of manhood, quite a looker. A heartbreaker. "Luke, who was that boy you were chasing?"

Luke and his two friends were throwing pocketknives into the ground. When he saw Jesse, he straightened to his full height, pleased to be culled from his posse. "He's new this year. Just a punk."

"What's his name?"

"Stick. Er is nix wie Haut und Gnoche." *He's nothing but skin and bones.*

"Actually, it's short for Yardstick," piped Ethan Troyer. " 'Cuz he beat Luke in a race on the first day of school by yards and yards." Luke stared at him in consternation, but it went unnoticed. "That's why Luke picked him as his project this year."

Luke jabbed Ethan with his elbow.

Jesse looked from Ethan to Luke, back to Ethan. "Project?"

"For a daily beating," Ethan said. "But Luke hasn't been able to catch him."

Luke shoved him. "Schtill sei," he ordered, "un schwetz net so viel!" *Be quiet and don't talk so much!*

A year ago, Jesse might have been interested in this school yard squabble. No longer. He returned to the issue at hand. "He sure looks fast."

"Fastest boy in school," Ethan said.

Luke lifted a fist to threaten Ethan just as Jesse's sister Ruthie approached. As soon as Luke saw Ruthie, he dropped his fist and straightened to his full height, ramrod stiff. His eyes were riveted on her. "Hey Ruthie," he said, but she didn't so much as *blink* in his direction as she passed.

Ruthie? Jesse's head swam. His sister, Ruthie?

Clearly, Luke wasn't accustomed to being ignored. His face turned red enough to ignite. For a few brief seconds, he looked completely humiliated.

Jesse saw it all.

David set out a Grocery Shower box on the front counter to collect food for Ephraim's family. This afternoon, he planned to stop by the hospital. Ephraim's condition had stabilized, but the doctors had said that he couldn't live without the ventilator. With great effort, Ephraim was able to communicate short words at a time. There was no doubt that his mind was clear. He had told his wife, Sadie, that he wanted to be taken off the ventilator and she refused. She didn't want to let him go. He told her he couldn't live like this.

One of the burdens on David's heart as a minister was to prepare God's people for a good death. Much of the world was suffused with a great fear of death, it seemed, if not actual denial of it. But there was another way to face death — by resting in the sovereignty of God. By trusting that one's life, though it may be short, would be complete.

Easier to say than to do — *that,* he knew.

The door opened and Gertie Zook and Lizzie King came into the store on a gust of cold air. They didn't notice David in the back of the store and continued their conversation. When he heard the word "tractor," he stilled to listen, his spirits sinking rapidly.

"I've lived through a church split before," Gertie said. "It's the same thing. A battle to hold on to the old ways or accept new ways. It never ends well."

Was that the battle of their church? David hoped people understood the issues were not so simple as the age-old fundamentalist vs. liberal battle. He wasn't trying to hold on to old ways for the sake of tradition but because he felt that the very foundations of the faith were getting eroded. Freeman was running the kingdom of God on his own terms. Every single decision he had made since he became bishop had been motivated by money.

Lizzie King noticed David was at the far end of the aisle and nudged Gertie to stop talking. David said good morning to them and asked how they were, but the conversation felt uncomfortable and forced.

After they left, he leaned his forehead

against the doorjamb. Anna would know what he should have said to those two women to reassure them that the church was not in danger of splitting into two factions. She always knew the path to draw people together. These were the moments when missing Anna went from its usual dull ache in his chest to a sharp pain. It seemed impossible that more than a year had passed since her death. At times it felt like she'd been gone for years, other moments he forgot she wasn't there. Last night, his dream about her was so vivid that it startled him awake. In the dream, he had asked her a simple question — what were they having for dinner? — and waited for her reply, eager to hear her voice, but she never answered him back.

Anna, he knew, had had a good death. Her life was complete. It was those left behind who struggled to hold firmly to that truth.

Jesse had made three bill collector calls in one morning, though only two were successful. He brought out the cash he'd been paid for Hank's buggy repairs and counted it again. He would've thought Hank would be more pleased about the money he was bringing in, but he didn't seem to care much about it. All he cared about was wooing Edith Fisher to the altar of matrimony.

If this were his money, he would make it work for him. Under the right conditions, he could double or triple it.

He made a quick detour into the drugstore. Ruthie asked — no, *ordered* — him to buy some bobby pins for the little sisters' hair, and he found it very aggravating to have to be in the women's beauty aisle, for all the world to see. He turned a corner looking for hair products and thought he caught sight of his sister Katrina just as she was leaving the store. He strode down the aisle to go after her . . .

And stopped dead.

On the glass door of the drugstore, the clerk was taping up a prominent poster about Stoney Ridge Founder's Day next Saturday, including a BBQ hosted by the town mayor. Including a hundred-yard dash.

Maybe . . . the right conditions for Hank's money had just arrived.

8

Early one morning, Katrina had taken the buggy to town to pick up a few things at the drugstore that couldn't be found at her father's store: toothpaste, dental floss, and a few other ladies' unmentionables, which she would have felt mortified to purchase at her father's store.

She had wandered the aisles for a long time, intrigued. So many of the items she could make herself or live without, but still, she supposed, there was something about store-bought things that made them seem special. And it would be easy to hunger for them, if she let herself. Like those tortoiseshell combs and barrettes, or those dainty gold earrings for pierced ears. Imagine how she would be looked at if she wore earrings to church one day! A Plain woman wasn't supposed to covet such worldly things, but she did.

She had noticed a sale on peppermint tea

and bought it, remembering it was Thelma's favorite flavor. Then, seeing the time on a wall clock, she hurried to pick up her last few purchases.

When she returned home, nearly noon, she made tea and took a cup to Thelma as she knitted by the window in the living room. "You missed a visit from Freeman," Thelma said. "He's showing more nephew-ly interest in me since Elmo's passing than he did his whole life."

"Still trying to talk you into selling?"

"Yes. Two weeks ago, the developers raised their bid. Freeman tries to have little persuasive talks with me, but I keep telling him I still won't budge from here. He's getting more persistent and I'm getting more impatient with his stiff ways. Today, he said the church needed the proceeds from the sale of the hill and I needed to go live in the Big House with that tribe of his."

"How did you respond to him?"

"I told him that my moss business was turning a tidy profit —"

A slight exaggeration. But there had been an increase in orders this week.

"— and that I had two employees to consider. That gave him pause." Her eyes smiled as she sipped her tea. "On a happier note, I saw your brother in church the other day."

"Yes. Jesse's back from Ohio. He's apprenticing with Hank Lapp to learn about buggy repairs."

Thelma froze, then swallowed her mouthful of tea. "Hank and Jesse? Now that's a curious combination." She took another sip of tea. "I always thought Jesse was a boy whose eyes were fixed on the horizon. Elsewhere."

Katrina looked up. "What makes you say that?"

"He seems to have an unsettled soul."

Katrina pondered that generous description. Yes, her brother did have an unsettled soul. Frankly, that phrase would describe her, as well. Maybe it was a family trait. But then, her father was a very settled soul. Her mother had been one too. "I'm going down to work in the greenhouse for a while."

"I haven't seen much of Andy today. If you see him, would you mind asking him to stop by the house?"

Through the window, Katrina saw Andy drive a horse and wagon toward the barn. "There he is now. I'll go speak to him."

She walked down the hill to Andy as he was unbuckling the horse's harness parts. Keeper spied her, wagging his tail at the sight of her, then galloped toward her. That dog, now he was a settled soul. He'd found the life he wanted.

The tops of the trees stirred with wind and Katrina shivered. Fall had arrived in full force.

He eyed her. "That color blue looks good on you."

Katrina ran her fingers over the hem of her sleeve. "This is the oldest dress I own."

"I don't care. It's still a good color." He held her gaze steadily, and in the bright, clear afternoon sun, his eyes were as blue as the sky behind him.

"Thelma wants to talk to you this afternoon."

"You look a little cold," he said, removing his coat and draping it about her in a gentlemanly fashion. "Is everything all right with Thelma?"

"Yes. Other than she's annoyed with her nephew. He wants her to sell and move in with him."

"Why does her nephew hold such sway?"

"He's the bishop."

Andy lifted his head in a nod. The one word, *bishop,* carried weight. "Ah. And she doesn't want to?"

"Not at all. She wants to stay put. That's

why she's excited to build up this moss business."

Andy lifted a heavy auger onto his shoulder as easily as if it were a bale of feathers and walked toward the barn in long strides. She followed behind him and leaned on the side of the open barn door, watching him set the auger against the wall. He straightened and turned to her, hands on his hips. "Would you like to take a walk tonight?" As he took a step closer to her, first one, then another, all thoughts flew from her mind, like swallows in the rafters.

Something about the direct way he met her eyes, and the slight, charming quirk of his mouth caused a stir at the base of her neck. Suddenly shy, she peeled his coat from her shoulders. "Thanks, but no. I just came down to tell you that Thelma wanted to talk to you this afternoon. That's the only reason I'm here."

"Katrina, hold on."

"I'd better go," she said. "See you later." And she left him, almost running.

Later that day, after visiting with Ephraim and Sadie, David was thoroughly spent. Sadie had agreed to Ephraim's request to be taken off the ventilator but she wanted to give time to allow their entire family —

both sides — to travel to Stoney Ridge to say their goodbyes. That was only fair to her, but knowing Ephraim as he did, he was sure he didn't want to delay this any longer than was necessary. Ephraim had always been a bustling, energetic man, always in motion. Now, his body was wasting away in the ICU. It was a heart-wrenching time for all involved.

David slapped the reins on the horse's rump to get the mare to pick up her pace. He tried to be home each afternoon as the girls returned from school, but he was running a little behind today.

After rubbing down his horse and giving her a few handfuls of oats, David gave his mare a parting pat, closed the stall door, and retreated from the shadows of the barn into the fall sunshine to stop short. He'd been so absorbed with Ephraim, as well as the disturbing murmurs of a possible church split, that he had never even noticed what a beautiful day it was today.

The temperature couldn't have been more than fifty degrees. The crisp air held a slight tang of burning leaves. Clouds above covered half of the sky like puffy balls of cotton. Later, he should bring the twins outside to see if they could pick out animals in those clouds. Last time, Lydie spotted an

elephant plodding across the sky and Emily
was sure she saw a buggy. He smiled. It just
occurred to him how those images summed
up his daughters perfectly — one so inven-
tive, one so practical.

When he started from the barn to the
house, he noticed Birdy Glick standing
down by the mailbox, shielding her eyes as
she tipped her head back. Each time he saw
her, she seemed to have her eyes peeled
upward. A timely reminder, he thought,
after spending the afternoon in the hospital.
Overhead, a gaggle of geese flew in
V-formation, two black ribbons in the sky,
heading south to Blue Lake Pond. He
brushed dirt off his pants and walked down
the hill to join her.

"Have you ever wondered why one side of
the V is always longer than the other?" she
said as he approached.

"I've never noticed."

"I've noticed," she said, "but I have no
idea why."

"I do know that the V-formation conserves
energy for the geese, but I don't know the
reason for that."

"Oh, that I know," Birdy said. "They face
less wind resistance and receive a boost of
air waves from those flying in front —
almost like being in a wind tunnel. The

farther back a goose is in formation, the less energy it needs in the flight. And an added bonus — it's easy to keep track of every bird in the group. It's a perfect metaphor for community, I've always thought."

Without realizing it, Birdy had just given him the ideal illustration for why the church should remain together. *Thank you, God.* He breathed it all in, deeply, and let it go, astonished.

When the geese had flown past, she dropped her hand and looked straight at him. "Is it true? You're not teaching baptism classes?"

"Did your brothers tell you?"

"No, I heard it from Gertie Zook. She seems to know everything in this town. My brothers don't reveal much to me about church business." She looked from his eyes up to the house, then back again. "Did you want to stop teaching the classes? Or did they tell you to stop teaching?"

"Let's just say, I didn't agree to teach the way they wanted me to teach the classes."

"Greatly abbreviated, is my guess."

"To be honest, yes. I believe that young people should be taught the fullness of God's words, of church doctrine. Not to pick and choose them. Thomas Jefferson used to take a pair of scissors to Scripture, cutting out the parts he didn't like."

"And you think that's what my brothers are doing."

She didn't state it as a question but he took his time answering. "Birdy, it's no secret that there's tension between your brothers and me. I don't want to put you in the middle of it."

"You're not. I'm asking for the truth. Is that what you think my brothers are doing? Picking and choosing?"

He didn't answer.

"So do I. My brothers would never let God interfere with the running of the church." Her harsh words surprised him, and his expression must have shown so. "Sorry to sound that way," she met his eyes, "but it's the plain truth." She heaved a breath. "David, don't let up on them."

"I'm trying to hang in there, but they don't make it easy."

Birdy, who to his knowledge did not have a mean bone in her body, patted his sleeve in approval. "Good for you." She smiled and said in a conspiratorial voice, "Well, it seems to me that our young scholars might benefit from a few lessons about Bible memorization by the minister."

David grinned, pleased, feeling cheered

179

up. "Well, put that way, how can I refuse?"

Some days are all ups and downs. September was drawing to an end with nice, clear weather, but the wind was practicing for winter. Jesse was not a big fan of winter. Nor was he a fan of his sister's cooking. Molly, always the hungriest of the hungry, had volunteered to take over kitchen duties in Katrina's absence and make dinner each night. Tonight was spaghetti noodles, very underdone, tossed with ketchup rather than spaghetti sauce. It was sorely lacking in flavor, virtually inedible, but Jesse's father ate every bite and made sure he appeared to relish it, pleasing Molly to no end.

Whenever Jesse complained about Molly's cooking, his dad would defend her attempts and say, "Every good cook begins somewhere. And this is Molly's somewhere."

Thankfully, Jesse's noontime meals at Fern's made up for Molly's meals.

"How is school going?" his father asked Lydie.

"Birdy's terrible hard."

"So are diamonds," he said with a fond swipe at the hair perpetually clouding her eyes.

"But one thing is good," Molly said. "She says she scorns the maxim that children should be seen and not heard."

"That's probably because she's single," Jesse said.

"And some big bug is attacking Luke Schrock," Emily said. "Nearly every day, he gets stung."

"He's starting to look like he's covered in polka dots." Lydie pointed to spots all over her neck. "Maybe it's a case of chicken pops."

"Chicken pox." Jesse looked up. "Just Luke? No one else." Interesting.

"Ruthie thinks it's a killer bee," Molly said.

"Hopes," Ruthie whispered, eyes on her fork. Jesse heard. So did their father. His gaze went straight to Ruthie, and stayed there, but she was studying a forkful of gray, limp, overcooked string beans.

"Jesse? Jesse, anyone home between your ears?"

Jesse startled, realizing his father was talking to him.

"I asked you how your days were going as a buggy repairman."

"Sorry, Dad. My thoughts were elsewhere." Pondering the mystery of Luke Schrock's personalized bug attacks.

"Just what is it you do all day there with Hank, besides keep him company?"

181

An apt question, not easily answered.

"This, that, and the other," he replied to his father honestly enough. He doubted that his father would be in favor of the bill collection aspect of his apprenticeship, thus he had decided it would be wise to avoid mentioning it. He held up his dish and plastered a smile on his face. "Molly, how about another helping?"

Molly beamed.

For the next few days, Jesse made a point to put himself in the general location of the schoolhouse around three o'clock. It took that long to catch Yardstick Yoder. When he finally cut him off in a detour and cornered him against a barn, Yardstick held his hands curled tightly into fists, his knuckles white, as if he needed to be prepared at all times to punch someone.

"Look, I'm not going to hurt you. My name's Jesse Stoltzfus. I just want to talk to you."

The boy was skinny as a broom and stood so rigid, he looked as if he might snap in two in a stiff wind. He scooped the floppy brown hair back from his eyes and met Jesse's gaze with a bleak one. He was even more gaunt-faced than he looked from a distance. "About what?"

Jesse had his answer ready, along with a slight smile. He nudged the boy's bony shoulder. "How'd you like to run in a race?"

Birdy watched the kinetic energy of the children on the playground, their happy shouts lifting up into the sky. Her eyes went to the bird feeder that was attached to a low point on the schoolhouse roof — safely away from misdirected balls and mischievous boys, but low enough that she could easily reach it to resupply with birdseed. Like right now, she realized, seeing how near empty it was.

In the coatroom, Birdy kept a container of sunflower seeds that she had grown over the summer just for the purpose of feeding her birds. The sunflowers took up most of her garden space, which her sisters-in-law teased her about, but she didn't mind. She loved birds, always had.

A year ago, Will Stoltz, who ran the Wild Bird Rescue Center, knowing of Birdy's bird interests, asked if she might be willing to lead local bird-watching tours. She was flabbergasted when he asked. And thrilled beyond words. She jumped in, loving every minute of it. Early dawn expeditions to Blue Lake Pond to spot a nesting pair of sandhill cranes. Tromping through the woods to seek out a yellow-rumped warbler. Climbing hills to catch sight of a ruby-crowned kinglet.

Then this last summer, Will Stoltz said her tours had developed a following and he wanted to increase tours for the fall migrating birds, plus give her a raise. She was as happy as she'd ever been. It felt as if she had finally found the one thing in the world that she was good at. Until Freeman told her — told her! never *asked* her — she would be teaching school this term.

Teaching school, she was convinced, would not give her the same satisfaction that leading bird tours did. She tried to explain that to her brother, but he wasn't listening. He never listened. It was a common characteristic in her family.

Birdy had always been surrounded by big personalities, starting with her father and mother, then her older brothers. Freeman was the firstborn, the oldest son. After him came five more boys, like stair steps. Then, when Freeman was twenty, her mother gave birth to Birdy. She had the daughter she'd always longed for.

But Birdy didn't fit, quite literally, the notion her mother had about having a daughter. She was ungainly, awkward, oversized. By the age of fourteen, she was an inch taller than her tallest brother. She preferred being outdoors, regardless of weather, to being stuck indoors with women's work. Her mother did everything well. Birdy did very little well. The harder her mother tried to make Birdy into her image, the more clumsy and self-conscious she became. Her mother passed when Birdy was twenty-one, but her awkwardness remained.

Birdy didn't know how or why or when it happened, but suddenly, in the midst of teaching school one day last week, she felt confident. Competent. Nearly as self-assured as when she led bird tours. For now, she knew that little schoolhouse was where she was meant to be. Even her clumsiness — a hallmark of her life — was leaving her.

She filled up the feeder and stepped back to watch the birds return to the feeder. Two little finches, one gold, one red, had lit on the feeder.

"Which is your true favorite?" His voice moved down her neck like a whisper. David.

He had said he would try to stop by after lunch to teach a Bible class one afternoon this week.

She swallowed. Her heart was pounding. He'd never stood so close to her. "I'm not sure." She smiled and gave a tiny shrug. "Depends on the day."

"If you could choose one bird to observe, which would it be?"

She swung around. He had asked just the right question. "Ospreys!" This, *this* was exciting! Unless she was leading a bird-watching tour, hardly anyone ever asked her about birds. "One of my favorite sights is to see a white-and-black osprey fly across a deep blue sky, usually with an unlucky fish in its talons."

Their eyes met, locked. There was something in his face that touched her like the flutter of bird wings.

He inclined his head. "Oh, I almost forgot. Would you like to come to dinner on Thursday? Katrina is bringing Thelma and wanted you to come too. Our Molly is learning to cook."

Is Thelma a chaperone or is he being kind? She nodded, holding his gaze.

"Is five thirty early enough?"

Something like hope bloomed in her chest. *Don't get excited,* said some cynical voice in her head, *he would never find you appealing.*

The atmosphere had shifted, the air grew taut between them. Then a ball came hurling through the air, breaking the moment. On legs that felt wobbly, she turned and went into the schoolhouse to pull on the

186

bell. Lunch was over, David would teach his class and go back to his life, and she was almost relieved. He was too much, the feeling was too much. But how do you stop a feeling once it begins?

Birdy peeked in the Stoltzfus kitchen at four thirty on Thursday evening — early because she was so excited — to find supper uncooked but Molly bent low to the opened oven. When she saw Birdy, her eyes filled with horror. "Teacher Birdy! This bird refuses to get cooked."

Pale and dry and flabby, the small turkey lay there in the roaster. Birdy rolled up her sleeves. "If I might make a suggestion, it is time to baste the beast."

Molly looked doubtful. "What does it mean to baste?"

"Allow me." Crouching where Molly had been, Birdy spooned the turkey's drippings over the breast and drumsticks. "There, now, that bird has no choice but to cook."

An hour and a half later, the bird was perfectly cooked. Molly was so excited that she screamed, which brought the girls running into the kitchen. As Birdy carefully placed the turkey on top of the oven, she had to admit, it looked pretty delicious. "And this, girls, is what happens when you baste a bird."

"Just the bird?" Ruthie said, giggling. "Or you too?"

Birdy looked down at herself. The top of her dress had greasy splatters from the basting of the bird, her face felt flushed from the oven, and she smelled of a roasting turkey.

And in walked David with Mary Mast hanging on to his arm. Mary looked at Birdy with the faintest frown of censure, then lifted a long elegant hand in a slight wave. Mary was so petite, her movements delicate and graceful, couched in femininity yet with undeniable strength, and Birdy found herself wishing she were more like that and less like . . . herself. But she gave them both her best grin.

The sound of his daughters' giggles, as they surrounded Birdy — who stood in the middle of his kitchen with a cock-eyed prayer cap and a grease-splattered dress — so startled David that he jerked to a stop.

"Hungry?" Molly said, still smiling, eyes darting between David and his guest.

"Always," David said with a smile directly at Birdy. Pink touched her cheeks, but they didn't flame. In fact, David felt heat in his own cheeks when she met his glance with a shy smile. But maybe that was just from being out in the sun all afternoon. Still, he was glad to see Birdy there, glad to feel the way she seemed to belong, glad to hear Ruthie and Molly and Lydie and Emily laughing with her.

He felt a tight squeeze on his elbow and realized he had forgotten all about the woman on his arm. Millie? Mona? Good grief, he couldn't remember her name! He didn't even know why she *was* here. He was about to lock up the store to head home for a special meal — Katrina had been unusually emphatic about having a family dinner tonight — and when he turned around, there was Mina.

Margaret? Mindy?

He gave her the beneficent ministerial version of his smile, which was low key and meant to be kindly. She was beaming at him, positively beaming, and walked alongside him all the way back to the house as if he'd invited her.

About halfway home, he discovered that Katrina *had* invited this woman to his house for dinner. It took until he reached the hill that led to his driveway for it to dawn on him *why* his daughter had invited this woman to his house for dinner. Hank Lapp's infamous letter to the newspaper.

And by the time he walked into the house, he was silently seething, then shocked by the sight of Birdy cooking at the old gas stove in his kitchen — she looked so *right* there, so comfortable and at home — and in the next second, he was filled with joy by the sound of his daughters' laughter. Laughter! How wonderful to see his girls smile — really smile, eyes and all. To laugh with ease. When had he last seen it?

He unlocked his arm from Mabel's, Monika's, May's? — *Arrgh, what is her name?* — and rubbed his sweaty palms off on his pants.

"Hello, Mary," Birdy said. "We met at church last Sunday."

Mary!

Before anyone had a chance to say another word, Jesse tumbled down the stairs and into the kitchen, the door swung open and in came Katrina, Thelma, and her new farmhand, Andy. Trailing behind those three was a big yellow dog, thumping his tail. And for the next few hours, the kitchen was filled with happy, noisy chaos.

It was the best turkey dinner David had ever eaten.

9

Katrina woke up and felt pretty good. Better than good. Great. Today, she felt great. The churning stomach she'd been suffering from wasn't bothering her, at least not like it had been. She had slept well last night too. She grinned. Maybe it was Molly's cooking. Or maybe her father was right — she'd had a lingering flu bug that was responsible for making her feel so poorly. The relief she felt over that thought made her want to skip and shout for joy. And on its heels came another happy realization: her father and Mary Mast seemed to have hit it off. He even offered to drive Mary home last night.

Katrina stopped by the Bent N' Dent to pick up a few things and was pleased to discover that Mary Mast had already dropped by and brought lunch for her father. The store smelled of that heavy vegetable soup smell, when the cook put in too much cabbage.

"Mary Mast's really something, isn't she?" Katrina said. From behind the front counter, her father nodded, his head bent over some papers.

He glanced up. "How come you didn't mention she was coming to dinner last night?"

"Didn't I? I guess it slipped my mind."

He went back to his paperwork.

"I noticed the moon was full last night."

"Was it? I hadn't noticed."

"Well, a buggy ride home under a full moon sounds awfully romantic," Katrina said in an encouraging tone.

Her father lifted his head and rolled his eyes. "Stop it."

"I mean it," Katrina said, "it does sound romantic. Dad, give her a chance. You never know. You might end up falling in love."

Her father looked up at her, shocked. "Don't be silly. I've got six children to raise, a store to run, and a church to care for. I don't have time to fall in love. I don't want to fall in love."

Katrina smiled. "Love isn't always about what you want. Sometimes it just is."

"Haven't I always said to let God write the love story?"

"Yes. Thousands of times. But who's to

192

say that a little help now and then isn't in order?" A mischievous little smile bowed her lips. "After all, that's why they call it falling in love, because sometimes you just can't help yourself."

Her father made an exasperated noise and went to the storeroom.

Katrina opened the door for some fresh air — that cabbage smell was revolting — and she noticed some students riding scooters past the store and realized that school had been dismissed for the day, so she hurried over to the schoolhouse. "It went well, don't you think?" she said when she found Birdy at her desk.

"Molly's turkey was delicious," Birdy said. "She seemed so pleased. All day today, she looked happy. I think having a success was just what she needed."

"Molly? Oh, well, I suppose so. But I meant the sparks that flew between Mary Mast and my father."

Birdy looked confused.

"Today she brought him soup for lunch at the store. Homemade vegetable beef soup." She wrinkled her nose. "Lots and lots of cabbage."

Birdy didn't seem at all impressed by that. "Sometimes, soup is just soup."

"Sometimes, but not this time." Katrina

rubbed her hands together. "I think there's something brewing there. Love."

"Don't you think she's a wee bit forward?"

That was certainly true. Mary Mast sat right down next to her father, in her mother's chair — which no one *ever* sat in. "My father — he needs someone like Mary. Someone who won't give up. He can be a little obtuse about matters of the heart."

"I suppose," Birdy said, though she seemed distracted.

"I should go before Thelma wonders what happened to me. I just stopped by to ask you for a favor. There's a lecture at the public library tomorrow night about astronomy that my father wanted to go to. When Thelma heard about it, she wanted me to take her — though I don't know why anybody would want to sit through a lecture about stars. Ruthie and Jesse wanted to go too."

Birdy leaned forward in her chair. "Why, it sounds wonderful!"

"Mary Mast certainly thought so. She invited herself along. So . . . I was wondering if you might —"

"I'd love to!"

"You wouldn't mind? Really? You don't mind babysitting Molly and the twins?"

Birdy did not move. "There's nothing I'd

rather do," she said, though Katrina thought her voice sounded strange. Sickly sweet.

And she was suddenly, overwhelmingly nauseated.

On Saturday night, when Birdy arrived at the Stoltzfus house to babysit, she found Molly grating a ginger root. "What are you making?" she asked as she put her coat on the hall stand.

With surgical precision, Molly filled a tablespoon with the grated ginger. "Gingersnap cookies." She lifted the tablespoon to tip it into the batter.

"Wait!"

Molly froze.

"Ground ginger is what you need," Birdy said. She opened cupboards to search for spices, hunting through little jars and containers until she found ground ginger. "Grated ginger will make sweet cookies taste like soap."

Molly's eyes went big. She took the ground ginger from Birdy and started to fill the tablespoon with it. Birdy grabbed the container from her. "Just a teaspoon will do. Ground ginger is rather powerful."

David stood by the kitchen door, an amused look on his face as he slipped his coat on. "Thank you," he mouthed to Birdy.

"My pleasure." She watched him walk down the pathway to join Jesse and Ruthie, waiting in the buggy, and tried not to give in to feelings of self-pity. A sin. And then feelings of envy for the lovely Mary Mast. Another terrible sin.

"Teacher Birdy?"

She forced a smile on her face and spun around. Molly held out the bowl of butter and sugar, whipped so much it looked like cream. "Does this look stirred enough?"

"Perfectly blended. I'd hardly know the eggs are in it."

Molly blanched. "Eggs?"

"Where is the recipe?"

Molly pointed to a splattered, worn index card. Birdy picked it up. "Is this your mother's handwriting?"

Molly nodded. "Some of the ingredients are splotched."

Birdy looked carefully at the weathered index card and the slanted, loopy handwriting. She would have expected it to be perfect, but it was dashed off, careless and sloppy, as if the writer was in a hurry and had someplace better to go. It made her like Anna more, to feel less intimidated by her memory. "There it is, I think." She pointed to a blurry spot. "Two eggs, beaten."

Molly rummaged for the eggs, so rather

than look out the window again, Birdy headed into the living area, sat down on the couch, and patted on either side for the twins to come join her. Emily sat on the far side, but Lydie snuggled next to her, looked up and linked her arm through Birdy's. "Why don't you have any children?"

Molly was in the kitchen, starting to bake the cookies. She poked her head around the doorframe and scolded, "Lydie! That is not a proper question to ask your teacher!"

Scowling, Lydie lowered her head. Birdy had to smile. In features and coloring, Lydie was the spitting image of her sister Katrina and had the makings of her brother's boldness as well. Emily, who kept inching closer to Birdy, had quieter looks and a quieter personality, more like Ruthie. Molly didn't really look like any of her siblings, other than her flaming red hair. Molly was just . . . Molly. "That's all right, Lydie. I take no offense." Birdy looked down and smoothed the little girl's hair. "You asked that because it seems as though I'm old enough to be a mother. Is that correct?"

Lydie shot Molly a guarded look, then nodded.

"Well, you're right," she continued. "I am old enough to have children. But the reason I don't is because I've never married."

Already seeing another question forming in the girl's mind, Birdy hoped it wasn't going to continue down that particular road.

"Why don't you get married?"

"Lydie!" This time embarrassment tinged Molly's scolding.

"It's all right," Birdy said with a wave of her hand. "She's just curious — which means she's thinking." She couldn't blame the little girl for curiosity, not when she possessed the same trait herself. Birdy was surprised at the warmth rising to her cheeks, and at how difficult the next words were to say aloud. "To tell you the truth, I've never had a man ask to marry me."

Lydie's brows pinched together and Birdy tried to imagine what question was coming next. "Do you love somebody?"

"Lydia Stoltzfus!" Molly shouted from the kitchen. "Come in here and wash dishes for me!"

Lydie sighed a grievous sigh, climbed off the couch, and trudged into the kitchen to get chewed out by her older sister. Grateful for the reprieve from such personal questions, Birdy patted the empty spot where Lydie had been and Emily scooted closer to her on the couch, not talking, just content to look through a book as she snuggled up. The crackling of the logs burning in the fireplace and the distant clank of pans in the kitchen sifted through the silence. Birdy's attention was drawn to the open window. Though dusk cast its purplish spell, it was still light outside.

This was what Birdy had imagined her life to be. Surrounded by children, loved by a fine man. She'd relinquished that hope years ago — or liked to think she had. Her gaze swept around the room, to David's desk in the corner of the room, piled haphazardly with thick books, to his winter coat that hung on the coat stand by the door. In moments like this, the distant heartbeat of the mother and wife she might have been started up again.

In the kitchen, she heard a frenzied conference of whispers between Molly and Lydie. Apparently, Birdy's lovelorn status was an issue Lydie wouldn't drop. In a loud voice, she finally said, "All I was going to say is that if she loves somebody, she should tell him so!"

Molly's voice went up an octave. "It's not your business who anybody loves or doesn't love!"

By now, Lydie was furious. She stomped upstairs. At the top of the stairs, she turned and yelled, "How's a body supposed to know if nobody tells 'em?"

Emily looked up from her book, mildly interested in her sisters' heated discussion. "Dad says Lydie and Molly can make mountains out of molehills, but I think they make molehills out of mountains."

"I think," Birdy said, "I think you both may be right."

Mary Mast had made no secret of her interest in David. He was flattered, though her persistence made him feel uncomfortable. Shouldn't the man pursue the woman? Mary dropped by the store nearly every day now to bring him treats. Sometimes, David felt like he had been tagged like a deer by a hunter.

But then, maybe he should take Katrina's advice and ask her out. Even Ruthie had been pushing Mary Mast at him last night.

What did people do on a date anymore? He hadn't been on a first date since he was twenty years old. And when would he even find time for a date? He had an entire church to worry about.

Of course he might not have a church much longer.

Later that afternoon, David found Birdy sitting on the porch of her little cottage. At first, Birdy didn't see him, so David caught the pensive expression on her face before she could mask it with her eternal smile. How could anyone be so cheerful? She was very sincere, and he had to admit that he always felt his spirits lift after being around her. But it still seemed amazing to think anyone could be so cheerful. He had spent time in her classroom. Those eighth graders in the back row could drain the joy out of anyone's day, even Birdy's. And yet, she remained upbeat.

She startled when she saw him and jumped to her feet as he walked up to her porch. "I've been summoned to the Big House," he said. And it was a big house. It had grown and spread like an Amish family, with attachments to the main house. That's where Levi's family lived.

"Ah, Freeman."

"What's your sense of this one?"

"He finds all kinds of things to object to." She laughed. "I always thought that taking on Freeman was like wrestling a carnival bear. You have to cross your fingers that the muzzle doesn't come off."

That was one of the things he was beginning to like most about Birdy — how she could find a reason to laugh at serious things, and suddenly it framed the issue in a lighter, more manageable way. "You do have a knack for saying unexpected things."

"Do I?" She snorted, in a very unladylike way, then her face flamed beet red. "I think my brothers would prefer if I said nothing."

"They just don't see you clearly. It's hard for families to see one another sometimes, don't you think? My older sisters still can't believe I'm a minister."

She tilted her head. "Do you enjoy being a minister?"

"Do I like it?" David couldn't remember a time in his life when he hadn't sensed God's hand on his shoulder. He had always taken Scripture seriously. He took Jesus seriously. He took prayer seriously. He loved helping people see the truths laid out in Scripture. He enjoyed caring for others who had needs and helping them find comfort in the Lord. Even as a boy, he had practiced giving sermons. It was as if he knew, deep down, he was going to draw the lot one day.

He couldn't imagine now *not* being a minister. Eight years ago, when he opened that hymnal and saw that piece of paper, saw that the lot had arrived for him, it felt like he had found a glove that fit his hand perfectly — a calling to the ministry. "Birdy, there's not a day that goes by when I don't thank God for the gift of drawing that lot." He glanced up at the Glick farmhouse. "Though less so on days when I'm summoned to face the bishop."

"That bishop isn't a tractable man on his best day."

"Was he always that way, your brother?"

Birdy bundled her hands in her apron as she considered his question. "Freeman is the eldest, and our father — well, he was quite the taskmaster. He put a great deal of pressure on Freeman. On the day our father died, Freeman returned from the graveside a different person. All stern and stiff and solemn, very much his father's son. I suppose . . ." She paused, as if to gather her thoughts. "I suppose it's all he'd known manhood to be."

That thinking made sense to David. Weren't we all what others expected us to be? A breeze came through the red cedar stands to swirl around them, and he saw her shiver, then rub her upper arms. He also saw her smile.

"He was sweet to me, Freeman was, when I was a child. More than twenty years separate us, but our birthdays were only a few days apart, and he used to say that I was the best birthday present he ever got. Each year, up until when he married, he insisted that we have a joint celebration. We would even decorate the cake together." She laughed. "It looked awful, a truly gaudy cake, but I'll always treasure those memories."

David wouldn't have expected to hear a tender word about Freeman, and it shamed him to think of how quick he was to criticize him.

"You came here to see Freeman, not to listen to me prattle on. And I have some third grade math tests to correct."

"You're doing a wonderful job as a teacher, Birdy. You seem to have an intuitive understanding of the children." He knew that his daughters loved her as a teacher, but he was impressed by the quiet control she had over the entire class. He could see that the students respected, even admired her, all the way from the big-eyed first graders to the narrow-eyed eighth grade boys.

His compliments set off a string of blushes. He wondered if one of the reasons she embarrassed so easily was that she'd never been given many compliments. All at once she clutched his arm hard enough to leave a mark. "Look, dear!"

This sudden term of endearment caught him by surprise. A mild panic rose. Had she read more into his words or actions than he'd intended? Yes, they were spending more time together lately, but only because he was teaching a Bible class at the school.

Good grief — she couldn't possibly be thinking that he . . . and she . . . why, it was unthinkable!

Then, thoroughly embarrassed, he saw the deer she meant, several does and fawns flitting through the stand of red cedars in the near distance.

Over in the Big House, Freeman and Levi sat on a comfortable green couch on one side of the room, David sat on a stiff wooden chair on the opposite side. Freeman leaned forward to begin, his long wiry beard tucked against his chest, his fingers steepled together. "David, I understand that you have been instructing the schoolchildren to meditate."

David wondered how word had trickled to Freeman so quickly, because he was certain that news hadn't come from Birdy. But it didn't surprise him; Freeman had eyes and ears all over the church. "I gave the students some suggestions about how to memorize Bible verses. Meditating on a particular verse, for example."

"And you meditate like this?"

"Yes. Of course I do." Oftentimes, as he would read the Bible, he would silently pray, confess, worship, untangle situations, and make resolutions. Sometimes he would just sit and listen. "Don't you?"

"I object to the practice altogether."

"As do I," Levi said.

David was confused. "Of meditating? You object to meditating on God's Word?"

"Of letting imaginations wander. Imagination is a gateway to the devil."

A gateway to the devil? "The human imagination is an amazing God-given gift. Our world is full of examples of its redemptive use."

Freeman wasn't interested in David's way of thinking. "You are leading young children down a dangerous path."

"By meditating?" David couldn't keep exasperation out of his voice. "Freeman, there are twenty-four verses in the Bible about meditating, mostly written by King David. It has deep roots in our faith. You'll never convince me that meditation is wrong. Just the opposite. I think meditating and stillness are antidotes to a hurried, distracted, noisy life."

"Meditation is far too advanced a notion for these young schoolchildren."

"But everyone starts somewhere. Years ago, when I first read about the idea of sitting still in God's presence, a good five minutes was about all I could handle. It's only after years of practice that I can be still for extended periods of time." These days, David found it didn't take long to reset his attention to the work of God. Attention on God's presence in his interactions with others brought a calm that helped him. He found he could be the father, neighbor, and minister he wanted to be — one who loved well. Whenever he found a moment or two, he would welcome God's presence. "How else do we teach our young people to tend and keep alive the inner fire of God?"

Freeman rose to his feet. "If you continue to go into the schoolhouse, it is to teach the children Bible verse memorization. Only that."

"Or?"

Freeman sighed. "David, must you challenge every single decision I make?"

"Yes. Yes, I think I must."

Freeman strode to the door and opened it wide. "Good day, David."

10

Andy stayed and helped Katrina clean up the mess she'd made after transplanting moss in the greenhouse for the first time. Dirt was everywhere, moss was everywhere, and Katrina was sticky from the heat of the greenhouse. "Go ahead and get cleaned up," Andy said. "We got a lot done today. I'll finish up."

She appreciated how Andy seemed to know what needed to be done and took the initiative to do it. She was learning a great deal from him and enjoyed working side by side. Not once did he criticize her, even when she dropped an entire tray of freshly transplanted moss. Sometimes, he almost seemed a little too good to be true. But then, maybe that's what knowing John had done to her. Made her suspicious of all men. Maybe Andy was one of the good guys, like her dad. But . . . maybe not.

As she turned to leave the greenhouse, he

said, "Would you like to go on a walk one of these nights? There's a harvest moon this week."

"Maybe," she said, but not promising. She smiled as she walked up to the farmhouse. But as she walked into the living room to say good morning to Thelma, who liked to start her mornings with a cup of tea by the warmth of the woodstove, she stopped short when she saw what was on her lap.

"Katrina, honey, you don't have to hide this. Not here. Not with me."

It was the little brown paper bag that Katrina had brought home from the drugstore a week ago. Inside was a pregnancy test.

Heart pounding wildly, Katrina couldn't make herself meet Thelma's eyes. "How did you find it?"

"I wasn't snooping," Thelma hurried to add. "Mornings are cold with the weather changing, so I went looking for my blue crocheted afghan. I keep it in the guest room closet, the room where you're staying. When I pulled the afghan down, that brown sack fell to the floor."

Katrina covered her face with her hands, but for just a moment. "I haven't had the courage to take it yet." She didn't want to know the answer. Then she sank into a chair and let her hands fall to her lap in a single, clenched fist. She glanced up at Thelma, expecting to see a look of condemnation, of judgment. But there was none of that in her eyes. Only compassion and concern.

Thelma's face was smooth and serene. "Well, I've had my suspicions."

Katrina looked up in complete confusion. "What? How? How did you know?"

She smiled. "You look green as my moss in the mornings and can't touch a bite of breakfast. You take long naps in the afternoons. I've had a baby myself, you know."

Unexpectedly, Katrina felt a wave of relief. The secret was out and she was glad. So glad. This was too big to bear alone. "I feel so ashamed, humiliated, sorry. And scared of the future, embarrassed by it."

"Honey, you're not the first girl to have a child out of wedlock and you won't be the last. Since the beginning of time, girls have given too much. No matter how modern the world becomes, girls still give up too much."

Katrina pressed her hands flat against her belly. "This may sound crazy to you, but I'm also a little bit . . . happy."

"Happy?"

She nodded. How could she ever regret

the single most perfect gift in her life? The zigzags of life were more puzzling than ever. "The accident caused so many internal injuries that doctors told me I would never be able to have a baby. I think that's one of the reasons I let things get carried away with John — it almost seemed like I was . . . like I was tempting fate."

"Maybe you were daring God."

"Maybe." Yes, exactly that, though Katrina hadn't realized it until Thelma spoke the words. God had taken so much from her, why shouldn't she take something from him too? But then, that completely backfired. Her gaze fell to her lap. She put a pleat in her apron with her fingers, then smoothed it out with her palm. "I'll pack up and move home."

"Oh no you won't! This is where you belong," Thelma said quietly, her eyes so filled with understanding and compassion that Katrina didn't deserve that it made her weep. She leaned forward to clasp Katrina's hand. "But, honey, if you are pregnant, you do have to tell John. He has a right to know."

She looked down at Thelma's knobby hand, covering hers. "He's engaged to someone else. Apparently, he's moved on." *I hate him, I hate him, I hate him,* she chanted in her mind. He didn't even know what he'd done to her life. And probably wouldn't care if he did.

"Maybe. Maybe not. But he deserves to hear the truth before he marries someone else. So go ahead and take that test. Find out for sure if there *is* something to tell him."

"The instructions say to take the test first thing in the morning."

"Tomorrow, then." She squeezed Katrina's hand. "And there's something else you should know. God has an uncanny ability to bring good out of the mistakes we make. Trust me on that."

Katrina felt a wave of worry wash over her, a wave that ended up — of course — in her stomach. And of course she had to make a quick exit and run to the bathroom, gagging on the way. She was so tired of feeling nauseous, tired of feeling worried and anxious and uncertain, tired of feeling tired.

First thing the next morning, Katrina carefully read the instructions on the pregnancy test box, did everything it said, exactly right, and waited. And waited.

When she saw the little pink plus sign emerge on the end of the pregnancy test stick, she sagged, sliding down the bathroom wall until she was sitting on the floor with her legs drawn up tight against her chest.

It can't be true.

But it was.

It was one thing to *think* she might be pregnant; it was quite another thing to *know* she was. She smothered her mouth with her knee and squeezed her eyes shut against the burn of tears, but they came anyway. They poured like hot rain over her face and down her legs. Poured and poured, until she was empty and full, both at once, of tears. For the longest time, she just sat there. Finally, she took some tissue and wiped her face, blew her nose, and slowly rose to her feet, leaning against the wall.

She was only nineteen years old, but she felt so weary, so worried, and so alone.

That evening, when she felt calmer, Katrina wrote a letter to John.

John, I got your message that you're engaged. I wish I could say that I was happy for you, but that would not be true. What is true is that you and I are going to have a baby. I'm about two months along. Count back and you'll realize it happened when I came to visit you in July.

She nodded and tried to swallow, but

couldn't.

I don't expect anything from you, John, but I want to do the right thing and let you know about the baby. Your baby. Our baby.

The emptiness inside her burned and burned. She was blinking back tears of — what? Betrayal? Loss? Anger?

All of the above.

She put on her coat and hurried down the hill to put the letter in the mailbox. The mailman stopped by early in the morning, and she didn't want to lie in bed tonight and talk herself out of sending it. It echoed as she dropped it in the yawning mailbox. She snapped the door shut.

Done.

From behind her, Andy said, "Want to join us? Keeper wants to walk."

She whirled, grateful for the darkness to hide the tears on her cheeks. Keeper sat politely by Andy's side, his dark eyes somehow steady and wise. She sank to the dog's level, scratching his chest. "You're a good ol' boy, aren't you?"

He lifted a paw and put it on her forearm, then leaned forward and very delicately licked her face. "I can see why you chose this dog," she said to Andy. "He has a big heart, doesn't he?"

He thumbed his hat back. "He knows he hit the jackpot. In just a few weeks, he's already spoiled rotten."

She straightened up. "Thanks for the offer for a walk, but I'm a little worn out. I think I'll go to bed early."

He spoke as if he hadn't heard her. "I can't stop thinking about your father's sermon last Sunday. About wakefulness — being the first thing. I keep wondering about it, about what he meant by that remark. I wondered if —"

Keeper barked, then ran off to chase something by the road and Andy went after him, ending their discussion, which was fine by her. She had other things on her mind than her father's sermon.

But that night, as she got ready for bed, Andy's wonderings about wakefulness kept stirring in her mind. It was the first thing, Andy had said. But to what?

She knew. She knew. Wakefulness to growing up. To facing facts, facing reality, facing the future, however complicated it looked.

One day later, Katrina went to the doctor, who confirmed what she had already figured out. She was almost twelve weeks along, and the baby's heartbeat sounded clear and strong — a whooshing *thump thump thump* sound that she tucked away in her mind to bring out when she felt overwhelmed and frightened at the thought of becoming a mother. That beautiful sound — it gave her strength and filled her with joy. There was a baby growing inside her! A healthy baby, the doctor predicted, who should arrive in April.

Two days later, Katrina was getting the mail for Thelma from the mailbox and heard the phone ring in the nearby shanty. She ran to answer it, knowing, somehow sure, that John was calling.

With a shard of ice sticking through her heart, she answered the phone. "Hello?"

"Katrina," John said. Hearing his deep voice through the line made the fine hairs on her neck rise. How she had loved the sound of that voice! "I got your letter."

Her heart was thumping wildly. "I thought you should know."

Silence rocketed down the line. "I think you're lying."

The accusation, the hostility, in his tone caught her by surprise. His words splattered against her face, cold and whole. "Have you ever known me to lie? Ever?"

"No. But you said you couldn't get pregnant, either."

That was true. She couldn't blame John alone for this situation. He never forced himself on her. She was a willing partner.

"I'm not letting you derail my wedding to Susie."

Reflexively, she hunched her shoulders, using an arm to cover her ribs as if he had struck her. Where had he gone, the man who had promised to love her forever?

"It's not gonna happen, if that's what you're thinking."

She squeezed her eyes shut. This was the side of him she hated, the cold, hard side, the man who could turn off all emotion and make her feel like a foolish girl.

Not this time.

"I'm not thinking anything of the sort." She took in a deep breath, closing her eyes against the reality of this moment. "I thought it was the right thing to tell you the truth, but I don't expect anything from you. I don't want anything from you. I don't need you." And she didn't. "I consider this baby to be a miracle. He or she is wanted and loved. Goodbye, John."

"Katrina! Don't hang up."

She waited. A half beat of silence.

"It is a miracle, isn't it?" His voice was hushed. "You said the doctors were sure you could never get pregnant."

This. *This* was how he wooed her — not the charm or the swagger or the persuasive words. His genuine wonder and awe at the unexpected. She remembered one time, on a hike, when he noticed a rare wildflower, a purple harebell. He had the same bewildered tone in his voice then as now, as if he couldn't believe what a gift he'd been given.

"Yes, John, it is a miracle. And every day I am going to hug this baby and tell him or her that very thing."

"Katrina, I am sorry. I did love you, you know."

She brushed her hand across her face, breathed again. "The thing is that love from you, John, is . . ." She searched for the right words and borrowed a phrase from Andy. ". . . it's pretty thin soup." And then she hung up.

For all her bluster, after the phone call, Katrina paced the road in front of the shanty for a full fifteen minutes, trying to pull herself together, to calm her racing heart and shaking hands, to erase the lingering effect of John's voice, his words. She was relieved and upset all at once.

"Everything all right?" Thelma said, looking up from her knitting when Katrina finally came back to the house. She watched

218

her over her reading glasses, needles click-ing along, her arm in the sling supported by a pillow so her hand was free to knit.

No, everything wasn't all right. Nothing would ever be the same again. "How am I going to get through this?" Katrina asked. "How will I ever manage?"

Thelma rested her knitting needles in her lap. "One foot in front of the other. One day at a time." She picked up her needles and started to click along again.

The taller the pile of money from outstand-ing bills grew for Hank, the less interested he seemed in the money. It drove Jesse crazy. How could Hank not care about money? Everybody cared about money! Everybody except Hank Lapp. The wad of money just sat there in his desk drawer, bundled with a rubber band. Something, Jesse felt, should be done with it. And after meeting Yardstick Yoder, he had a plan to double Hank's money.

Jesse enjoyed competition of any kind. It started in the fifth grade, when he made a wager with his seatmate over how strong he was. Strong enough, he said, to snap the pointer of infamous Teacher Edna into two pieces. The teacher kept a pointer at the chalkboard that doubled as a means to whack the knuckles of misbehaving children. Mostly, Jesse. The day before, he had carefully replaced the pointer with a dowel he had found at the hardware store and painstakingly hollowed out, then stained to match the appearance of the original pointer. At the opportune time, Jesse spoke out of turn — something that never failed to set off Teacher Edna and make her reach for her pointer to come after him. He extended his palms for a whacking but, upon impact, the pointer broke apart.

Jesse had it all worked out, but the horrified look on Teacher Edna's face surpassed anything he could have imagined. It inspired him to embellish the moment: He screamed and wailed and carried on as if every bone in his hand had been smashed. The next day, he came to school with enormous bandages wound around his hands. Teacher Edna never again used corporal punishment. Jesse won his first bet, the admiration of all the scholars, and Teacher Edna treated him carefully and cautiously, as if he might have brittle bone disease.

In the sixth grade, Jesse organized a betting pool among the upper grade boys. Each one contributed a dollar and the "pot" was awarded to whomever scored the most points on an upcoming exam. By age twelve,

Jesse had discovered greyhound racing. By age fourteen, he had found the pony track. At times, he had amassed sizable winnings, but they never lasted long. There was always another race beckoning to him.

Jesse heard talk of a man in Stoney Ridge who was known for placing bets, a man who could be found at The Chicken Box, a dive bar at the edge of town. A few days before the Founder's Day Picnic, Jesse went to The Chicken Box. Sitting in a corner of the bar, he found a small man, thick-necked, with a body like a brick privy. Domenico Giuseppe Rizzo. Also known as Domino Joe.

Jesse sat down next to him, hat brim tucked over his face, his back to the bartender. He wasn't old enough to be in a bar.

Domino Joe sized him up with a tilt of his head. "What's up, kid?"

Jesse got down to business. "I believe you have the wherewithal that I'm looking for."

Domino Joe squinted to hear, as if Jesse was speaking in a foreign language. "Huh?"

"I heard you are the one to know how a man could place a bet."

"Think so?" Domino Joe scanned the room nervously. Satisfied that no plainclothes policemen were nearby, he whipped out a much-used notebook.

"What's your pleasure? The boxing matches?"

Jesse shook his head. A boxing match was anathema to a Plain man. "Never that. I have my standards. I have something in mind that requires no violence. The boys' Hundred-Yard Dash at the Founder's Day Picnic."

Domino Joe scribbled down some information in the notebook, then extended a palm to Jesse. "Let me see the color of your money."

As Jesse peeled out his twenty dollar bills, temporarily borrowed from Hank Lapp's neglected bundle but soon to be replaced, he caught sight of a Plain man sitting at the bar next to an English man, handing papers back and forth, talking animatedly. After Jesse shook hands on the deal with Domino Joe, he went to the door and pivoted around, curious as to who that Plain man could be. The church in Stoney Ridge wasn't big, and it was getting smaller by the week. The fellow's back was to Jesse, but then he turned to speak to his companion and Jesse recognized his profile: Andy Miller, Thelma Beiler's new hired hand.

In the morning Katrina awoke, for a moment forgetting. Then she jerked into wakefulness and it all came flooding back. Today was the day she was going to tell her father about the baby. She pulled the sheets over her head, wishing she could just stay in bed and sleep the day away . . . but she'd done that long enough.

One foot in front of the other, Thelma had told her.

She climbed from bed and began to get ready for the day. This day. Would her life always seem branded by this day? A before and an after.

She stopped by Thelma's door but didn't hear any movement yet. In the kitchen, she pulled out a bowl to whisk eggs for breakfast but soon found there were no eggs in the refrigerator. She grabbed a shawl that hung on a peg by the kitchen door to head down to the henhouse. She crossed the yard, passing through the deep shadow cast by the barn and the morning frost crackled beneath her shoes. At the sight of Andy emerging from the barn, her steps faltered.

His hat brim hid his eyes, but his mouth was smiling as he strode toward her. "I was just heading to the house, hoping for a cup of hot coffee to warm my bones on this cold morning."

"That room in the barn must get cold."

"A little brisk."

"Why didn't you say something? I'll bring down some extra quilts." She felt his gaze on her face and forced herself to meet his eyes, but for a moment neither said anything. Then she looked over her shoulder toward the henhouse. "I was just getting started on breakfast when I realized we were out of eggs."

"I haven't seen much of you the last few days."

She shrugged. "You always seem to be off on the other side of the hill." She pointed to his boots, caked with mud.

He stamped his feet to shake off the mud. "Muddy on that hill." He took a step closer. "It's nice to see you out and about." He tugged on one of her capstrings. "Hope you're not avoiding me."

"No." She shook her head so the capstring slipped away from him. "No, I just have had a lot to think about."

"I'm not such a bad listener myself." He reached out for her hand and opened the palm, lifting it to his lips for a soft graze.

She closed her eyes. It felt so good, his warm lips on her hand. Having a man give her this kind of attention.

Katrina, no. Not now. This won't give you what you need. That voice — it might not have been audible, but it was unmistakable.

Clear, calm, to the point. A chill started at her neck and trickled down her spine. How many times had she heard her father say, "The God who spoke, long ago, still speaks." Was this what her father meant? A voice . . . a God . . . who knew her name?

She yanked her hand away, startling him. "Andy, I don't want you to get the wrong idea about me. I only want . . ."

"Friendship. You only want friendship." His dark brows knitted together, staring at her as if he was trying to figure her out.

"Yes." No, but yes. She wanted to reach out and brush his hair out of his eyes, to touch him with the same gentleness he had touched her. Instead, she twisted her hands in her apron. "There's a reason for that. I've been hiding something from you, from everyone." She took a deep breath. "I'm going to have a baby."

For a long, miserable moment, he stared at her, as wide-eyed with wonder as he ever got. "How long have you known?"

"Officially, just a few days. Unofficially, I've suspected for a few weeks." She peered upward at him. She listened inwardly, waiting for the voice again, but she felt only a simple sense of rightness. Sorrow, too, for all that was lost to her.

She glanced at him but he didn't say

another word, only gave her that unreadable gaze, so she started toward the henhouse. "I just needed to tell you why I can't get involved with you."

He skimmed his hand over her arm. "Wait."

She stopped.

"I'm sorry. Kinda hard to switch gears that fast. You've got to give a fellow a little time to process that information."

The silence lengthened and Katrina let it. She was still trying to process the news herself. She looked up at him, vulnerable and exposed. She didn't even realize she was crying until he took her in his arms and said, "Go on now, get your cry out."

She clung to his coat and let the tears fall as he held her, stroking her back. And after a while he rested his chin on the stiff pleats of her prayer cap and held her closer. Soon, though, she stepped away and wiped the tears off her face. When would these endless tears stop flowing?

"If a friend is what you need, then a friend is what you'll have.

He looked down at her with eyes that were warm and concerned.

"I could definitely use a friend. Especially today."

"You can count on me." He looked so

solemn, so serious, that she felt a slight grin quiver on her lips. Seeing it, his eyes sparkled, and an answering grin lifted his mouth. "Why today?"

"I'm planning to tell my news to my father."

She started past him as he tugged on her sleeve and asked, "Are you sure today's the right day to tell your father?"

"Yes. Absolutely. I don't want to delay it any longer."

"Maybe it's slipped your mind. Today's the Founder's Day Picnic. Everybody and their grandmother will be in town."

11

Yardstick Yoder was loping back and forth at the edge of the field of contestants like a stray keeping his distance from the herd. Jesse went over to lend encouragement and found he needed some himself after a closer look. Yardstick seemed as restless and anxious as a riderless horse. His strawlike hair hadn't been combed in days and his clothes were dirty and wrinkled. Bending down to him, Jesse urged in a low voice: "Run, Yardstick. Run like the wind."

"Huh? How does wind run?"

Ah, he was a literal-minded fellow. Jesse tried a more concrete motivational tool. "As you run, imagine that Luke Schrock is right on your heels, trying to catch you to beat you up."

"That's not hard to imagine," Yardstick said stoically.

Jesse patted Yardstick's thin shoulder, then hurried over to the sidelines, looking worriedly at the big boys in the race. Each one made two of poor skinny Yardstick. He wondered if he might have made a mistake, especially when he thought of the sizable sponsoring fee he had to put up to register Yardstick. But then again, he had seen Yardstick run. The boy was lightning on two legs.

Catching Domino Joe's eye, Jesse stepped over to speak to him. "I'll bet he wins by at least a dozen yards."

"What?" Domino Joe said. "A racehorse couldn't do that." He glanced at Jesse. "You want to put some greenbacks behind that prediction? Double or nothing?"

Jesse thrust a hand out to shake on the deal.

A warning whistle blew and Yardstick bolted for the starting line to join the other entrants. Eleven of the dozen boys bent over in a determined crouch, while Yardstick just stood there, fidgeting nervously from one foot to the other. Then the starter's pistol fired, and Yardstick was in full flight while the others were getting their speed up. He ran as if devils were pursuing him with red-hot pitchforks. He ran however fast it is a boy can run. Down the track he flew, leaving the puffing boys in his wake.

Not a moment after Yardstick sailed past

the finish line, Domino Joe appeared at Jesse's side and loomed in on him. "Kid, we got some talking to do. I'm gonna need you around this weekend."

Jesse smiled. "What do you have in mind?"

The day started cold but became warmer as the sun floated up the sky. A perfect day for the Stoney Ridge Annual Founder's Day Picnic, Katrina thought, glad she wasn't in town for it. Fern and Amos Lapp had arranged to stop by Moss Hill to pick up Thelma and Katrina in time for the picnic, but at the last minute, Katrina opted out, insisting that she had some things she needed to take care of at the house.

She felt grateful for the unexpected solitude of this day. She needed a break — from both those people she wanted to avoid and the one she liked too much for her own good. She needed time to sort things through. The phone call with John, the talk she needed to have with her father soon — not today, not Saturday because she knew Mary Mast planned to stop by the store, and then it would be Sunday. Surely, this kind of news did not need to be delivered on the Sabbath. Even though it was an off-Sunday, her father deserved a day off from troubles. Soon, though, she would tell him.

And then there was Andy. Something was happening between them, something within her. It was an unsettled feeling, something she was not prepared for and had not imagined she would feel again. She didn't *want* to feel it again.

But then, her life had turned upside down and she suspected the unsettled feeling was only partly due to the presence of Andy Miller.

Restless, she decided to take a walk in the midday sun, and remembered that she had promised extra quilts for him. She chose the warmest quilts she could find, stacked neatly in the guest room closet, and carried them down to the barn. Andy hadn't complained — though she had noticed that he never complained, even after working long hours in the rain — but his little room at the back of the barn must be getting bitter cold in the mornings and nights. And this was still autumn! Imagine how it would feel in mid-January.

When she reached the barn, she opened the door and called his name. Thelma's buggy horse shuffled in its stall, a few sparrows flew through the rafters, but Andy didn't answer. That wasn't unusual. He often disappeared for long stretches, full days, working on different sections of the hill. She breathed in deeply, enjoying the thick, musty scent of alfalfa hay. She knocked on the door to his room to make sure he wasn't inside and waited a moment before opening it. She set the quilts on the bed and took a moment to look around, curious about Andy. Fascinated by him.

And yet there were very few signs of him. Very little evidence that anyone even lived in this room. His shaving brush was next to a small mirror, hung on a nail in the wall. She lifted the brush, breathed in the smell that reminded her of him. She closed her eyes, imagining herself and Andy . . .

Stop it! Stop it now, Katrina Stoltzfus. How ridiculous. This was hardly the time to allow herself to be interested in a man.

She pivoted around to leave and noticed a trunk stored under the bed. Ignoring a pang of guilt for snooping, she bent down and pulled it out. *Locked.* She looked around for a key but heard a loud blasting sound in the distance — a gunshot? — and quickly shoved the trunk back under the bed. She left the room and hurried outside, waiting a moment for her eyes to adjust to the bright sunlight after the dim barn. She heard another gunshot go off and decided it must be coming from some Founder's Day event. The sound of the gunshot startled Thelma's buggy horse and set the chickens to clucking.

Katrina started slowly up the hillside path. She passed some hens that were exploring the grass for grubs, walking as if on sharp stones, fussing like old women. When she reached the top of the hill, her favorite spot, she flopped down on a moss-covered rock and looked up. The sky was filled with swiftly moving, wispy, feathery clouds. Up here, the wind was blowing, and she had to tie her capstrings under her chin to keep them from blowing in her face. Yet the wind brought with it its own silence, she thought, until you began to wonder whether it was the wind you were hearing or the beating of your heart.

It was a good place, this rocky hill. It had been a good place for Thelma and Elmo, and it was providing a way for Thelma to remain on it.

She watched a hawk ride the wind. The hawk banked suddenly and flew straight off, like a shot arrow, into the sky. When it disappeared from sight, Katrina lay back and closed her eyes. She heard another gunshot and wondered if her father and sisters were having fun at the parade. She knew Jesse would be finding a way to have fun. She hoped it was legal.

The strange, unsettled feeling was still with her; curiously, it made her aware of just how attached she was growing to the piece of earth upon which she lay, that particular hill of moss, that particular tiny patch of Stoney Ridge.

She knew she was at a great crossroads in her life, that important decisions were facing her, ones that would affect her and her baby for the rest of their lives. She had no doubt that the bishop would either insist she and John marry — and that wasn't about to happen, seeing as how he was engaged to another girl — or give up the baby for adoption. She felt fairly confident that her father would intervene and let her choose her own path.

Which was what? What was it that she wanted to do? She asked herself the questions and could not think of any answers. No solutions to her problems. All she knew for sure was that she had made an unholy mess of growing up.

Tears filled her eyes and overflowed, spilling down her face, infuriating her. She had to stop this crying! She wiped her face with her apron, rose to her feet, and walked to the top of the hill, then pivoted around to gaze at the hillside of rocks, blanketed in emerald-green moss.

To the sky at large, she announced in a loud voice, "Show me! Show me that you are really here. And where I'm meant to be. And what you want me to do."

The word "cherish" emerged in her mind; it was as simple as that. Some deep instinct within her asserted itself; an instinct to cherish another person, to cherish the land. Something, someone — God? — had given her an answer.

A warm breeze blew over her face. She would find a way — somehow, some way — to buy this land from Thelma. She would raise her baby here. She could care for Thelma as she grew older.

Spirits lifting with every step, she nearly skipped down the hill toward the house. This time, she eyed the yard, imagining flowering shrubs along the foundation of the house. She eyed the old shed, imagining it as a gift shop for plants. She imagined a new, large greenhouse, replacing the old one with its broken windows. Cheerful potted flowers on the porch. She imagined herself happy, playing in the yard with her little girl. Or maybe her little boy? She thought it was a girl. Hoped it was.

There was a lot to do, but the challenge fired her with eagerness. She'd never had this feeling before — a certainty, a positivity, a fire in her belly. Never! Not even for John.

She chuckled . . . and the sound of her own laughter was so foreign to her ears it made her heart hammer. She tilted her head back and squinted at the sky, letting freedom and happiness overcome her. She chuckled again, feeling the wondrous thrust of the sound against her throat. How long since she had felt such happiness? How long since laughter had spilled out of her? How long?

Everything, she sensed, was going to be all right. She had her answer.

After the Founder's Day Hundred-Yard Dash victory, Domino Joe developed a keen interest in Jesse and his protégé. Domino Joe made it possible for Yardstick Yoder to run in any Hundred-Yard Dash that was included in every nearby town's fall gathering over that weekend: Pumpkin Fest, OktoberFest, Harvest Fest, if there was a festival of any kind — and there were plenty in Lancaster County — there was a race to be run.

It was working out nicely for everyone: Domino Joe found gamblers who had a keen interest in racing, Yardstick received a cut of the winnings, Jesse got an even more generous cut. Everybody won.

Until the last race.

It was late on Sunday afternoon, and Yardstick Yoder didn't show up to run in the race as he had promised. Suddenly Jesse found himself owing Domino Joe a rather sizable sum of money.

Domino Joe, it turned out, was merciless.

If Jesse didn't cough up one thousand dollars within one month's time, Domino Joe implied, in quite a nasty tone, that he would send some of his people to shatter his kneecaps.

At that pronouncement, Jesse rubbed his knees, keenly aware of how fond he was of his knees. He was in way over his head and didn't know where to turn.

It was distressing to Jesse that riches kept eluding him — he needed to do something about that — but for now, he had more pressing matters on his mind. His knees, for example. He was scooting his way to the hardware store to pick up some equipment for Hank when he passed right by the Sweet Tooth Bakery. A cinnamon roll sounded nice right about now, especially after Molly's inedible scrambled eggs this morning. He parked his scooter on the side of the building, and suddenly felt as if he wasn't alone. He glanced over his shoulders and there were two of them, big and bigger.

Domino Joe's goons. The kneecap smashers.

"Jesse Stoltzfus," the big one said. His head was round, with tiny eyes and a bulbous nose. "We'd like to have a little chat with you."

Jesse swallowed. "Certainly, gentlemen. Let's go inside." Where it was safer. Where there were witnesses.

"We like it out here," the bigger one said. "Nice and private." He had a broad nose and a high forehead and a long throat with an Adam's apple that was too prominent. He sized Jesse up with a tilt of his head. "So you're the one who owes Domino Joe some money."

"One month, he said. And don't forget October has thirty-one days in it." On top of everything else, Jesse was mortified to hear his voice jump an octave.

Swish, and then *bang!* All three of them jumped like spooked schoolboys.

A Plain man towered in the doorway, the flung-open door still quivering on its hinges behind him. "What's going on out here?" He reached one hand into his coat pocket and pulled out something shiny and metal, something Jesse had never seen before.

Something the man gripped tightly in his fist.

All at once there was more space around Jesse, both goons stepping back from the circle of authority the man seemed to bring with him. Why was that? This fellow was a Plain man, half their age, hardly a physical match against two conscienceless goons.

"Clear out of here," the man boomed, "and I mean now."

The pair cleared out, but not without pointed glares at Jesse's kneecaps that sent a deep chill down his spine. By the time he turned back around, the man was nowhere to be seen. But it occurred to him who this Plain man was: Andy Miller.

David had been at the hospital since Sunday afternoon. Ephraim and Sadie's entire extended family had arrived and gathered to say their goodbyes. Surrounded by his loving family, Ephraim was taken off the ventilator. His lung muscles were too paralyzed to work to breathe, so he labored hard to get air. Those he loved wrapped around his bed, watching him struggle to get air, praying that each breath would be his last and his soul would be released from his broken earthly shell. Everyone was prepared for this moment.

What no one had been prepared for was that Ephraim's heart was young and strong. The afternoon turned into the evening, which turned to morning, another day, and still he labored to breathe. Gasping, choking. He was suffocating to death.

It was a heart-wrenching thing to watch, especially for his wife and son. Not a single relative — over twenty packed into the small room — left his side. David stayed through the night and into the morning, but felt he had to leave for a few hours to open the store. He planned to return to the hospital as soon as Bethany Schrock arrived for her shift at noon.

Around nine thirty on Monday morning, David left the hospital in a taxi and went straight to the store, surprised to find Katrina waiting for him by the door. "Morning, sweetheart." He greeted her with a warm smile but she didn't return it. She seemed . . . all business. Even the bow was tied tight under her black bonnet. But she wasn't as tired looking as she had been looking lately. In fact, her eyes were bright and clear.

"Dad, there's something I need to tell you. I thought we could talk privately before the store opened."

Finally, she was ready to talk. David had

known she returned from Ohio that weekend in July with a broken heart, but he could tell her heart wasn't mending. If anything, the heartbreak had seemed to deepen with time. He wanted to do something to make it better, to make her better. "Okay. Let's go inside." He went right to the coffeepot but she waved him off.

"You'd better sit down for this."

They went to the storeroom and he pulled out a chair for her, then sat across from her. "What is it, honey? You seem so troubled."

Katrina untied her bonnet and took it off. She placed it on his desk, took a deep breath, squared her shoulders, and lifted her head, though she kept her eyes on her black bonnet. "I'm . . . going to have a baby. John's baby."

For several moments, David said nothing, his mind struggling to grasp this new information. Dazed, he sank back in the chair. He knew something was wrong — but not once did this option cross his mind. Not once.

"Say something, Dad."

He'd bent his head as she spoke, and now he looked up. Tears rose in his eyes, and his throat ached. Moments came back to him, in swirls and glimpses, strange disconnected

241

details. Katrina as a newborn, then a toddler, struggling to walk, tying her shoelaces. Katrina, playing happily in the backyard, putting her soft arms around his neck for no reason at all and saying, "I love you, Daddy." His mind pictured her on her first day of school, then years later, when he went into the emergency room and saw her still figure lying on that gurney, sure she had died along with Anna. A deep sense of loss rose up in him, so forceful, woven of so many memories.

Too much. Too much. David was on the verge of weeping. He pushed it all back: the accident that affected Katrina so profoundly — emotional scars that were every bit as real as the physical ones, the powerful rushing love he felt for his daughter. David stared at his girl, his little girl, his firstborn. He felt as if someone had bushwhacked him.

"Dad, I know it's wrong, a sin even. I regret what we did. But I'm not sorry about having a baby. I didn't think it was possible . . . and what if this is the only baby I will ever have? To me, this baby is a miracle." She paused and looked at him. "Please say something. You look so pale."

He struggled for breath to respond to her, knowing all that was hinging on this moment . . . for her, for the baby's future, for them.

And then he pictured Ephraim Yoder, struggling for breath in a hospital room. A reminder of the fragility of life, of focusing on what was truly important. He rose to his feet, pulled his daughter close to him, and kissed the top of her head. The wonder of it grabbed him, gave him the strength he needed, and he smiled. "You're right. A baby is always a miracle."

She clung to him in a way she hadn't since she was a little girl. For a long moment they stood there, father and daughter, until she pulled away and walked toward the window. "I'm not going to marry John. Or rather, he is not going to marry me."

That, David felt, was a great relief. "Did you want to?"

"I thought I did. I thought we both wanted that. I was sure of it. But I was wrong."

"He knows about the baby?"

"Yes. And he made it clear it didn't change the fact that he was going to marry Susie." She had been staring out the window, but now she swung hard around to face him. "You know what he said? That he was sorry. *Sorry.*"

David went cold inside. He believed in nonresistance, believed it with his whole core, but at this moment, he wanted to hurt John. He clenched his fists and breathed in and out slowly. With great effort, he kept his voice level and calm. "Sounds like you don't believe him."

She shrugged and crossed her arms, eyes filling with tears. "John doesn't matter anymore."

He smiled and gathered her back into the circle of his arms. "We'll get through this together. I promise." He put his finger under her chin and tipped her face until he was looking into her wet eyes. "And did I ever make a promise to you that I didn't keep?"

"I don't remember."

"You would remember if I did."

"Dad, there's one thing I am sorry about. Disappointing you. You don't deserve this, and I know there will be repercussions."

"Katrina, there's not a person on this planet who doesn't have regrets about choices they've made. The important thing is to make things right with God."

That was the wrong thing to say, he could tell by the way she tensed up and pulled away. But it needed to be said to her, as a father, as a minister. This was between her and God. A turning point, he hoped. Katrina had never had the strong faith of

Anna or him, but she knew where the source of their strength came from.

She reached for her black bonnet on his desk and started to put it on, then lowered it and held it in front of her, chin tucked low. "Since Mom died, it's been like a long night that never ends. Sometimes I think God asks for more than I can give. Der Herr gibt und der Herr nimmt." *The Lord gives and the Lord takes away.*

"It might seem like that at times, but he also gives us more than we can receive. This baby, for example."

Her voice dropped to a whisper. "Dad, do you think this baby is a gift? Do you really?"

"Oh yes, Katrina. A great gift." A thought occurred to him. "Well, what do you know? I'm going to be a grandfather." He smiled at that thought. The first smile of many, it dawned on him, over this new life.

Relief swept over her face, then just as quickly, it was gone. As she put her bonnet on, she said, "Dad, do you think people will talk?"

David reached out to straighten her bonnet. "Of course not," he said, not at all certain.

12

Thunder sounded in the distance. The clouds had darkened the day. The rainstorm that was threatening to move in this afternoon suited Jesse's mood perfectly.

Life had taught him you have to do what you have to do. Aware that he should get down to business, he decided to pay a call to Andy Miller at Moss Hill.

He hadn't gone far when lightning lit the sky, followed closely — too closely for his liking — by a crack of thunder. A sprinkle hit the back of his neck as he swept along down the road on his scooter. The sprinkle turned to an icy cold shower, making Jesse think twice about the wisdom of his errand.

At the little house, he barely rapped on the door when it opened wide and Fern Lapp stared back at him. She seemed amused. "You look a sight. Like a mouse washed down the drainpipe."

That woman was everywhere at once. She

said she was sharing a cup of tea with Thelma, but her expression at the sight of Jesse seemed to imply that she knew he was up to no good. "Does your employer know you're traipsing around the countryside?"

"But I was out doing an errand for Hank —" He stopped himself. Some questions scare off words. Why was he trying to explain himself to Fern Lapp? Jesse felt it wouldn't be worth pointing out that Hank wasn't much of an employer — he seldom repaired anything, nor had he taught him a single thing about buggies. Jesse had to admit, Fern Lapp was the one responsible for keeping him on his toes every second . . . though she was not exactly easy on the nerves. "Since I was in the neighborhood, I thought I'd drop by to say a quick hello to my dear sister."

"She is a dear," Thelma said, peeking around Fern's shoulder. "But she has gone to the Bent N' Dent to speak to your father. Andy might know when she's due back. He's down in the greenhouse."

Excellent! Out the front door he went, past Fern Lapp's cold eye, to the greenhouse near the barn. Thunder blasted overhead. Thunder meant lightning, and here he lay in a prime location for a direct hit from a lightning bolt. He started to run toward the greenhouse. Thunder cracked louder, closer. A flash of lightning lit up the noonday sky.

He burst into the greenhouse, gasping for breath. Andy looked at him, startled, as did his big yellow dog. The dog came flying down the aisle with a threatening bark, but Andy gave a sharp whistle and the dog stopped in its tracks but blocked the aisle, staring Jesse down. He decided to stay by the door until the dog realized he was friendly.

On both sides of the greenhouse were flats of soft green moss, at various stages of growth. The sight of it was mesmerizing, truly beautiful. But Jesse needed to stay focused on the purpose of his task. "Sorry to interrupt you."

Andy cocked his head. "If you're looking for your sister, I dropped her off at the Bent N' Dent to talk to your dad."

Jesse took off his hat and twirled it in a circle. "Actually, you're the one I've come to see. I don't think we've been properly introduced. I'm Jesse, Katrina's brother."

"I know who you are. And you know who I am, otherwise you wouldn't be here." Andy whistled again and the big dog returned to his side and lay down. "Still a little spooked from your friends at the Sweet Tooth Bakery?"

Everyone seemed to be an expert on Jesse's countenance today. "I'd never met those two before."

"Really." Andy fixed a look on him as if he didn't quite buy his story. "My grandmother had a saying — 'Gleich und gleich gsellt sich gern.' " *Birds of a feather will flock together.*

This wasn't going well. Jesse tried a more direct approach: honesty. "I seem to be in a bit of a tight spot and thought you might be able to help me."

A crashing thunderbolt rolled across the sky overhead. "Tight spot?"

"A long story. Suffice it to say that a bet went south."

"Goons tend to have long memories."

And didn't Jesse just know it.

He had a tendency to draw the attention of goons the way syrup drew flies. A few months ago, back in Ohio, he had made a bet with the wrong sort — so grumm as me Hund sei Hinnerbeh. *As crooked as the hind leg of a dog.* The race had been fixed, Jesse later realized, but his favored horse — quick as greased lightning — hadn't gotten that information and won by two lengths. The bookie was not happy to have to cough up a large winning, and Jesse thought it expedient to depart his aunt's home that very day.

"What makes you think I'd have any experience with goons?"

"For starters, the way you scared off those two earlier this morning."

"They were just trying to intimidate you."

"It worked."

"Their boss wants his money."

"So I've been told." He rubbed his kneecaps. "Another reason I thought you might be able to provide some help is that I've seen you at The Chicken Box."

"Oh, that place." Andy lifted one shoulder in a careless shrug. "I just go in now and then to grab a hamburger."

Right. That wasn't what the meeting seemed like to him. Andy had sat next to an English man and the two were huddled together, talking in earnest. And perhaps Jesse was mistaken — highly doubtful but there was always a slim chance — but while he was scootering around town on bill collection errands, a car had passed him on the road a few times, driven by that very English man, with Andy in the passenger seat.

"What were *you* doing at The Chicken Box? Aren't you underage?"

"That's where my bookie hangs out."

Andy groaned. "Not Domino Joe. Of all the bookies in the world, you picked

Domino Joe. He doesn't forgive and he never forgets."

Jesse nodded. "The very one."

"How much do you owe him?"

"One thousand dollars . . . by the first Sunday of November."

Andy let out a whistle. "Any way you can drum up the cash? Maybe you can ask your father for a loan."

Jesse shook his head. "No chance at all. My dad is completely preoccupied with someone at the hospital who's dying." He moved in on Andy and tried to keep a tenor of desperation out of his voice. "If I could just have a little more time, I can make good on what I owe Domino Joe." Enough time for Jesse to track down Yardstick for one more race. All or nothing. Preferably, all. He glanced cautiously at Andy, inclined to play an all-or-nothing hunch of another sort entirely. During church on Sundays, he had seen Andy gaze at Katrina as if he had her made to order. "My sister has spoken so highly of you. I felt sure you'd be the one who could help me."

Andy hesitated. He was weakening. "What do you want me to do?"

"Perhaps . . . you could talk to him for me? Put in a good word." Wisely, Jesse stopped talking and gave him room.

251

Andy frowned. "Wait here. I'll be right back." He made a dash in the rain from the greenhouse to the barn, disappearing into the yawning open door. Happily, the dog trotted behind Andy, his tail high. Someday, Jesse would like to have a good old dog like that. A loyal companion.

While waiting for Andy to return, Jesse wandered up and down the aisles of the greenhouse, marveling at the sheets of moss growing in flat wooden containers, carpets of emerald green. Moss was something he'd never given any consideration to before, and yet here, it was strikingly beautiful. When he had first heard that his sister was going to stay with Thelma to help her with a moss business, he thought it was a joke. Now, looking up and down the rows of growing moss, he thought it was brilliant. A much less dangerous business venture than a Hundred-Yard Dash.

Moments later, Andy came back to the greenhouse, his fist lifted in the air. "It's been years since I needed to resort to these."

Brass knuckles.

So *that's* what he reached for in his coat pocket outside of the Sweet Tooth bakery. *That's* what scared off those goons. "Seems like a strange thing for a Plain man to have."

Andy grinned. "One of the many reasons

to not bend at the knee yet." He handed them to Jesse to try on. They fit across the back of his hand cold and secure. "If you show them off at the right time, you won't ever have to use them. All they're meant to do is to intimidate Domino Joe's goons right back. Give you the upper edge."

Jesse was doubtful, but he was willing to try anything to keep his kneecaps intact. Still, it didn't solve his primary problem. "And you'll talk to Domino Joe? Try to buy me a little time? Get him to call off his goons?"

Andy sighed a doubtful sigh. "I'll do what I can."

Jesse's spirits soared. "Thank you, Andy. I'm indebted to you."

"I haven't done anything yet."

In his puniest voice, Jesse said, "Can I count on your discretion? You won't say anything about this —"

"No reason to."

Hugely relieved, Jesse jammed the brass knuckles against his other palm and yelped in pain.

"You have no idea what you're doing, do you?"

He looked up at Andy in surprise, relieved to see not censure in his expression but rather an understanding light in his eyes.

He couldn't quite stifle a small grin. "Absolutely no idea at all."

The grin faded, however, when he thought of Domino Joe and his goons, waiting for him around every corner. He rubbed his knees again as he walked out of the greenhouse, ready and armed to face his foes.

From the smell and feel of the air, tonight would bring the first hard frost. Birdy closed the schoolhouse door behind the last student — Luke Schrock had to stay after today for another misdeed — and turned back to take a fond assessment of the little room. It continued to surprise her that she enjoyed her role as teacher. More than enjoyed. She loved it, loved waking up in the morning, loved hurrying to school to start the day.

She'd always thought of herself as a student — after all, she loved to study birds. But never as a teacher. And yet she was actually competent in the role. Perhaps her brother had done her a favor: he'd given her the unexpected discovery that she had a gift for teaching.

This little piece of property had some pull on everyone in Stoney Ridge. Everyone she could think of had something at stake in this school. Her brothers, as school board

members. Along with them, the men of Stoney Ridge who had built the snug
schoolhouse. The mothers who sent their
hearts out the door every morning. And
now . . . here Birdy was, pulled in to teach.
And loving it!

It mystified her, how life had its twists and
turns. It delighted her.

Birdy went to her desk to finish up the
grading of seventh and eighth grade essays.
The door opened and she didn't even look
up, sure it was Luke Schrock, who had a
habit of forgetting his hat and coat. He
never remembered until he was halfway
home, then he would blast into the
schoolhouse and grab them, then blow out
again. Without lifting her head, she said,
"You have to stop doing this!"

She braced herself for the stomp of his
feet, but none came. When she looked up,
there was David Stoltzfus, standing in the
back, a slightly amused and puzzled look on
his face. She jumped out of her chair and it
tipped backward. She hurried to pick it up
and then knocked over her mug filled with
pencils. They went clattering. She gathered
the pencils on the ground and stuffed them
back in the mug, silently berating herself.
Her awkwardness had improved in the last
few encounters with David — she hadn't

done anything clumsy during the two times he had come to speak to the class. It only seemed to happen when she was acutely nervous, like now.

David didn't budge from his spot. He patiently waited until she had recovered from everything . . . but embarrassment.

"Um, hello, David. I wasn't expecting you today." He took a few steps toward her. How could a person's eyes be so true, so beautiful? And — could it be more unfair? — thick dark lashes framed those eyes. Trying not to think of her own rather ordinary eyes, she refocused. She reminded herself to breathe normally.

"Sadie Yoder asked me to bring you the death message of Ephraim."

"Oh." Birdy sank down in her chair. It wasn't unexpected news, but it was still so sad. So very, very sad. "So that's where Noah's been today."

"Yes. Ephraim was taken off the ventilator yesterday afternoon, and passed away around noon today. Sadie called me at the store to let me know the news. I was planning to go back to the hospital this afternoon, but that won't be necessary. She said they're all heading to the house."

"How is Noah doing?" He was a solitary character, that Noah. Lean and lanky and not at all interested in school or in making friends with the other children.

"Quiet. Sad. Surrounded by lots of family." He smiled. "Last night, gathered around the hospital bed, the entire family sang hymns. I think it was . . . a good death for Ephraim." He crossed his arms over his chest. "The viewing will be tomorrow and Wednesday, and the funeral on Thursday."

"So no school on Thursday."

"No school on Thursday," he repeated. He frowned in thought, then looked up. "I think you said something about a bug attacking Luke Schrock."

"Yes, yes I did. It's been a frightful thing for him." Her eyes lifted to the corners of the ceilings. She was sure the bug must live in the back of the room near Luke's desk.

"It only strikes Luke, you said."

She nodded, but she didn't dare move in case she knocked something else over.

"Have you ever noticed what's going on when Luke gets stung?"

"No, not really."

"Is there any chance that my daughters could be involved?"

"Your girls? Why, no. No chance at all. Lydie and Emily sit up front. Molly is over there. And Ruthie —" she pointed to the far row — "she's on the opposite side of the room."

David walked over to Ruthie's desk and turned to look at Luke's desk. "What I meant was — do you think the younger girls might have been the focus of attention for the children while Luke was getting stung?"

Birdy thought back to what was happening during today's bug attack event, but she didn't feel comfortable describing the circumstances to David. It had been Molly's turn to read her short essay to the class. The assignment was to finish the prompt of "My Favorite —" and write a two-paragraph description about something they liked.

Molly had stood by Birdy's desk and read the title, "My Favorite —" and before she could finish, Luke shouted out, "Food! The more, the merrier!"

Molly burst into tears and *zap!* The insect stung Luke. The entire class erupted into chaos. The boys ran to examine Luke's newest injury, the girls surrounded Molly to offer comfort. It took quite a bit of time to settle the students back into their seats. This time, Birdy had Luke stay after and sweep out the schoolroom.

The reason Birdy didn't want to tell David the story was because Molly's story was, indeed, about her favorite food. Ice cream.

She realized that David was waiting for her answer. "It is . . . possible . . . but . . ."

David strode over to Ruthie's desk, lifted the lid, moved some books around. He stilled, and held up a peashooter. "Aha. I think this might explain a few things."

Birdy's mouth went wide. "But . . . how . . . when . . . ?" How could she not have noticed? What kind of teacher was she? How obtuse! How mortifying. And, more importantly, what must David think of her?

But David wasn't thinking about Birdy. He was holding the peashooter in both hands and snapped it in two, a clean break. Then he put it back in Ruthie's desk and closed the top. "If you don't mind, I'd like to keep this between us. It would be good for Ruthie to think you're on to her. She's sneaky, that daughter of mine. Anna used to say we had to 'outfox the fox' with Ruthie." He took his hat off and fingered the brim. "Birdy, I'd like an honest answer. Do my daughters get teased often?"

Slowly, Birdy nodded. "Mostly Molly. The twins look after each other."

He raised his chin and nodded wisely, as if to say, *Ah, I see.* He didn't seem to be surprised. "Molly has a naïveté that makes her a target. Always has."

No wonder Birdy had a soft spot for

Molly. How well she understood her. Birdy had been teased endlessly throughout her school years. If it wasn't because she was a head or two taller than most everyone, it was her fascination with birds. She used to bring crumbs in her pockets to school and wander off to a quiet place during lunch to lay the crumbs in a circle around her. She would sit as still as a stone until one bird, then another, ventured close. She learned to imitate birdcalls and could summon them as effortlessly as other children whistled for their dogs. Eventually, certain birds learned to trust her and would perch on her open palm to eat crumbs. That was the year her formal name, Betty, was altered to Birdy. The boys meant to insult her but she loved the nickname and it stuck.

David worried his hat in a circle. "Well, hopefully, the mysterious bug stings have been stopped before Ruthie put Luke Schrock's eye out." He thumped his hat back on. "I better not keep you. So long, Birdy." They smiled at each other and a moment of subtle appreciation fluttered between them.

"David, before you go, what made you think Ruthie was the culprit?"

"On Saturday, Mary Mast mentioned that she used to teach school. She remembered a boy shooting off a peashooter in her class. It seemed like something Ruthie might do to protect her sisters from getting teased. She's tricky, that Ruthie. Quiet but effective."

Birdy's heart sank. Mary Mast was not only lovely, but she was clever. And David had spent time with her on Saturday. Apparently that lucky woman, whom Birdy knew would swoop in one day to win David's heart, had arrived. A fresh wave of envy rolled over Birdy.

God forgive me, she thought, ashamed of her uncharitable thoughts.

Later, when David was finishing up a few extra dinner dishes that the girls had missed, he thought about the peashooter in Ruthie's desk. He wished he could share that story with Anna. Knowing his wife, she would have laughed and laughed to hear it. She was such a woman for that kind of thing, finding amusement in their children. His hands stilled in their scrubbing, and he shut his eyes. He could hear her voice as if she were standing in the kitchen beside him. She would have said that peashooter solution sounded just like Ruthie; she found a way to get the job done — that of silencing Luke Schrock — and avoid any blame. For

261

a moment, the memories of Anna were so sharp they took his breath away.

He heard a heavy clump on the porch as Jesse jumped onto it from the walkway, splattering icy mud all over the porch. Then the kitchen door squeaked open and there he was, hungry as a bear and full of interesting news. David shook off his melancholy, grateful for the gift of his son.

Wouldn't you know, no sooner was Jesse prepared to face down the lurking thugs of Stoney Ridge than they ceased lurking. He kept one hand in his coat pocket at all times, and one eye peeled for errant thugs. But even when he deliberately dawdled on Main Street, passing the time of day in front of the Sweet Tooth Bakery, he could not draw them out.

He had Andy Miller to thank for that, no doubt. It was as he indeed hoped, that Domino Joe and his goons were wasting no further time on him. Which was a lucky thing, because Jesse was growing fond of this little charming town. With the exception of Fern Lapp, most people were softening toward him as he became acquainted with them. He found that if he offered to do a stray task that housewives wanted to dodge — clean out a clogged drainpipe or empty ashes from a cookstove — it brought him an invitation to stay for the evening meal. With Molly's cooking being what it was, he happily accepted all invitations.

But he kept the brass knuckles with him at all times, just in case. His concealed weapon was at the ready, and there was never an occasion to use it. A huge disappointment.

13

Thursday was Ephraim Yoder's funeral. The service would be held in the Yoder's barn, so David went early to see if there was anything he could do to help get ready. The Yoder farm sat in one of the most picturesque settings David had ever seen. A hill rose up behind it on the west. To the south, a broad meadow was dotted with Jersey dairy cows, placidly cropping grass as calves gamboled around their mamas. Beyond that a wide stream created a natural barrier to keep the cows from straying. David heard the rush of water over stone as the creek twisted and bent into thick woodland. A big barn stood to the south of the house, with a corral of horses grazing on lush grass. A broad porch stretched across the front of the house. Rocking chairs were perched along the porch, as if waiting for visitors to come calling.

As soon as David arrived, he went to the

barn to make sure the benches were in place and, indeed, they were. Someone had seen to it: neat rows lined up evenly in the center of the barn. He glanced at his watch. Still a half hour before others would start to arrive. He sat on a hard backless bench in the back row — the men's side — and looked across the rows to the opposite side — the women's side. It felt good to gaze upon the many benches, to think of and pray for all who would be sitting on them soon. How he had grown to care about them over this last year!

Today, the entire church would stop business as usual for the day — school was canceled, his store was closed, even farmers who needed a sunny day like today to harvest hay would forego the chore — everything stopped. People young and old would come together to worship God and to thank him for the life of Ephraim Yoder. And to bury Ephraim in the cemetery down the road. The last thing they could do for their friend.

David looked again at the benches in the barn, facing each other. These benches were a reminder that when everyone came to worship, they weren't isolated individuals but a family of God. They came to worship not just to see and hear but to pray and praise God with one another. As a community.

This. This was the Plain life he loved so much.

David soaked up this moment of quiet, of stillness. Just being here in this beautiful silence was an act of worship. An aspect of the Amish life that he loved most dearly was that solitude and silence were normal conditions of everyday life. Whenever he went into town, he felt barraged by noises: people talking on their cell phones, the squeal of car brakes, the earsplitting sirens of emergency vehicles. Last time he went to the post office, a county worker blew leaves off the sidewalks of Main Street with a gas-powered leaf blower. A man couldn't even hear himself think!

To David's way of thinking, there was an intimate connection to God in silence. Silence created an open, empty space where he could become attentive to God, as he was right now, where the useless trivialities of life began to drop away.

This. This was his life. The life he loved.

After the burial of Ephraim, and after the lunch that would follow, and assuming there was an opportune time, David planned to tell Katrina's news to Freeman, Levi, and

Abraham. David gathered all of his stray thoughts and pushed them aside so that he wouldn't be distracted during the preaching of his sermon.

He rose to start preaching, but soon his eyes went to Katrina. She looked scared. She had left the hymnbook open on her lap as if trying to cover up what was weighing on her mind. He felt a surge of protective love toward her, wishing that he could shield her from all she would be facing in the coming months.

And suddenly his mind went blank.

Despite hours of prayer and preparation, his sermon gathered in a hard knot just below his heart and refused to budge loose. That sudden expectant silence fell over the church, almost a breath-held quiet, as if the worshipers had sucked in their breath in unison and were afraid to breathe out again as they waited. The silence stretched, broken only by the bleat of a lamb in the barnyard. David's throat tightened up, threatened to close off completely. Of course, as long as he kept his eyes closed and his head bowed, people would think he was praying instead of panicking.

Indeed, he was praying. With more urgency and anxiety at every passing minute. He waited for some words to come, but his mind remained blank. A few people began shifting restlessly on their benches as the wait stretched out too long. His prayer got more frantic. *Help!*

Then, from the back of the women's benches, came a dramatic, elaborate, enormous, over-the-top sneeze and everyone looked around to see who had sneezed. He knew even before he looked up that it was Jesse, helping him out with a distraction, and David couldn't keep himself from smiling. Into his mind popped a picture of Jesus at the tomb of Lazarus. Words began to form in his mind, one after the other, then complete sentences, then paragraphs, and soon, as always, the Lord took over and filled in for what he lacked.

Hours later, after the burial of Ephraim Yoder, David was the last to leave the graveyard. He wanted to make sure everything was as it should be: no piles of uneven dirt or stray leaves left on top of Ephraim's fresh grave. He scooped up some remaining piles of dirt and dumped them beyond the fence, then leaned on the shovel, gazing out over the sleeping land. There wasn't much to see, though there was.

Here in this plain, unadorned graveyard lay the keepers of the faith. Each rough-hewn granite marker looked just like the one next to it because, even in death, no one should stand out as better than another. He felt a great responsibility to these keepers of the faith who had faithfully run the race the Lord had marked out for them. Now it was his turn to carry the torch for them, for all the members of the church, for the next generation.

No, there wasn't much to see here, though there was.

It was always a curious thing to Jesse to see how serious and solemn people were during a funeral service, all the way to the graveside, but the minute that cold body was dropped in the ground — *plunk!* — it was like the sun rose after a long dark night and everything was back to business as usual. As people made their way back to the Yoder house for lunch, he overheard several conversations about lame horses and broken buggy wheels and how too much rain this year was spoiling their hay harvest.

Freeman Glick cornered him, as he had a habit of doing, to give him a short sermon of admonishment and warnings. One of the subtexts in virtually every one of Freeman's mini-sermons was "Liquor has never passed my lips." Jesse heard it frequently.

Today's dour warning from Freeman took

a more funeralish turn: "And when your earthly body is dead and gone, and your soul will meet God face-to-face, will he say to you, 'Well done, my good and faithful servant'?"

These encounters with Freeman always left Jesse stuttering and tongue-tied. He hardly knew he had a soul. Mostly, he had hormones.

While he was recovering from that odd encounter with Freeman, Miriam Schrock swept past him and gave him a brightening glance, and he smiled gamely back. Maybe this was only a mild degree of thawing out from her, but it greatly improved his mood.

Jesse sat with his back against a tree, watching buggies leave, wishing his father would hurry it up. There was some kind of important discussion going on between the church elders and he just hoped it had nothing to do with the Founder's Day Hundred-Yard Dash. Plus, he was getting hungry again.

He saw Danny Riehl help Miriam Schrock climb into his buggy. A pang twisted Jesse's gut, and he knew it wasn't hunger. Thinking of Miriam Schrock with someone else didn't set well. All the brightness left Jesse, like clouds swallowing up the sun.

And then he spotted Yardstick Yoder down

by the barn and jumped up to go talk to him, to try to find out why he had blown off that race on Sunday afternoon, and did he have any idea how much trouble his carelessness had caused Jesse? Even if the goons had been called off, it didn't mean his debt had been forgiven. Or maybe it did? He liked to hope so but he doubted it. He hadn't forgotten Andy's assessment of Domino Joe: he never forgot and he never forgave. Unconsciously, he bent down and rubbed his kneecap.

He picked up his pace to pin Yardstick down, but the boy saw him coming and took off running. Jesse's good mood disappeared as quickly and completely as Yardstick.

After lunch, after families started for home, David found Freeman and Levi, then they all pulled Abraham away from a discussion with Hank Lapp over the use of divining rods as a means to find water, and the four men went up to the porch to have a conversation. David sat on the farthest rocker and leaned forward. He didn't plan to beat around the bush — just tell them the truth. "I learned recently that my daughter Katrina is expecting a baby." He could feel their rapt attention waiting for him to try to explain the unexplainable.

Freeman, Levi, and Abraham exchanged looks of surprise. And then Freeman started in. "Do you know who the father is?"

"Of course," David said, letting the implied remark pass. "Of course. But that doesn't matter."

Freeman leaned forward in the rocker, his feet making a thudding sound. "It does matter. We'll make him marry her."

"No, we won't," David said slowly and firmly. "He's engaged to someone else."

Abraham, always the peacemaker, lifted a hand. "I know of a couple who've been waiting for years to adopt. They'd be wonderful parents."

David had anticipated this suggestion. "It's an excellent option, Abraham, but Katrina has decided she wants to raise the baby. Our family will help. And no doubt in time, Katrina will find the right man to marry and that man will become the child's father."

Freeman let his rocker dip backwards, hands folded in his lap. "Well, David, you seem to have one family problem after another, don't you?" He looked happier by the minute.

Jesse picked up a broom and began to sweep the buggy shop when a *clank!* rang out and he froze. His nerves shot back up to high alarm, the threat of goons never absent. Fumbling for the brass knuckles in his side pocket, he stopped when he got a full look at what had made the noise.

Hank squatted down to pick up a tool he'd dropped. "Something's not quite right around here. You've got ears like a mule deer when it comes to what's going on in this town. Catch me up."

Jesse hesitated. He dreaded any direction this conversation might take. Exactly what kind of "not quite right" did Hank mean? There were all kinds of rumors racing through town. A word here. A word there. It could come from anywhere. Rumors were things with wings.

Did he mean the news of his sister's unwed venture into motherhood? He'd barely been able to digest the shocking news himself. His father had told them all Sunday evening. "Girls, you're going to be an aunt, and Jesse, you'll be an uncle. Katrina and her little one will need all of us." The twins were ecstatic, as was Molly. After they went to bed, his father had something else to say to Ruthie and him. "Our family is going to face a storm over this. Katrina, especially. We need to stay strong, to not let hurtful words affect us. Trust me, words will come

273

at you that will feel like darts." He had been looking pointedly at Ruthie when he said that. "But I don't want either of you to defend our family. We will let the Lord be our shield."

His father's words had been a portent. The news about Katrina Stoltzfus, the minister's wayward daughter, was spreading like wildfire through town, thanks to the wagging tongues of the Glick wives.

But Jesse doubted Hank would join in with the town's gossips. More likely, he was referring to something that hit closer to him, such as the bill collecting income that Jesse had lost due to the absence of Yardstick Yoder in a critical race. A prickle of inevitability started climbing up his backbone. Smiling thinly, he blinked at Hank with innocent eyes. "What exactly do you mean?"

Hank went to the point. "I've heard rumors that the church might split into two."

Ah, *that*. Jesse had heard similar grumblings and murmurings. Still, he met Hank's report with uncertainty.

"The progressives and the conservatives. We're already half the size we used to be, so even if it's an even split, right down the middle" — Hank made a slashing gesture

— "that means that each church would be down to a quarter. Or something like that. I've never been good at subtraction."

"Fractions," Jesse said distractedly. "And you did just fine."

"SO . . ." and Jesse jumped at Hank's loud tone. You'd think he'd be accustomed to Hank's erratic bellows by now. "What about the split? Is it going to happen?"

"Hank, I honestly don't know."

"But you're Jesse Stoltzfus! The minister's son! You're supposed to know everything that goes on in this town."

Yesterday morning, he would have thought the same thing. Today, he was surprised by everything that went on without his knowledge. He was slipping.

It was past seven in the morning. Katrina rustled through the straw in the roosts of the henhouse, searching for eggs. She found one and added it to the two she already cradled in her apron. It was slim pickings today. Thelma's henhouse was home to a dozen Rhode Island Reds, good laying hens for a backyard flock, but one or two were always slipping away to hatch a clutch of chicks. Mostly, if they left the safety of the henhouse at night, they met an untimely demise. A fox, a raccoon, a dog. Enemies.

A shiver went down her back. That's just what the bishop said would happen, in yesterday's sermon, if anyone were to leave the Amish community. Perhaps nothing as dramatic as an untimely demise, but surely, the world outside would be a lonesome and fearful place. Full of enemies.

Oh, why was she filling her mind with such grim and dour thoughts on this beautiful morning?

She hurried back across the yard, one hand cradling the eggs in her apron, the other swinging out for balance. The wind filled her skirts like sails, pushing her along. When she came into the house and didn't see Thelma in the kitchen or living room, she crept down the hall to her bedroom and found her door slightly ajar. The older woman was still buried in her covers, snoring lightly. Katrina left her alone and decided that she would walk the hillside without her.

The morning was perfect. The word "splendid" wafted through her mind, lit from behind with sunshine. The sky was clear as far as she could see, stretching over the rolling green fields. A pair of hens waddled behind her, as if in deep conversation, and the sound of them made her smile. What did they have to talk about, those hens? Bordering the vegetable garden, the hives were alight with buzzing bees and Katrina gave them plenty of space. She wondered how anyone got used to handling something that could, and most likely would, hurt you. Sting you. She'd have to figure that out, she realized, if she were to stay here.

Was she going to stay?

As she walked along a path that Thelma and Elmo must have made over the years, Katrina realized she could seriously imagine living here, that somehow she would find a good life here. She crested the hill and turned around in a slow, easy circle. She looked at the sky, at the little house below, at the small barn and greenhouse, and finally at the sea of rocks and moss. It felt so . . . familiar, so welcoming, so safe. This place was becoming her home. Yes. Yes! She was going to stay.

She went back down the hill and noticed that the doors to the greenhouse were propped open. She gave a whistle and Keeper bounded out, running to her for a greeting. Soon, as she expected, Andy emerged from the greenhouse. "Good morning," he said cheerfully. His hair was tamped down beneath his hat this morning. "What are you up to?"

"Andy, I'm going to ask Thelma if I can buy her property." Not that she had any idea where she would procure the funds for such a buy.

He didn't speak for a moment. "Really."

"I know, kinda silly, since I have no idea what I'm doing, but I really want to do it."

"Not silly at all." But he didn't sound convinced. Or look convinced. In fact, he looked as if a sudden headache came over him.

Maybe she was as scatterbrained as everyone said.

And maybe this was a scatterbrained idea too.

Her confidence started wobbling, until she took a deep breath. "I think I might be able to make this work, for me and for Thelma. I think I can take her ideas, like the one about the gift shop in the shed, and actually make it work. I can see it in my head, as if it's just waiting for us." She stopped, watching carefully for a sign of encouragement from him. Anything. "From the look on your face, you think it sounds crazy." And he would be right. What did she really know about this moss business? Her knowledge was an inch deep, like the substrate used for transplanting moss.

He looked straight into her eyes. "I

think . . . I think you can do anything you set your mind to."

She smiled, slowly at first. "Andy, I think this could be a place I can stay, a place I want to stay, make a home for me and the baby."

What she didn't know, she could learn. She *would* learn. "And here's something else. I think we should rename the greenhouse. I think it should be called the mossery."

"The mossery? So be it." His eyes lit up with amusement. "Come on," he said, putting his arm around her shoulders in a companionable way. "Let's go have some breakfast with Thelma and enjoy the day. There's time."

The next time Katrina had a reason to go to town, she made a point to visit the public library. Andy had made a casual comment about the environmental solutions that moss provides and she wanted to do some research on her own. To her surprise, she discovered all kinds of information about moss that she didn't know . . . but should. She read about a new trend in having a lawn of moss instead of grass. She'd always assumed that moss only grew in the shade, and only facing north. Not true. There were varieties of moss that grew in sun and in most any area. Sogginess was the only thing it couldn't survive. No wonder Thelma's steep hill provided ideal conditions for natural moss to grow.

Something else Katrina learned: Once certain mosses were established, they could withstand extreme temperature — high winds, heat, and cold. They required no chemicals, no fertilizers, no pesticides, which meant no runoff that could affect groundwater. And no mowing. She could hear her brother Jesse shout out, "You've sold me!" on that piece of news.

Moss doesn't have a dormant period and doesn't die back during winter. She smiled. Imagine a green lawn of moss during a bitter cold January in Pennsylvania.

Then she came across a news story that made her gasp loudly and brought a frowning look in her direction from the head librarian. "Green Roofs Are Gaining Support around the World" proclaimed the headline. In Europe, moss was being used on roofs and finding great success — it was a trend that was spreading in the United States, though there weren't enough suppliers.

She read on about the benefits of a green roof: moss provided excellent insulation.

Because moss doesn't have roots, just rhizoids, the required soil needed very little depth. "Engineering concerns for weight load were virtually eliminated by using moss," she read.

Moss Hill could do this! There was already an established need and they — well, Andy, anyway — could figure out how to fill it. She made a copy of the article and hurried back home to share it with Thelma and Andy.

She felt happier and more excited than she had in a long, long time. This moss farm — *moss,* of all things — it meant something to her.

As she climbed into the buggy, she drove down Main Street and thought she caught sight of Andy in her rearview mirror. He was crossing the street, talking to an English man she didn't recognize. But then she realized that was impossible — Andy was working in the mossery when she left for the library. She had the buggy. And Keeper wasn't with him. Keeper was *always* with him. Plus, he wouldn't leave Thelma alone on the hill if Katrina were in town. He was very protective of Thelma.

And then she wondered why she was thinking about Andy so much. She was conjuring him up in places he wasn't! What was *wrong* with her? Hadn't she decided that a romance was not a good idea right now . . . for oh-so-many reasons?

When she drove up the hill to Moss Hill, Keeper greeted her halfway down the hill, barking his big, deep bark, wagging the whole back half of his body. She drove the buggy to the hitching post by the barn, with Keeper trotting along beside the horse. When she climbed down and tied the reins to the post, she turned to the dog and said, "Hey, buddy," and held her hands out, waiting.

He sat politely, his feathery red tail sweeping back and forth across the ground. "Good job." She gave him the reward of her hands on his body, scrubbing his back, rubbing his ears. "You're the best. But even you couldn't have gotten a smile out of that cranky librarian."

Where *was* Andy? And then she saw him, striding out of the barn with his work gloves on. "I'll put away the horse for you," he said. "You've got company." Only then did she notice a horse and buggy waiting by the far side of the barn.

"The bishop and his shadow are waiting to talk to you."

Katrina had to admit Freeman Glick pulled

no punches. He told Katrina that her father had informed him of her situation and she would need to be baptized as soon as possible. Levi was going to teach the fall class and expected her to attend on Sunday. And then the two men left.

Katrina watched the Glick buggy head down the hill. Freeman never gave her a chance to respond. She knew the bishop well enough to know that he was using shame to manipulate her. But she also knew that he wielded enormous power in their church. What if she didn't want to be baptized right now? But if she didn't get baptized before the baby was born, what would that mean for being a part of the community? Would she and her baby be unofficially ostracized?

She dug her nails into her palms. She would not cry again. Not again. She had done enough crying in the last few weeks to last her a lifetime.

Thelma came up behind her and put a hand on her shoulder. "Every now and then, you find yourself in a situation you'd never have chosen in a million years. Something you can't believe you've done or been a part of. I know that's how you feel right now."

It was. All that and more.

"Freeman said I was a sinner."

Thelma frowned. "Well, so is he. So am I. You're not a bad person. You're just going to have a baby. You are not going to hang your head, got it?"

A little of the heat drained out of Katrina's cheeks. She nodded. "It's just that . . . they're telling me what I have to do to make things right in the eyes of God, and I do want to do that. Of course I do. But my father has always told us to wait until it's real before we get baptized. I'm just not there yet."

"It'll all get worked out in due time." Thelma then fit her hand over Katrina's. It was bony with thick knuckles, but soft. "One day at a time, right?"

"Yes. You're right."

"Have I mentioned that I'm so glad to have you staying with me?" Thelma hobbled off to the kitchen to check on the stew that was simmering on the stove top. She could move around as quietly as a cat, even with her cane.

Katrina picked up her spine and her chin and her fragile sense of self. Her people weren't ones for overt displays of affection, but she couldn't help calling out, "And have I mentioned that I love being here, Thelma Beiler?"

Thelma peeked her head around the doorframe of the shoebox kitchen. "No, but I thought so. Still, I'm glad to hear it."

14

Birdy sat across the room from the man she most admired and tried very hard not to feel self-conscious. How she wished she'd worn her turquoise dress today — someone told her once that it suited her coloring nicely. She didn't know that David would be dropping by to teach a class today, and here she was, wearing her drab brown dress. She reminded herself that it didn't really matter how she looked. But it did.

David stood by her desk, drawing the children into a story, and Birdy tried to keep her mind on the important topic of Bible memorization, and not on how deep his voice was, exceptionally deep, yet warm and kind.

"I know an old, old, *old* bishop who has an incredible ability to recite long passages," David said. "Apparently memorization didn't come naturally to him. He decided that memorization is like working a muscle

— the more you exercise it, the easier it becomes. So he worked at it every day, and he found some tips that helped."

David's instructions to the class were simple: "Let a passage find you. When you hear a verse that appeals to you, scribble it down on an index card. Tape it to your door, or rubber band it to your scooter handlebars so that you can whisper the lines on your way to school."

He passed out index cards and rubber bands to each row. "But it isn't about just gathering information. And for what? To impress others? To feel clever and smug? Never! You must ponder the meaning and significance of each verse. Truly living a few lines is better than memorizing a hundred. You all know Bible stories about Pharisees in Jesus's time who could recite Scripture but never let it enter their hearts."

David picked up a piece of chalk and wrote on the blackboard:

Thy word is a lamp unto my feet
and a light unto my path.
                              Psalm 119:105

He pivoted around. "How many of you have walked in the dark with a flashlight?"
The entire class raised their hands.

"How far have you been able to see?" He looked around for a volunteer, found none, so called on one. "Noah Yoder?"

"Only as far as the flashlight's beam spreads."

"And how far is that?"

Noah squinted. "I guess, what's right in front of you."

"Exactly! Sometimes in life, that's as much as God lets us see of the future. Just a few feet ahead of us. And the Word of God is like that flashlight beam, showing us which path to take." He pointed to the chalkboard. "I want you all to write that verse on your index card and try to memorize it this week. Next week, I'll quiz you to see who has it memorized." He grinned and looked at Birdy. "There might even be a prize."

The children scribbled down the verse. "There's one more thing my old friend the bishop told me. He said that if memorizing takes such a long time that you feel as if you're chiseling words in granite, then to rest easy. Any idea why?"

No one had an answer. No one except Luke Schrock. He raised his hand and Birdy cringed. She never knew what would tumble out of Luke's mouth on any given moment. David gave him a nod and Luke stood at his desk. "I guess 'cuz words chiseled in granite will never disappear."

David smiled. "Well done, Luke," and the boy preened like a jaybird.

Birdy dismissed the children to have a recess on the playground and they thundered out the door like a herd of wild beasts. David picked up the extra index cards and stuffed them in his coat pocket.

Birdy fiddled with her hands, searching for a subject to put off his departure. "Did you have a particular prize in mind? For next week?"

"I think Molly wouldn't mind making some baked goods for a prize for students who memorize the verse next week . . . though —" he hesitated — "judging from the look on your face, as if you found a mouse in your soup, maybe that's not such a good idea."

An unladylike snort of laughter burst out of Birdy and she felt her face grow oven-warmed. "I know Molly's been working very hard on her cooking. But perhaps she might want to come to my house on Saturday afternoon and we could bake something together. I have a new recipe for pumpkin chocolate chip muffins I've been wanting to try."

Those beautiful eyes of his lit up at that

news. "Molly would love that, Birdy." He picked up his hat.

End of subject.

"Thank you again for taking time to teach the children."

"I enjoyed it." End of subject. He put his hat on.

"I liked the part about putting a rubber band around the note card on their scooter handlebars," she added hurriedly.

"Thanks."

End of subject, again. He walked toward the door and she followed behind. On the porch steps, David and Birdy stood a moment, shoulder to shoulder, studying the children. A closeness stole over them, binding them. Their gazes met momentarily. "Birdy, where do young people go on dates around Stoney Ridge?"

"Dates?"

"Yes. If a fellow wanted to take a woman out on a date, where would they go?"

"At this time of year?"

"Yes. Soon."

Oh. Birdy's heart sank. Again, Mary Mast loomed large. "I suppose, if the weather cooperated, they would go to Blue Lake Pond for a picnic." Her favorite place in all the world.

David grinned. "Perfect. That sounds just perfect."

The next Sunday was a church day. A glut of buggies and wagons lined up along the rim of Sol and Mattie Riehl's pond by the time Thelma's buggy arrived. Andy dropped Thelma at the door to the Riehl farmhouse, but Katrina had remained in the buggy. As Andy squeezed their buggy into an open spot, a young boy came galloping up to them. He was supposed to unhitch the horse and lead it out to pasture, but when he caught sight of Katrina, he skidded to a dead stop. His eyes grew wide, his mouth hung open, his face turned a dozen shades of red as he stared stock-still at her.

It was the first time Katrina was part of a church event since she had told her father that she was going to have a baby. This was the first time she realized that everybody knew, everybody was staring at her, and not in a good way. Shame pressed down on her again. For a moment, she felt as if she might faint. She hadn't thought this through — the story of her life!

Knots of men and women stood gathered in the morning sun, waiting for that invisible signal when they would file into the front doors of the barn for church to start.

Andy helped her out of the buggy and walked with her toward the farmhouse.

Halfway there, she froze. "Maybe I should just go home," she said to him, and turned around to leave, but of course she couldn't really leave, much as she wanted to. No Plain person ever missed a preaching just because she didn't feel like going.

"Absolutely not," Andy said in a calm voice. "Look at me, Katrina."

She raised miserable eyes, hoping Andy would see that she desperately wanted to get out of there and help her back into the buggy before her knees buckled from under her. "I can't do this."

"Yes, you can," he said in her ear. "Think of this as the wild beast you're facing in the Roman Coliseum. You're in the lion's den. When you get inside, you sit up straight. Stare back if anybody stares at you. *That's* how you scare off a wild beast."

That, Katrina thought, and a fierce weapon in your hand.

"I just . . . I never thought of how this would feel. I'm not prepared to face people. I'm just barely beginning to figure things out myself."

"You don't have to have it all figured out." His mouth took on that teasing look of his. "You'd be surprised at how many people here don't have it all figured out, either."

Maybe so, but their humiliation wasn't quite as public as hers.

She gave the bow of her bonnet a straightening tug, then smoothed her hands over her skirt. She didn't need to look around to hear the hiss of whispers start up around her, even in her imagination. Ears buzzing, face burning, she kept her head down. Her throat felt like it would close completely, and when she did lift her head, she caught the sour look of Edith Fisher giving her a once-over. "Why is it that here, coming to church, is where I feel such shame?"

"Maybe that's what's supposed to happen," Andy said thoughtfully. "A few weeks ago, your father said that part of coming to worship is to bring our shame to the altar."

Bring our shame to the altar. A wheel clicked over in her mind. Until that moment, the fact that her father was a minister had never held any resonance to Katrina. It was a flat word without depth.

Bring our shame to the altar.

She saw a tiny ray of light break through the messy crack of her life. She took a deep breath and found her chest didn't feel as tight as it had; she could breathe a little easier.

"You're not alone in this, Katrina. If you'd just lift your head, you'll see what I mean."

She raised her head to see her father, brother, and sisters, her friend Bethany Schrock, and behind them trailed Birdy, with her arm supporting Thelma, all coming down the path to welcome her to church.

A small thing it was, really, a small moment in this long morning ahead of her, and yet it made some broken part of Katrina begin to feel whole again.

Jesse thought Sunday church went fairly well, all things considered. His father and sisters went home right after lunch was served, but he stuck around to see if his presence could curtail any Stoltzfus gossip. Just as he thought there might be a dim but hopeful chance that Katrina's news might be swallowed up and digested by everyone, that they had moved on to other topics of conversation, a police car drove up the driveway. Sheriff Hoffman eased out of his car. Everyone stilled and quietly watched to see what the sheriff wanted. It turned out, what he wanted was a who. Jesse Stoltzfus, in fact, he announced in an overly loud voice. For questioning about a gambler known as Domino Joe.

Submissively, Jesse got in the back of the squad car. He tried not to notice the stunned look on Miriam Schrock's face as the sheriff closed the door. The car was backing up to turn around and was getting ready to pull out when somebody started banging on the trunk. "Wait a minute!"

Andy Miller leaned toward the sheriff's open window and said something to him, then opened the back passenger-side door and jumped in next to Jesse before he slammed the door shut.

Jesse stared at Andy. "You want to go to the police station with me? Why?"

"Because you need some help. Whatever you did, I'm pretty sure you'll incriminate yourself."

"But I didn't do anything to Domino Joe! I haven't even seen him, or his goons."

"Shhh!" Andy glanced up at the sheriff in the front seat. "Slip me the brass knuckles when the sheriff isn't looking," he whispered. "They're illegal in the state of Pennsylvania."

What? *Now* he tells him that? "I left them at home. I didn't think I'd need them at church."

"Good. Don't say another word until we get you a lawyer."

At the Stoney Ridge police station, Sheriff

Hoffman took Jesse into his office for questioning while Andy was told to wait in the lobby area. Apparently, Domino Joe had been arrested. This sheriff was a talker, and he took particular delight to describe the circumstances that ended in the arrest of Domenico Giuseppe Rizzo.

The Lancaster County Fair had started last weekend, the sheriff explained, and the Lancaster County Police Department had come up with a clever sting to collect fugitives with outstanding warrants. The "Lancaster County Lottery Commission" had sent out thousands of letters, claiming to be distributing millions of dollars in excess lottery funds. The winners were instructed to present identification at the County Fairgrounds. Those who received a letter arrived at the fair to find a balloon and streamer-festooned building. They were called, one by one, into separate rooms to receive their surprise. Uniformed officers explained the hoax and arrested the befuddled fugitives.

"And so that's where Domino Joe and his thugs have been?" Jesse asked incredulously. "In jail?"

"Yup," Sheriff Hoffman said. "That's where he'll be cooling his heels for a good long stretch. The LCPD served 53 felony warrants and made 29 arrests. His is going to stick."

"Then, uh, why am I here?"

"I was the arresting officer for Domino Joe. In his coat, I found a notebook with your name in it. Looks like you had a streak of good luck, and then your luck ran out. I also found this." He took an envelope out of his top drawer. "There was one thousand dollars in it." He tossed the envelope across the desk. Jesse's name was scrawled on the envelope. Jesse picked up the envelope and opened it. Inside were ten crisp, new one-hundred-dollar bills.

He tried to keep all signs of alarm smoothed out of his expression. "Am I under arrest?"

The sheriff took his time answering, so long that a bead of sweat ran down Jesse's back. "I happen to know your father. He's a good man. So this one time, Jesse Stoltzfus, you've got a pass. Next time your name crosses my path, I won't be quite as understanding." He pointed to the door. "Now, get out of here before I change my mind."

"Yes, sir, thank you, sir." Jesse couldn't get out of that office fast enough.

But waiting out in the lobby area, seated next to Andy Miller, was Jesse's father. Jesse opened his mouth to explain, but his father held up a hand. "Andy's filled me in. Are you free to go?" At Jesse's nod, David stood up. "Then let's go home."

There was a thick silence in the buggy riding home. Jesse sat in the backseat of the buggy, utterly still, sifting through the different defenses he could provide, but whenever he started to say something, he thought twice. His father's jaw was clenched and he shifted in his seat, leaning forward almost prayerfully. Long out of experience, when his father took on that particular stance, Jesse knew it was best to remain silent. Andy sat up front, his eyes glued to the road, providing nothing beside companionship. Finally, his father broke the silence. "One question, Jesse. I only have one question and I want the honest truth in an answer. Do you know who Yardstick Yoder is?"

"Of course. A few weeks ago, I saw him run and asked him to be in the Hundred-Yard Dash at Founder's Day. Dad, he is *fast*. Fastest boy I've ever seen. I saw him run, and I got carried away. Downright greedy. I see that clearly now."

"Did you ever, *ever*, think to ask what his real name is?"

Such a thought never occurred to Jesse.

"Yoder is a common name," he offered up weakly.

"Yardstick's name is Noah Yoder. His father was Ephraim Yoder. He missed Sunday's race because he was at his father's bedside in the hospital, watching him pass away."

"Oh," Jesse said. Oh, oh, oh.

The success of Jesse's bill collecting took a noticeable downturn after he had been unceremoniously hauled away in the sheriff's car on Sunday. For the last two days, whenever he knocked on a farmhouse door, no one answered, though he heard sounds of scurrying feet inside.

He started to feel more paranoid. Each time Jesse passed a farm he imagined that people were watching him from behind their curtains, wondering what he was up to. He asked his sister Ruthie if she thought people might talk. "Of course people will talk," she said with certainty. "People always talk. Especially about preachers and their families. As if they weren't human like everybody else."

These people of Stoney Ridge — they had memories like elephants. Another reason why Jesse wasn't cut out to be a minister's son. He preferred people who provided him a large margin of grace. Or forgetfulness.

His father insisted that he tell Hank the truth. Jesse had been avoiding that inevitable conversation — even hoping he could scrounge up the money he owed him this week. But after two full days of fruitless bill collecting, he knew he couldn't postpone it any longer. He had to come clean. And then, perhaps, move far, far away to make a fresh start from his messy life. Prince Edward Island, perhaps.

Feeling at his lowest point, he happened across Miriam Schrock in town. He slowed his scooter and, for once, she actually stopped to speak to him.

"You're an interesting person, Jesse Stoltzfus," Miriam Schrock said. "Most interesting." A smile flickered in her eyes, and then it was gone and she went on her way. Yet for Jesse it was enough. Being interesting was a good thing in his book. He felt himself smile in return and then heard himself laugh.

Instantly, Jesse's gloominess lifted.

By Tuesday evening, David realized that the Bent N' Dent store had far fewer usual customers than the previous week. By Friday of that week, sales for the week had declined by two-thirds. It troubled him to ponder why, but his hunch was confirmed

300

when Gertie Zook and Lizzie King came into the store. A whisper fanned like a breeze across the store. "A man who can't control his family certainly can't be expected to lead a church."

"Gertie," Lizzie scolded, "stop your gossiping."

Gossip. The whisper in the wind.

Gertie Zook was the worst gossip among their people. She'd been sticking her meddlesome and inquisitive nose into others' affairs for so long that the Plain had started calling her Grapevine Gertie to her face. She didn't seem to mind, but then she did have quite a few grapevines in her garden and David sometimes wondered if she just didn't understand the pun.

As David rang up their purchases, he kept his smile steady. Sometimes, though, he wanted to just grab people by the shoulders and give them a good shake until they realized what was important.

Saturday dawned so bright and sunny it almost made David forget the gloom of the previous week. He walked around the store, coffee cup in hand, trying to decide where to start the day's work.

He heard the sound of a horse and buggy in the parking lot and peered out the window to see who had arrived. Mary Mast climbed out of the buggy and hitched her horse to the post. His first customer of the day, which he took as a good sign. He watched her smooth out her apron and straighten her bonnet — a habit Anna had too. He felt a little catch in his throat, but he swallowed it back.

He had succumbed to Katrina's urging and given some thought to courting Mary Mast. He didn't know her well, but she had a pleasant nature and seemed to enjoy his children, and she was certainly appealing. Most of her appeal, though, was that she seemed interested in him. Quite, quite interested. After Katrina had brought her for dinner that one time, she had dropped by the store every other day though she lived two towns over. But this week, her visits had stopped and David noticed.

Last evening, he left a phone message for Mary Mast, inviting her to go on a picnic tomorrow afternoon at Blue Lake Pond. He said it might be one of the last warm days before winter settled in for a stay, so they should enjoy the good weather while it lasted. It had been a long time since he'd noticed a woman, and he gave thanks to God for this budding relationship. It was a welcome distraction from the more serious issues he faced.

As she reached the front steps, she paused for a moment in the morning sun, and he was caught by her attractiveness. She had a pair of the nicest lips he'd ever seen on a woman — full and wide. David pulled open the door for Mary, giving her a warm smile. "Good morning, Mary. Can I talk you into a cup of coffee? Fresh brewed."

Mary smiled in return, but it didn't quite reach her eyes. "No, but thank you, David."

Something wasn't right. He felt awkward and uncertain. "Is anything wrong?"

Mary put her hands together. "Is it true? About your oldest daughter? Being . . . with child?"

Good grief. Had such news traveled two towns over? "Yes, it's true."

"And she's not going to marry the father?"

"No. He's engaged to someone else."

"So she's going to raise the baby alone?"

"She's chosen to raise the baby. But she won't be alone. I'll be helping her, so will the rest of the family. And the community. I have a hope and prayer that there will be a wonderful man in her future who will come alongside her and be a father to her child." Unexpectedly, an image of Andy Miller came to mind. He was quite touched when he learned how Andy had intervened with the gambler and paid off Jesse's debt.

Intuition whispered there was something between Andy and Katrina, some fledgling attraction. He had noticed from the first that Katrina was entirely herself around him — something she had never seemed to be around John.

Mary Mast tucked her chin against her chest. "It must be awful — having this sort of scandal in your family. Being a minister and all."

David felt his neck turn red, and the fingers of his right hand clench involuntarily. "I feel what any father would feel about the situation. I don't deny that the news gave me pause. But my soul is glad."

She lifted her eyes. "Glad?"

"A child always brings joy."

"And then . . . your son, Jesse . . . I heard he was arrested for the murder of a gambler."

"Murder?" How had that rumor circulated? "No murder, no arrest, but he was brought in to the police station for questioning."

"And one of your other daughters — she tried to blind a boy in school?"

"What? No. Ruthie never tried to *blind* Luke, she was just trying to teach him a lesson — never mind. It's a long story."

"And then I heard the worst thing of all.

That you encouraged a man in the hospital to be . . . ," she searched for the right word, ". . . euthanized."

"What?" If the death of Ephraim Yoder wasn't so tragic, nor so fresh and raw in his heart, he would have laughed. Ludicrous! How did rumors like these get started? Who was behind them? And how and when would they end?

Mary seemed to have that answer. She bit her lip. "David, there's talk of having you quieted."

David made a raw, gasping sound. *Quieted.* It was the Amish way to have a church leader removed. Silenced. Other bishops would come in for a hearing, to listen to the charges laid against him by the church members. If they decided there was enough evidence, a minister or bishop could be replaced.

"I came by to let you know that I won't be able to go on the picnic tomorrow."

He swallowed, trying to get past the lump in his throat. "Not tomorrow? Or not ever?"

"Not . . . ever."

"I see." But he didn't. Not really.

"I'm sorry, David. I had a hope there might be something blooming between us."

"So did I, Mary. I had a similar hope. But I've learned that there's far more to the

Christian life than getting it right. There's living it right. Living it means working through the ordinary stuff."

"What you're dealing with isn't exactly . . . ordinary." She looked down at her hands, which were twisted in a knot in her apron. She unclenched them and smoothed out the bunched material. When she raised her head again, there was resolution in her eyes. "Being a minister's wife —"

Wife? Who said anything about getting married? All David had in mind was a picnic. A stain of color spread along his cheekbones.

"— it's just more than I can handle. I believe that a minister's life should be beyond reproach. And . . . I must say . . . your family seems to have more than the usual amount of problems. I'm sorry to say that I'm not ready to face the controversy you're about to encounter."

He felt himself flush a little as he opened the door for her. "Well, thank you for coming by to tell me personally."

As he watched her horse and buggy drive down the road, he felt himself unable to shake the pall Mary's visit cast. He had observed a quieting once before. He remembered thinking that the minister under fire had a look on his face as if he were having his skin peeled off in strips. Where would this conflict with Freeman end?

And one thing he chided himself over: he had never asked the Lord if Mary Mast was the one. It was just like last spring, when he embarrassed himself by asking to court Rose Schrock when she was already involved with her neighbor Galen King. He hadn't asked God about Rose, either.

Never again. The next time, he was going to let God write the story.

15

In the last month, Jesse had learned a great deal about his employer. Hank Lapp was utterly affable, and utterly lacking in ambition. On top of that, he had a bad back, and believed that many chores were too strenuous to do very often. He applied that same principle to organizing, sweeping, dusting, rearranging tools, ordering supplies, bill collecting, and taking inventory. It was all too much work.

Hank had a soft spot for children. In his pockets, he carried Smarties candy, which he gave away when a child skinned his knee or fell for some whopper of a fish story he told.

Also, Hank didn't like to talk about money.

On a cold day in late October, Jesse arrived at the buggy shop to make a full confession to Hank about the unfortunate disappearance of funds. Hank was tinkering on a buggy that had a broken axle.

Say it, Jesse. Just say it. "Hank, there's something I need to tell you." His forehead was slick, his hands were sweating, his heart was pounding. He took a deep breath and exhaled the words, as quickly as he could. "I lost all the money I collected for you in a gambling debt."

Hank exchanged a wrench for a hammer. "That's just the reason I avoid gaming, myself. I always seemed to come out on the wrong side of a bet."

Another thing Jesse had discovered about Hank was that his conversation came off the top of his head and out his mouth seemingly without passing through his brain. Jesse tried again. "Hank, I lost everything."

"Wer nix hot, verliert nix." *If you have nothing, you won't lose it.*

Jesse sighed. "Your money, Hank, not mine. I lost all of your money."

"I'm not deaf. I heard you the first time. Second and third time too."

Was it possible that someone in this town forgave a Stoltzfus? "That's it? You aren't angry? Aren't you bothered?"

"Nope."

"Hank, I lost over one thousand dollars. Of *your* money."

"Easy come, easy go."

Jesse was confused. He held a different view entirely on money. It didn't come easily and yet, he had to admit, it did go easily, with alarming speed. "Why aren't you upset?"

"Mighta been if you told me yesterday. But today, nothing could bother me."

"Why today?"

"You won't believe it," Hank said, as if he'd just been waiting to tell Jesse his news. "SHE SAID YES."

"Who said yes?" Jesse said. "And what was the question?"

Hank smacked a hand to his desktop, a sound like a shot, clearly disappointed in Jesse. "EDITH! She said she'd marry me."

"Marry you?" *You?*

"Yup. Two weeks from today. Turns out Fern was right."

"You mean . . . about women liking kindness and sweet gestures?" That was a new thought for Jesse.

"YES! Last night, Edith and I had a long talk. She wants me to give up the buggy repair business and come help her with those chickens. So I'll be handing over the buggy business to you."

"Me?" *Me?*

"That was the plan, all along. To give you some skills that you could make an honest living out of and turn from your life of crime."

"But . . ." *But, but, but . . .*

"NO NEED TO THANK ME, son. Someday, you'll be doing the same thing for a wayward boy in your own life. And the news gets better. Fern said you're to move into this apartment over the buggy shop. I think she's finally warming up to you. Either that, or she wants to keep an eye on you."

Suddenly Jesse was looking ahead into the terrible future. But one thing he had learned in his sixteen years, sometimes it was wise to bend before the gale. "And keep me straight."

Hank's good eye skimmed over Jesse. "Well, that might be too much to expect." He turned back to the buggy he was working on, then spun around. "Almost forgot. Fern wants you up at the house. She's got a long list waiting for you."

"A long list?"

"To ready the farm for the wedding!" He grinned. "Edith thought it was too much to have it at her place, what with her boy Jimmy's heartless abandonment, so Fern volunteered Windmill Farm. Less than two weeks and she wants this place cleaned from top to bottom. Spick-and-span."

Again? Jesse thought, scratching his head.

It seemed he had just finished doing that very thing.

It was the time of year that Katrina loved the best, October sliding into November. She loved the way the light angled, illuminating valleys she never noticed the rest of the year. Today was a beautiful wedding day for Hank Lapp and Edith Fisher, the sun was overhead in the sky.

Her happy mood was jeopardized after an encounter with the Glick wives, just as she and Andy and Thelma arrived at Windmill Farm. She was helping Andy unhitch the horse when the Glick wives strolled past, looked Katrina up and down with disdain, and one of them said, "Wann'd dich amme schwatze Kessel reibscht, waerscht schwatz." *Rub up against a black kettle and you will become black.*

Katrina blanched a little at such a rude remark, irritated to know that people in town had been talking about her. But, she reminded herself, how could they not? Stoney Ridge was a small town. Everybody knew everybody else's business. She'd been guilty of it herself from time to time. No matter how she felt about it, people were going to talk about her and the baby, at least until some newer and more interesting gossip came along. She kept her head up. She wasn't going to let those two steal her happiness. And she did feel happy.

After the initial shock of discovering that she was going to have a baby, Katrina decided to focus on the fact that this little one was surely a gift from God. Once she'd made up her mind about that, she couldn't understand that anybody else might not feel the same way or take longer to reach the same conclusion. She understood the responsibility and challenges that lay before her, but that didn't stop her from being thrilled by this miracle child.

Bethany waved to her and hurried to the buggy. "I've been waiting for you."

Andy squeezed Katrina's shoulder. "Go on. I'll finish with the horse."

As they walked toward the house, Bethany looked at her friend. "What's up with you two?"

Katrina swayed. "Nothing." And something. "You look especially happy today."

She grinned and lifted her chin toward the house. "I got a letter from Jimmy Fisher."

"He didn't come back for his own mother's wedding?" She knew Bethany had hoped this event might draw him home.

"He just got a job and couldn't leave." She rolled her eyes. "As a cowboy." She leaned closer to Katrina. "He wants me to come to Colorado."

"Are you going to go?"

"I told him I would only go as a married woman. I'm no fool." Her eyes dropped to Katrina's midriff, and she gasped and covered her mouth. "I'm so sorry, Katrina. Please forgive me."

"You're right. I *was* a fool. No longer." She looped her arm through Bethany's. "All is forgiven."

Katrina's gaze took in all the women, gathered in clusters in front of the house, at the men who gravitated toward the barn, the children who played in the yard, and then went beyond. A thousand times her eyes and heart must have taken in such a scene. It was all the same and so was she. She hadn't changed at all, not at all.

After the very long wedding ceremony, everyone enjoyed a traditional wedding lunch of turkey and celery roasht, potato salad, chow chow, coleslaw, pickled beets, four-bean salad, applesauce, sweet rolls, every jam imaginable, pies, cookies, and cake. And punch.

Freeman Glick said it was the best punch

he ever had, and that his wife should be sure to get the recipe. Jesse, being the kind and thoughtful fellow that he was, a true servant, made sure that Freeman's glass was never empty.

Meanwhile, a rumor started to circulate among the older boys that someone — no one knew whom, though Luke Schrock's name was tossed about — had spiked the punch with vodka.

Freeman spent the remainder of the afternoon "resting his eyes" in his buggy, snoring loudly.

After returning home from Hank and Edith's wedding, Katrina wondered if events like today made Thelma feel sad, aware of her widowhood. As she started to get supper ready, Thelma sat on a chair placed at the kitchen door threshold. There wasn't room enough for two to work in the shoebox kitchen, so this had become their evening ritual. Thelma would keep Katrina company while she cooked or vice versa.

"Do you miss Elmo terribly?" Katrina asked, mashing up hot potatoes with a fork.

"In many ways, I do. An important part of my life ended when he died. But I must say that it's not such a bad thing to have the final say-so in my own life. Elmo was a wonderful man and he thought he had my best interests at heart, but he was always keeping things from me. He said it was to protect me, maybe that's true, but I always thought it had more to do with his mindset that women were meant to cook and clean and bear babies, but we didn't have the mental hardware to manage more than that."

Katrina brought her a cup of peppermint tea.

"When Freeman first told me I had to sell my property, in the same tone of voice Elmo would give me at times, something woke up inside of me." Thelma gave Katrina a mischievous little smile. "I snapped at him and told him I would be making my own decisions from here on out. That shocked him! I don't think he's had many women tell him what's what." She laughed.

Katrina added hot milk and butter into the mashed potatoes and whipped it all together. What was it about most men? Were they born knowing how to use a certain tone in their voice to make a woman feel foolish and inconsequential while professing to have her best interests at heart? Or did they pick it up from their fathers and older brothers? Katrina's father had always supported her, made her feel important and capable, but he seemed to be an exception to the general inclinations of his gender.

John had known that certain tone well and had adopted it whenever she had a differing opinion from his. Maybe if he'd encouraged her a little more, maybe she'd have been a little more confident . . . Maybe a lot of things.

But one thing was sure, like Thelma, Katrina had learned how to say no.

She saw Andy stride up to the house for the evening meal, Keeper trotting behind him. She couldn't help herself from comparing the differences between John and Andy. She never had to say no to Andy because he didn't push her. She didn't feel manipulated when she was with him. She knew that he was attracted to her. Many times throughout a day, he would find her wherever she happened to be on the farm. Just checking in to see if she needed help, he would say, but she knew he had missed her. He had a tender way of looking at her, just at her, that tugged at her heart: his smile deepened, his eyes warmed.

She knew Andy would like to kiss her if she'd let him — but after that one time, when she told him no and why, he never tried again. But kissing wasn't all he wanted. He liked to talk to her too.

John had never been much of a talker. Well, no, that wasn't quite right. He talked plenty, and he was always joking around. At first, she'd liked his lightheartedness; it was a breath of fresh air compared to the sadness that filled her home after her mother's death. He seemed so upbeat, filled with big ideas, and it was flattering to have an older man like him pursue her.

But looking back, she realized that he never talked about things that mattered. And listening? He never listened to her. It was a one-way conversation. No, hardly even that. It was a monologue.

Andy liked to listen to her ideas about the moss farm. Many times, after supper, he would stay and help her with the dishes, then they would sit in the living room, warmed by the woodstove, and work on plans for expanding Moss Hill. He would take her thoughts seriously, like changing the name of the greenhouse to the mossery. He never referred to it as a greenhouse again, only as the mossery. A small thing, really, and yet it was meaningful to her. He listened.

Now that she thought about it, if she measured it just on word alone, Andy talked considerably less than John ever had. But he managed to say a whole lot more.

■ ■ ■ ■

On Sunday evenings, Birdy went up to the Big House for supper. She was helping her sisters-in-law in the kitchen when she heard snippets of conversation between Freeman and Levi in the other room. She stood by the doorframe, unnoticed, to listen more closely.

"I never thought we'd be facing this kind of thing," Levi said.

"No, but I'm not at all surprised," Freeman said. "David's far too independent-minded. If we wish to destroy a weed we must pull it up by the roots." Freeman clapped his hands against his knees. "I'll make a call to a couple of bishops I'm friendly with — Isaac Fisher in Gap, and Sam Smucker over in Leola. They'll help get him quieted."

Birdy gripped her elbows, hugging herself to stifle a sudden chill. This was wrong, what they were planning to do. Wrong and malicious and deceitful. When her brothers noticed she was standing by the door, they abruptly stopped their conversation. Freeman's gaze swept over her, holding her quiet and still and frightened, and then he smiled. The way he could go from that hard look of a moment ago, his eyes all flat and cold, to the way he was now, warm and friendly. It disturbed her, but she only blinked innocently back. "Supper's almost ready," she said in the sweetest tone possible.

All throughout the night, and over the next few days, Birdy wavered about what to do. She felt that familiar pluck in her chest, a need to make sure everyone else was happy. But after she heard her brothers discuss that they were setting into motion the process to have David quieted, she knew the time had come to do something she should have done months ago.

Katrina went into the mossery and found Andy transplanting moss. She smiled at his concentration, the comma of his body arched over the shelf, his precision in placing the gathered moss into the substrate like he was creating a picture of mosaic tiles. His face was nearly perfect in profile — the high brow and angled cheekbones, his strong Roman nose and full lips. So very handsome.

Keeper, curled up by Andy's feet, scrambled up to meet her, his tail wagging like a flag. Andy straightened. He stared at her for what seemed like forever. She was having a hard time meeting his eyes, the way he looked at her lately. Then came one of those unexpected and dazzling smiles. "Morning."

All business, she reminded herself. *Keep everything all business.* "I just received a call from a florist in Lancaster. She wondered if Moss Hill could provide reindeer moss for a wedding this weekend."

"Well," he answered, drawing out the word long and slow. "First of all, reindeer moss isn't a moss, it's a lichen. And if anyone does provide it for her to use in a wedding, he should be drawn and quartered."

"Why?"

"It's endangered in most states. It's very slow growing, takes thirty to fifty years to recover after it's been removed or trampled on. Reindeer and caribou rely on it for their winter diet. It's highly nutritious. They can smell it through the snow and paw down to eat it."

Katrina put her hand up in the air to stop the lecture. "Thank you, Professor Miller. I'll tell her that we can't provide reindeer moss and that she should be ashamed of herself for depriving animals of their winter food."

He laughed, a soft laugh. "Tell her we've got something even better. A specialty moss called Hedwigia. Looks somewhat similar to reindeer moss but she won't have to feel guilty."

"She needs two trays by Friday morning."

"Sounds good. She can even come get them today and put them in the refrigerator for a few days. They'll keep fresh."

"I'll let her know."

He stared at her again in that intense way he had, his head slightly tilted.

"What? Is there something else you've thought of?"

A trace of color rose under his fair skin. "To be perfectly honest, I'm still thinking how much I'd like to kiss you."

She flushed, looking away. "No." Yes.

He read her mind and took a step toward her and leaned his head close, but she reacted without thought. "No! You mustn't." She put her fingers against his mouth and felt as if she got a spark from touching him, like you might get if you pressed your fingertips to a window during a lightning storm. She took her fingers off his lips the instant she had touched him, but the strange tingly feeling remained. "Andy, any girl in town would be flattered by your attention."

He backed up a step, studying her as if he didn't quite know what to make of her. "Any girl except you?"

She conceded with a tilt of her head. "Not me. Not right now. It's not a good time to start something. Not for me, not for you. I think it's best to stop it before —"

"Right." He held up a hand, shaking his head. "We're not even involved."

Yet. She heard the word clearly in his head.

On Saturday morning, David had barely opened the Bent N' Dent store when Freeman Glick burst in the door. "There's going to be a Members' Meeting after church tomorrow."

"Good morning to you too, Freeman." David tried not to show any reaction, though he could feel his whole body and soul tense up. "Any particular reason?"

Freeman sucked in a deep breath and closed his eyes. "David, I think you know why we've come to this point."

"Actually, I don't."

"It's my duty to inform you that you will be asked to confess your sins before church on Sunday."

"Which particular sins are those?"

Freeman drew in another deep breath. "Neglecting your children."

Not controlling them, he meant. Pretending they weren't separate and unique individuals who had their own journey of faith to discover. "Freeman, have you ever had a herding dog?"

"Yes, but what does that have to do with anything?"

"My father raised sheep and always counted on a border collie to help him with the sheep."

Freeman sighed.

"A smart herding dog never nags or drives or frightens the sheep, never nips at their heels or rushes them. It goes back and forth from the rear, gently guiding the sheep into the fold."

"Your point?"

"My point is that I've always considered it to be an illustration from the natural world of good parenting."

"Well, maybe that's the problem right there. You're letting a dog guide you." He leaned forward with a sneer. "And just look at the results."

"Freeman, I don't deny that Anna was a better disciplinarian than I am. I'm not a perfect father, not by any means. I can certainly confess to making mistakes as a parent. But neglecting my children? That, I don't agree with."

"That's the sin that's been laid on you."

That's the one you can build a case on. David was aware there were a number of rumors circulating around and that he was not held in high regard in the church right now; the balance sheet at the store gave credence to that fact. But Freeman, as bishop, would have the most influence over the Members' Meeting on Sunday. He'd been trying to get rid of David for a long time now and, at last, he'd found what seemed to be a legitimate way to oust him.

David crossed his arms against his chest. "And just what will happen if I don't confess to the sin of neglecting my children?"

"Then we will have you quieted." Freeman strode out of the store, leaving only the sound of the bell ringing on the door.

So. The rumor was true.

That evening, after he read stories to the girls, David worked on his sermon — possibly the last sermon he would ever give. The text for that Sunday would come from the book of Exodus, the life of Moses. He kept sensing a distinct impression: power through weakness. God chose Moses, a man who showed little courage and less wisdom. A man who responded to God's divine call with five different excuses. A weak man. God used a weak man to shame the strong

— Pharaoh and his multitude of armies.

David sat back in his chair and thought of how often that very principle displayed itself throughout Scripture: God's power operates best in human weakness.

He read, then reread this moment from the book of Exodus, when Moses and the Israelites faced the Red Sea in front of them, Pharaoh's pursuing army behind them: "And Moses said unto the people, Fear ye not, stand still, and see the salvation of the Lord, which he will shew to you today: for the Egyptians whom ye have seen to day, ye shall see them again no more for ever. The Lord shall fight for you, and ye shall hold your peace."

A wave of understanding washed over David's mind. This was what the biblical phrase "wait on the Lord" was all about: committing our Red Sea situations to God in prayer, trusting him, and waiting for him to work. God alone could part the waters. And he could hold on to his peace.

He went outside to look at the stars. He lifted his hands toward the night sky, handing to God the outcome of tomorrow's Members' Meeting. Again, that one verse of Scripture filled his mind: "The Lord will fight for you and ye shall hold your peace." A gentle hush of God's Holy Spirit overtook him and he could hardly speak. He hadn't felt God's presence like that in a long, long time.

If Freeman wanted to have David quieted, so be it.

16

There was an atmospheric condition known as earthquake weather, a blanket of stillness that forecasted a shaking up. This day felt like such a day to Jesse.

After church on Sunday, everyone who wasn't baptized — mostly children — was asked to leave and wait outside. Ruthie had organized a softball game in the yard for the children while the young adults gathered at a picnic table. "It's times like these that I think I should just go ahead and get baptized," Katrina whispered to Jesse. "Freeman is making Dad his scapegoat and I can't do a thing about it."

That was enough for Jesse. He slipped away quietly and walked the perimeter of the house, stopping when he spotted an open window. Just what he had hoped to find. He peered cautiously over the sill and saw the backs of the four old sisters from the Sisters' House, sitting like pigeons on a telephone wire. He waved to Katrina from the corner of the farmhouse. "Hsst! Kumm mol!" *Come over here!* When she started toward him, he cupped his mouth and whispered, "Bring Andy!"

Katrina and Andy walked over to join Jesse. He put a finger to his lips to be quiet. "I can hear everything," he whispered, crouched beneath the open window. "Freeman is explaining why Dad needs to confess and mend his ways." Jesse was insulted. "Why, it's because of us! *You and me.* We've veered off the straight and narrow path, Freeman is saying."

Katrina was amazed. "Did you truly just figure that out now, Jesse Stoltzfus?"

Andy sat down, his back against the house, his head tilted to the open window to listen. Katrina crouched down next to Jesse.

"David Stoltzfus," they heard Freeman say, "do you refuse to make things right?"

"What exactly do you want me to do?"

"Your daughter must get baptized, right away. She needs to marry the father of her baby."

"Katrina is not going to marry him."

"Why not?"

"He's engaged to someone else and, apparently, that young woman is also with child."

Katrina gasped, her eyes wide with shock. "Jesse, did you know that?"

Jesse shook his head. "I didn't. I would have said so if I'd known! Aunt Nancy must have told him."

"My daughter will make her vows when she is ready," she heard her father say. "I can't think of anything worse than to force baptism on a person."

"What about that son of yours? He's lost to the world, and you do nothing about it."

"Lost to the world? He's only sixteen!"

"He gambled away Hank Lapp's life earnings."

"Jesse will be making a full restitution to Hank Lapp."

"JESSE AND ME ARE ALL SQUARED UP," Hank piped up.

Jesse smiled. "He's a fine fellow, that Hank Lapp."

Freeman had a differing opinion. "Jesse Stoltzfus spiked the punch with the devil's brew at Hank and Edith's wedding. He was seen doing it."

"By whom?" Jesse whispered. He had been so careful.

"Hush!" Katrina said. "I can't hear what Dad is saying."

Apparently, neither could Freeman. "So," he said, "you have nothing to say for yourself."

"No," David said. "I have no defense."

"Well, then," Freeman said. "There's nothing left for us to do but to call for a vote to have you quieted."

Jesse climbed on the sill to peer into the window, searching past the sisters of the Sisters' House, over the rows of white and black prayer caps to see the front bench, needing suddenly to see his father. He noticed that his father's knuckles were white where they clenched at his side, and his arm muscles were taut, as if poised to jump. Jesse wished he would.

"Get down, they'll see you," Katrina whispered.

"Not a chance," Jesse said. Everyone's attention was riveted on Freeman and his father.

Then he saw Birdy stand up. "But there is something else," she said.

Jesse saw several worshipers shift their bottoms on the hard benches to turn to her.

"Speak up, Birdy," Freeman said. "No one can hear you. Do you have something to lay against David?"

"I said, there is something else," she repeated, projecting her voice with effort.

"But it's not about David. I have something to confess. I have kept some information from all of you. My brothers took part in a sinful deed. A few months ago, when we voted to nominate a new bishop, they fixed the lot in the hymnal so Freeman would receive it and not David Stoltzfus. They put lots in each hymnal, but Freeman made sure to pick it up first."

Suddenly the very air itself seemed suspended with tension, the way it felt in the time between a strike of lightning and a blast of thunder.

After some moments, Freeman found words. "Sie verschteht ken Buhn davun." *She doesn't know a thing.*

"But I do. I saw you do it, Freeman. You and Levi. And I'm ashamed that I did nothing. Der Verhehler is graad so schlecht as her Schtehler." *The concealer is just as bad as the stealer.*

"Schtehler!" Freeman walked right up to her. His breathing was strident, the wool of his beard quivered. Jesse saw it all. Freeman pointed a stiff finger at her. "Narrisch!" *Foolish!* His lips twisted hard with revulsion. "Narrisch, narrisch, narrisch!" His big farmer's hands were clenching and unclenching rhythmically, his powerful chest shook.

332

"I'm only ashamed that I didn't say something on that day."

"How dare you accuse me of such a thing?" His voice roared, as if shouting her down could make his own words truer.

Thelma rose slowly to her feet and Jesse saw people crane to look at her. "She dares," Thelma said in a shaky voice, "because she's telling the truth. She dares because she's much braver than I've ever been. It's time to bring it all out in the open, Freeman, and admit something that should have been told years and years ago." She looked around at the worshipers, who were all staring back. "This terrible deed goes back further than Freeman and Levi. It started with my Elmo," she said, nearly choking over her husband's name.

The quiet that followed was immediate and complete, as if the very heart of the earth had suddenly stopped beating. Yet it seemed to Jesse as if he could still hear Birdy's words ring in his ears: he fixed the lot. Freeman fixed the lot.

"It was wrong from the start," Thelma said, "and I told Elmo as much but he wouldn't listen to me. It started after Bishop Caleb Zook passed, and there was a dearth of good leadership in our church. Elmo thought it was best to keep the leadership in the family. He fixed the lot when he was nominated to be bishop, then he brought in Abraham as deacon, then Freeman as minister. He didn't see what it would do, down the road. Elmo could make himself believe that fire wasn't hot. Just like you can, Freeman. You've all become imposters, and it started with Elmo."

Jesse glanced behind him to exchange a shocked look with Katrina. He turned to Andy, but his head was bowed down, his chin tucked low on his chest.

Freeman's voice was shaking in rage. "Elmo did what he felt led to do. Just like I've done."

"But you never asked yourself who was doing the leading," Thelma said.

"Now you listen to me," Freeman said in a voice that was low and fierce, a tone unlike anything anyone had ever heard him use before. "All of you listen to me. I'm not going to let you undo all the good I've done for this church." He marched to the door, stopped, and bracing his hand hard against the frame as if he needed it to hold himself upright, he turned back. "I've only tried to do what was best for this church." But then his arms fell to his sides, and something seemed to collapse inside of him, like a rotted tree.

Levi stood as if his body felt too weighted to move. Slowly, he turned and followed his brother. The Glick wives stood and brushed past them and through the door as if they couldn't get out fast enough.

At first the congregation sat slightly stunned, afraid to move. Even the infants sensed the need to remain quiet and still. David had never witnessed anything like this. His heart felt bleak with the knowledge of a thing he could hardly bear to accept. Thelma leaned forward, her forehead resting on her folded hands. Murmurs swept the congregation and the room began to buzz like a hive; some were softly crying. Everyone looked to David, waiting for him to say something to help them make sense of what had happened, but he had no answers.

Slowly, David rose to his feet and stood in the middle of the room. "This church," he said in a tone that hurt to hear, even to his own ears, "has been dealt a great blow. I don't know how this will all unravel, but I do know this: we do not shoot our wounded." He admonished everyone to pray for Freeman, for Levi, to not gossip or tell tales. To pray for the church as it moved forward to correct the wrongs. What he didn't say aloud was that he desperately wanted prayer for wisdom and discernment for himself as he sorted out church discipline over this disturbing revelation.

Abraham walked up to David, his head bowed in sorrow. "I never knew. I . . . never knew what they'd done."

"Of course not, Abraham. I would never have thought it of you. No one would."

"We'll talk later this week," Abraham said sadly. "I'd better get on home to milk the cows."

The way of life was strange. Terrible things happened, earth-shattering things, and life had a way of moving right along like it always had. Their little church was rocked to its core today, and the cows still needed milking and stomachs needed filling up with supper. David watched the deacon walk away, his head bowed, his shoes scuffing the floor.

"How did this happen?" Amos Lapp asked, mystified, after he made his way to David. "How could this have possibly happened?"

"I don't know the answer to that," David said. "Some things are just beyond understanding."

Pride. The fruit of hell. That surely was the only explanation.

■ ■ ■ ■

Instead of going home after church, Birdy went to the schoolhouse. Her haven. She sat at her desk in the dusk of late afternoon, not bothering to turn a lantern on, wondering what she would face when she finally gathered the courage to go home. She tried to pray for Freeman, for Levi, but found that she felt empty of words.

She watched a jaybird land on the feeder outside the window and frighten off the smaller birds, and she wondered if that was what her brothers seemed like to others. Like jaybirds.

No. Thelma had called them imposters, and she was right.

The door opened and she braced herself, then relaxed when David walked in. "I thought you might be here."

"I'm not quite ready to go home."

He took a few steps into the classroom and leaned against the doorframe, one booted foot crossed over the other, his hat dangling from his fingers. "Well, Birdy, you're a wonder," David said, in a voice that sounded as if he really meant it. "I can only imagine how much strength that took for you."

"Out of me, you mean." She felt thoroughly exhausted. "I know it was the right thing to do, but somehow, it doesn't feel very good right now."

"That's one of the disturbing effects of sin. It ripples through to everyone." He walked up to her desk. "The way you handle yourself, and your teaching, and everything that comes your way . . . I respect you, Birdy. I really do."

She felt as though she should say something in return, but she didn't know what to say. Instead, she ducked her head, glad for the semidarkness that hid the blush of pleasure she felt rising on her cheeks. "Another first," she whispered.

"Excuse me?" David said, tipping his head to one side.

"Nothing," she replied, not knowing how to explain how much the word meant to her. Never before had she earned a man's respect. Until this moment, she had not realized how much she had desired this. "Thank you, David."

He nodded and they stood together in the empty schoolhouse, listening to the silence. It was nice to have this moment of rest, to feel tired but peaceful, knowing she had done the right thing. And it was good to have David to share this moment with.

"What will happen to our church?"

"Honestly, I have no idea," David said. "I suppose it will depend on what Freeman and Levi choose to do next. I hope . . . they will stay. One thing I've learned in life, we're all just a few choices away from becoming just about any kind of person. Good or bad."

She saw a muscle tick in his cheek. He lowered his head slightly, so that his long, thick eyelashes shielded his eyes. "Well," he finally said, "seems like everything is under control for the moment. How about if I walk you home?"

She liked David. That wasn't a surprise considering that she loved him, but this was different. She liked him too. She appreciated his quiet humor and solid good sense, his character, the way he talked to people with authority but never a hint of arrogance. She liked the way he treated his children too, the way he listened to them. And she liked that he could admit when he'd been wrong. She felt comfortable with him. Now they were friends, and friendship was what she needed. She felt like she could be satisfied like this, just walking silently, matching her steps to his.

When they reached the road to the Big House, she stopped and turned to him. "I can get home from here, David." The last thing this long day needed was another difficult encounter between Freeman and David. He seemed to understand, because he didn't object. He reached out and squeezed her arm, as if offering moral support.

Birdy took the last few hundred feet of her journey at very slow speed, partly because it was getting dark, but mostly to give herself time to mentally rehearse the possible menu of Freeman's reactions and think up responses to each. The thing to do, she concluded, was to keep things light and cheerful.

By the time she walked up the driveway to the Big House, she felt ready to face her brother. But her confidence waned when she saw Freeman waiting on the porch of her little house, frowning with his arms crossed over his chest, looking exactly like he used to when she was a teenager and had stayed out past her curfew. A thud of anxiety punched her rib cage. She held her breath before deciding to get it out and over with. "Hello, Freeman."

He ignored her greeting. "Why? Why would you do this to me?" He stood in front of her with his chin jutting forward and his hands on his hips, demanding an answer.

Birdy had only slept a few hours last night

and was too tired to keep up the pretense of cheerfulness. It obviously wasn't going to work anyway. She had expected Freeman to shout, to lecture, but instead he just stood there, staring at her with an expression of disbelief tinged by something deeper and harder to pinpoint — betrayal and profound disappointment. It was harder to take than a harangue.

It surprised her, in a way, to see him look so intensely at her, almost as if he was seeing her for the first time. So often, she realized, he looked right through her as if she wasn't really there.

She struggled to find words to fill the silence and break the uneasiness that lay between them. "Freeman . . ."

"What kind of sister are you? What have I ever done to you that you would shame me?"

"It had to stop, Freeman. You were trying to quiet David when he did nothing wrong. You were the one who did something wrong."

"And you couldn't have come to me in private? Du hot mich yuscht fer en Narr ghalde." *You just made a fool of me.*

She brought her shaking hand up to her forehead. *I'm tired,* she thought. *And scared of him.* "I thought of doing so. But if I had come to you in private, would you have done something about it? Or would you try to convince me that I was foolish and mistaken? To try to make me believe that I hadn't seen what I know I saw?"

He said nothing.

"The problems you have with David Stoltzfus are because you can't control him like you can everyone else."

Freeman thrust his face into hers, so close she felt the hot breath propelling his words. "I've had a bellyful of him and you both." His jaw bunched, then he pushed out a hard sigh. "You are to leave this home and never return," he said in that cold, cold voice. "Your father's home."

She held her hand out to him. "Freeman . . ." He looked at her, then through her, before he shoved off from the porch and walked across the yard, leaving behind an arctic silence.

She watched him walk away, the gait of an old, ill man though he wasn't old or ill, and the sight of it touched her heart with pity. She had known that revealing his deception would anger him. She hadn't realized it would hurt him.

Katrina had thought she was over John. She was sure of it. And then she heard her father say in the Members' Meeting that John and Susie were expecting a child, and she realized that John had been going out with Susie while he was also going out with her. No, not just going out. He was *sleeping* with her. And an anger started to simmer inside her, steadily, until it was red hot and glowing. She hated John, hated him with every fiber of her being. And a part of her hated herself too, for being so naïve and trusting. So stupid! She missed every signal he gave off, ones that she could see as plain as day now.

The week she visited him in Ohio and he said he had to attend a wedding of a relative, though he didn't invite her along. Or that visit where he spent all day Saturday helping someone repair a fence. At the time, she wanted to ask him, *In the pouring rain?* But of course she didn't. She never let him know she was sad, or disappointed, or angry. Because if she did, he might stop loving her.

And wasn't that fear a red flag too? She never truly trusted him with her heart. She saw that clearly now too.

She wished she could see him, just once, to look him in the eye to force him to consider things from her perspective. To tell him how she felt, make him understand what he'd done to her, what he had stolen from her and how it had changed her life. But knowing John, he would somehow turn it all around and place the blame on her. She could hear his voice in her head: *I never remember inviting you to visit me in Ohio. You just told me you were coming.* And that was true.

No, there was no point in wishing she could tell John how she felt, so instead, she stuffed it inside. Deep, deep down, and tried to ignore it.

When David had prayed for God to open his eyes, he hadn't meant he wanted to see all this. Early the next morning, as early as he could muster the girls to get ready for school, he paid a call to Moss Hill to ask Thelma some questions. When he knocked on the door, he was surprised to discover Birdy at the door.

"David! You're a sight for sore eyes."

David didn't mention that he'd been thinking the same thing about her. Nor did he mention how the unexpected sight of her had caused his heart to race. Why was that? Lingering emotion, he concluded, from yesterday's tumultuous event.

"Freeman told me to leave," she volunteered before he could ask. "So last night, I packed up and came over to Thelma's, and she welcomed me in."

"He made you leave," David recited mechanically. How much more damage would Freeman inflict? When would this stop?

Remarkably, Birdy seemed unperturbed by being ousted from her childhood home. She was as cheerful as always. He had to hand it to her: she was the most resilient person he'd ever known. She had . . . joy. True joy.

Over his shoulder, she noticed the girls waiting in the buggy. "I'm sure you're here to talk to Thelma. I'll go outside and keep the girls entertained." She gestured to the living room. "Thelma's in there, having a cup of tea by the woodstove. Go on in and I'll bring you a cup." She turned, then pivoted around. "Oh, I forgot! You're a coffee drinker. I'll make a fresh pot."

"Birdy — don't go to the trouble."

"No trouble at all." And she whisked away.

Thelma, it seemed, was expecting him, despite the early hour. She was dressed, sitting in her rocker by the woodstove. The room smelled of peppermint tea.

"Morning, Thelma. Your tea smells good."

"It settles my nerves. Sit down, David. Katrina and Andy went to town early to make a delivery to a florist for a wedding. Now's a good time to talk."

Birdy brought a cup of coffee to David. "One lump of sugar, one dollop of milk, yes?"

"Perfect."

"I'll be outside with the girls, then."

"I'll drive you to the schoolhouse with the girls in a few minutes, Birdy."

He watched her as she put on her coat and bonnet and headed outside, then he turned his full attention to Thelma. "Why did Elmo ask me to come to Stoney Ridge?"

"We heard you preach when we were visiting family in Ohio. Afterwards, I told him that this terrible deception with the lot fixing had to stop. That I believed you were the one who could put a stop to it. To my surprise, he invited you to move to Stoney Ridge. It was the only time he ever listened to me." She took a sip. "Though, I have to admit, it all turned out differently than I would have expected. You can thank Birdy for that. I wouldn't have had the courage to do what she did. She was absolutely right. Der Verhehler is graad so schlecht as her Schtehler." *The concealer is just as bad as the stealer.*

"Both of you were put in a terrible situation. Do you support your husband or

346

brother? Or betray them? I don't know what I would have done if I were in either of your shoes. No one does."

He heard laughter outside and walked to the window. Birdy was helping Molly and the twins fill a bird feeder and hang it on a tree near the house. Ruthie remained in the buggy, reading, with her feet propped up against the dashboard. Molly saw him and waved, then ran to the window. She cupped her mouth and shouted, "Birdy is going to set one up at our house too, and we're going to compare notes on how many birds we see at the feeder this winter!" Then she ran back to join Birdy and the twins by the tree. David was studying Birdy in a new light and found he liked what he saw.

Birdy made Molly feel important. She made all the children feel important. And now him.

One morning, after they had finished their walk around the property, Katrina and Thelma sat down for a cup of peppermint tea. "I'm so disappointed that Mary Mast and my father's romance fizzled. It seemed to be going so well, and then —" Katrina snapped her fingers — "it was over. Done."

"It's just as well. She didn't have the hardiness to be a minister's wife. It takes a very special woman, after all this." She waved her twig-like hand in the air.

"Don't I know it." Katrina sighed. "Back to the drawing board."

"Hardly necessary. Your father only has eyes for Birdy."

Katrina looked at her in surprise. "What?"

"Yes. And she for him. I don't know how you keep failing to notice."

Katrina considered Thelma's observation. On one hand, she was relieved to think that her father might have set his sights on someone, but she was shocked by the thought of Birdy. *Birdy Glick?* Like everyone else, she considered Birdy, in her early thirties, to be on the shelf and there to stay.

How curious!

"Speaking of fizzled romances, what's going on with Andy?"

Katrina ignored Thelma's insinuation about a fizzled romance, but she had no explanation for the sudden change in Andy's demeanor. It started on Sunday afternoon, on the buggy ride back to Moss Hill after the Members' Meeting. Andy seemed preoccupied and withdrawn.

Over the next few days, he barely said a word to her and Thelma. He ate his meals up at the house, like he'd always done, but otherwise kept to himself. Usually, he would disappear off to the moss fields for large chunks of time, but he was sticking close to the house.

Katrina saw him drive himself hard all day long, tackling all the hard, dirty jobs that no one ever wanted. He mucked out the horse stall, tarred the roof of the chicken coop. He replaced the broken windows in the old greenhouse and set the foundation in place for the new one. He replaced rotten gateposts in the paddock and repaired the loose shingles on the barn roof. He mended all the fences, dug postholes by hand, and brought in an additional supply of feed and hay. The barn loft was as full as it possibly could be.

Katrina's chair made a loud grating noise in the quiet room as she pushed away from the table. She picked up the empty teacups. On the way to the kitchen, she paused at the window and watched Andy stride from barn to mossery, Keeper trailing behind him. She stood so close that her breath fogged the glass and she had to set down a teacup to wipe it clear. Andy stopped for a moment, his head up and slightly tilted, as his gaze took in the entire hillside, and something about him in that moment pierced Katrina's heart.

"He's battening down the hatches like

we're about to face a hurricane. Guess he senses that winter's on its way." She hadn't heard Thelma come up behind her; she jumped at the sound of her voice so close to her ear.

"Maybe so," Katrina admitted. *Or maybe he's planning to leave.*

17

The next morning, Andy didn't come up to the house for breakfast. Through the window, Katrina didn't see any sign of him or Keeper, so after Birdy left for school, she walked down to the barn and paused outside Andy's door in the back of the barn. Steeling herself, she knocked briskly. She waited, but no one answered. She placed her hand on the door and opened it a few inches. Through the crack she glimpsed the made-up bed. She opened the door and walked inside. Andy's shaving brush was gone, so was the little mirror hanging on the wall hook. She crouched down to look under the bed. No locked trunk.

There was no note. No nothing. He was gone.

She let out a sigh of utter disappointment. What a fool she'd been to let herself start liking him, even to think he was something more than he appeared to be. It was all because of his dazzling smile and teasing manner. And because he'd reminded her, in some strange way, of her own father. She felt more disappointed than she could've imagined. And angry too. Angry at him, angry at John, angry at Elmo, angry at Freeman, angry at most men in general.

She felt like a teapot that was starting to whistle. Steamed up, under pressure.

She drove over to Windmill Farm and found Jesse propped up against a buggy without any wheels, reading a book called *The Idiot's Guide to Buggy Repairs.* "Where do you think Andy would be?"

"Andy?"

"Yes. I need to find him. Quickly. Where would he go?"

"He's been known to frequent The Chicken Box."

"What's that?"

"It's a dive bar."

She put her hands on her hips. "And how, Jesse Stoltzfus, do you happen to know that?"

Jesse shrugged. "Word gets around." He put down his book. "I'd better go with you."

"Then hurry it up."

A light rain started as Katrina and Jesse drove to The Chicken Box at the edge of Stoney Ridge. Keeper was under the porch, his leash tied to a pole, and barked when he saw the horse. The horse pricked its ears and tossed its head, as if it knew that dog. She told Jesse to stay in the buggy, hitched the horse to a porch railing, and went over to pat Keeper. After the dog settled down, she smoothed down her apron, tucked the stray hairs beneath her prayer cap, adjusted her bonnet, took a deep breath, and went inside. She'd never been in such a place before, never even looked inside one.

She pulled open the door and stopped on the threshold, blinking against the sudden darkness after being outside. It took awhile for her eyes to adjust to the dimness. There were large television sets placed on every wall, a visual bombardment. Rank smells assaulted her: stale sweat, beer-soaked floorboards, the musty smell of peanuts. A huge mirror on the far wall caught and reflected Katrina's image. In front of the mirror was a long, high, narrow wooden bar polished to a glossy sheen. Two men sat before the bar: Andy and an English man. A hush fell over the noisy room as she walked over to him. She felt the eyes of everyone on her.

Near Andy, she coughed politely until he glanced up at the mirror and saw her standing there. He whirled around when he recognized her, his eyes widened in disbelief. She could hear his breath scraping in his throat. "Katrina! What are you doing here?" He steered her outside into the daylight.

Outside, she jerked his hand off her shoulder, took a deep breath, rose to her feet, squared her shoulders, and said, "You left Thelma's without so much as a by-your-leave. Why?" She was surprised her words sounded so everyday, as if she were discussing a new customer order for moss or what she was going to fix for supper, when underneath her words, she was seething.

Katrina's question hung in the air. He had yet to take his eyes off her. He didn't seem to be breathing. "I didn't know how to tell you goodbye. Either of you."

She rolled her eyes, disgusted. "I thought you were different. You're just like John. You think you can do whatever you want to do and waltz off without a thought for those you leave behind."

She saw him swallow hard. "I had plenty of thoughts about those I left behind."

"Then, you've got some explaining to do."

He rubbed his hand through his hair, as if wondering where to begin. He put his black felt hat on his head, all business. "Have you ever heard of doodlebugs?"

"It's a divining rod. Hank Lapp has one he uses to find water, though I don't think it's ever worked."

"That's one kind of doodlebug. But it's also used to describe oil prospectors."

"Oil?"

"Yes. It's kind of an old-fashioned term. My grandfather used to doodlebug. He taught me how to look for oil traps. Geochemists use much more sophisticated equipment today, but it's the same principle of using sound waves to discover if there might be a structural trap below the surface."

"A trap?"

"A large oil pool."

"So *that's* what you've been doing on Thelma's property? When we thought you were gathering moss to transplant, you were . . . doodlebugging?"

"Yes. No. I mean, I was gathering moss. But I was also surveying the hill to look for traps."

"Why here? Why now?"

"A rocky area like Moss Hill is a likely candidate for a discovery."

"I don't understand why." As he started to open his mouth, she added, "The short version, please."

A smile lit his eyes. "Okay. The short version. Geologists have found that moss in high places can mean an abundance of trapped oil or gas beneath the surface. It's a precious commodity. I wanted to get to it before any other oil exploration company got to it."

"So you preyed on an unsuspecting Amish widow."

The light faded from his eyes. "No. It was nothing like that. I was contacted to survey the hill."

"By whom?"

Andy hesitated, waited until a car passed, then quietly said, "Elmo."

"Elmo?" Elmo Beiler?

"Right before he died. He knew the church was in trouble and he must have had a pretty good idea that he had buried treasure on his property." He glanced at her, eyebrows raised. "He found me, Katrina. He found *me.* He asked me to keep quiet about what I was doing, to not let his wife know what I was up to when I was drilling on the hill. I promised him I would if he would sign all the paperwork before I even started the work — permits, options to lease the land, royalty agreements. I know the Amish are good for their word, but I also wanted to protect my interests. Elmo couldn't afford to pay me to doodlebug, so he offered me a percentage of whatever the oil trap brought in. That sounded more than fair to me. Then, unexpectedly, he died . . . and I got greedy. If I could find an oil trap on that hill, I would make a fortune for myself. For Thelma. For your church. But I needed a reason to get on that hill. When I saw the ad for a handyman to start the moss business, I knew that was my ticket in."

"And does it have an oil trap?"

"Yes. A large structural trap. A bonanza."

"How? How did you find it without anyone noticing? I would think you'd need equipment or machines or computers or . . . I don't know. It just seems crazy that we wouldn't have noticed."

"Not if you know how to doodlebug. I drilled holes with an auger about twenty feet down, all over the hill, and then shot bullets down the hole to create sound waves."

Gunshots. Those were the sounds Katrina heard on Founder's Day. And that's why he was always going to town for new auger bits. And why his boots were caked with mud. He'd been digging holes.

"Kind of a crude way to explore for an oil trap, a slow way, but it's just as effective as modern geophones."

"So you've done what you came for.

That's why you left." She looked over at The Chicken Box. "That man inside. The one you were talking to, was he the land agent?"

"Yes, he's the land agent. But I told him I couldn't find an oil trap on Moss Hill."

She lifted her chin, skeptical. "Why? Why would you do that?"

"I've been asking myself that same question. Why would I walk away from a small fortune? Partly, I suppose it's all that time I've spent in church, listening to your father talk about wakefulness.

"When Elmo died, the right thing to do would have been to tell Thelma the truth or rip up all that paperwork. I've done nothing but lie to you, to everyone, for the last few months. I was on that hill for all the wrong reasons. When I heard Thelma call Freeman an imposter last Sunday, I couldn't stomach what I was doing another minute. I've become just like my grandfather — full of lies and hypocrisy. I'm the imposter, Katrina. I'm the pretender."

A panic gripped her chest so tightly that she was sure her heart had stopped its beating. She didn't know what she had hoped for from this encounter, but she couldn't have imagined this . . . confession. How had she missed this? It was just like being with

John — she saw only what she wanted to see. How naïve. No . . . how stupid! "Were you once even Amish?" She practically spit the words.

"Yes and no. My grandparents were. I lived with them in western Pennsylvania for most of my upbringing — that's where I learned to speak Penn Dutch." His gaze fell away from hers. "It's late," he said, barely hearable. "Your brother looks like he's ready to go."

"Let him wait." She had to finish this, all the way. She made herself look at him. "So was I just part of this game you were playing?"

"No!" He pushed the word out on a sharp expulsion of breath, and she saw regret in his eyes. "You musn't say that, you mustn't think it."

She was feeling feverish inside, all shaky and sweat-sticky and cold. "I don't know what to believe about you, Andy. Everything I thought about you seems to be a lie."

"You've shown me how much more there could be to my life."

She gave him a look as if she didn't believe a word he said.

"I came to the Beilers' to make some money — it was just another deal. And then I met Thelma. She reminded me so much

359

of my grandmother — she even looks like her — that it . . . it shook me up. Then you arrived. At first, I thought . . . I lucked out. A beautiful girl just showed up, out of the blue." He gave her a soft grin. "And you wanted nothing to do with me, which only made me more interested, even after you told me why. But I watched you as you were figuring out what to do . . . how you were going to face this. You didn't take the easy way out. You kept surprising me. Shocking me, actually. It was like someone held a mirror up to me, to show me how far I've strayed from the boy my grandmother believed me to be." He dipped his head so his hat brim would hide his eyes. "I know life hasn't turned out the way you thought it would. But you're making a life for yourself and the baby. I've seen how much you've grown to love Thelma's farm. I couldn't take it all away from you, from her. From both of you." He took a step closer to her, but she shook her head, stepping back, moving out of reach of his touch. His eyes glittered with hurt. "I am so very, very sorry, Katrina. More than you could ever imagine."

"Where are you going? I mean, do you have any idea what you'll be doing . . . ?" She'd nearly said *with the rest of your life.*

His shoulders lifted in a shrug. "I'll get by. I always do."

"Before you leave town, you need to go to Thelma and explain all of this. She believed in you. She trusted you. And she's grown to love you like family."

Just barely, he stifled a gasp. "What do you think I'm made of?"

Clay, she thought. Pliable, moldable, soft. Unfinished and unrefined. "Apparently, more than you think of yourself." She made another decision. "There's one more thing I want you to do — return to Thelma all of the paperwork Elmo signed. And any findings you have about the oil trap on her property. Oh . . . and the name of that land agent."

He looked confused. "Do you think you'll get oil wells constructed on Moss Hill?"

"All I'm thinking is that Thelma is the one who should be informed about what's on her property, so she can make her own decisions about it."

His eyes steadied on hers. "Katrina, listen to me. My feelings for you are genuine. It was never my intention to hurt you."

She felt suddenly depleted, almost faint. "You might not have intended to," she said, "but it happened anyway."

She walked back to the buggy and started

to climb in, when he was suddenly there to steady her, with his hands grasping both her arms. As she settled in the buggy, he let his arms fall to his side.

Then he turned and walked away in the rain, his head bent, his shoulders hunched and wet.

She let him go.

The store was still chilly on Saturday morning, but sun streamed in through the window, which David took to be a good sign. He started the coffeemaker and washed out yesterday's mugs while he waited for it to brew.

Coffee in hand, he went to his desk in the storeroom to pay bills. The store's income had dropped alarmingly over the last few weeks, though this last week, it was back to normal. He'd had a goodly number of customers over the last few days, church members who wanted to show their support. The balance sheet wasn't good, but at least it wasn't hemorrhaging as it had been.

The bell on the top of the store door clinked. David downed the last of his coffee and walked out to greet the customers. Along with a burst of cold air came Jesse, followed closely by the newly married Hank Lapp. The two of them came in grinning, grinned at each other, then grinned at David some more as they strode to the front counter.

"What's got you looking like the cat that swallowed the canary?"

"We been thinking," said Hank as if it was something new. "But first, I need some coffee." He rubbed his hands together. "It's cold out there. Supposed to snow tonight."

David filled a mug with coffee and handed it to Hank. "I'm surprised you're out and about after just a week of married life, Hank."

"Edith said that living with me is an acquired taste and she needs a little time to herself to fully appreciate it. So I went on over to Windmill Farm to see how Jesse was getting on."

"I see," David said, trying to look serious, but he was swiftly losing his battle to contain a smile. He turned to his son, happy to see him. Jesse had moved into Hank's empty apartment at Windmill Farm a few days ago, after Fern Lapp gave it a thorough cleaning, and David missed him sorely. Hank had implied that Fern was not entirely unfond of Jesse, and that with Jimmy Fisher away, she needed another wayward youth to reform. David understood. For all his son's flaws, he had a way of endearing himself to

363

others. When Jesse walked into a room, the place lit up. "Son, how are you doing in a place of your own?" He took a sip of coffee.

"Gaining weight with Fern's good cooking." Jesse patted his stomach. "She's a tireless taskmaster."

Good for Fern, David thought. Boys edging up to manhood needed to be kept busy and tired, in that order. Wann die Aerwet mol gschafft is, is gut ruhge. *Rest is easy when the work is done.*

"Dad, we think we've figured out a way to breathe new life into the store. Make it the go-to place for shopping in Stoney Ridge."

"I see," David coughed out. "Actually, I don't. What exactly do you have in mind?"

"We're thinking that if we can build up customer service, we'll build customer loyalty."

"Such as?"

"First off, have you ever thought of adding a delivery service to the Bent N' Dent?"

"Huh." Sometimes women would telephone their order in and ask for a delivery. "It's not such a bad idea."

Both heads bobbed at his response, gratified that he was catching up. "I thought up JUST THE RIGHT BOY for the job!" Hank bellowed.

"Yardstick Yoder?"

"Exactly." With that, Hank sat back and slurped his coffee, ready for all due praise.

"We've got all kinds of ideas for the Bent N' Dent," Jesse said, an eagerness in his voice that warmed David's heart. "Delivery service is only one of them. We're thinking of adding a deli, offering meats and cheeses. And fresh sandwiches on homemade bread."

"Who's going to make the bread?"

"Molly! We've got a whole bakery planned out — fresh cinnamon rolls, breads, the works."

"Molly?" To David's surprise, he liked these new ideas . . . but Molly as the baker? That might have to be reexamined.

"She's improving, little by little. She even remembered to add yeast to last night's rolls."

"And chairs!" Hank piped in. "Next spring, we want to put lawn chairs and picnic benches out front so folks will linger."

"Hank and I can handle the whole thing for you, Dad, don't worry none."

David had not really started to, until Jesse said that.

David hadn't had more than four hours of sleep at a stretch in the last week. And yet he knew that if he lay down, he wouldn't be able to sleep. He felt anxious and unsettled, filled with a nervous energy. He closed his empty fingers into a fist, dropped his head down, and closed his eyes, thinking. His mind was too filled with thoughts of what to do about Freeman and Levi to grant him rest.

And then there was Birdy. It appalled him that Freeman had told her to leave her home. How was it possible that her brothers made her seem so dispensable, so unimportant? How could they fail to see what he saw in her — a lovely, kindhearted, strong-willed woman who had more courage than he had ever imagined? He couldn't understand it, but one thing he knew for sure: those brothers didn't deserve a sister as fine as Birdy. But then, David thought, neither of them had ever looked at their sister as a being of substance, something separate from them. They'd never thought to wonder if she had feelings, dreams, desires of her own.

How was it that every single man in town was not in hot pursuit of her? David reminded himself how young Birdy was and realized he didn't actually know how young that was. He could ask Thelma, but age was a touchy subject with Thelma. Besides, even if he didn't know Birdy's age, it was obvious she was too young for him. Or was she? He could just imagine the talk around town if he asked her out. Of all the women in this world, he was interested in Freeman Glick's sister.

Was he interested? Was that why his heart started to pound when he saw her at Thelma's the other morning? Or why, when she spoke up in church last Sunday, it was everything he could do to keep himself from reaching out to pull her into his arms. The more he knew Birdy, the more he wanted to know. Such a realization stunned him. Stunned and delighted him. It felt so right.

He figured a man could spend a lifetime trying to understand everything she was, and that he'd like to do exactly that. But first, this time, he wanted to hear a word from God. *Lord, give me a sign. If Birdy is the one, show me. Unmistakably.*

He climbed in bed, turned out the lamp, and immediately fell asleep.

Katrina was in the mossery when she heard Thelma call her name. She looked up. "Andy came to the house earlier today, when you were at the store. He told me . . . all about it. Everything. Starting with Elmo contacting him last summer."

"I'm so sorry, Thelma."

Thelma lifted her head. "I'm not. Andy helped me make a decision about something. I haven't known what to do, not really, not until today."

"About what?"

"Katrina, you love this place, don't you?"

"Yes. In fact, I've been trying to figure out a way that I could make you an offer for it someday. And have you stay here, of course. We'd run Moss Hill together. I just . . . haven't quite figured out how to come up with the cash. There hasn't been a good time to ask my father."

"No, he's got his hands full."

"But maybe, someday, if you can wait for me, maybe I could buy it from you."

Thelma reached out for her hand. "I've got a better idea. I'm going to give it to you now. It would be your farm."

"What?" A scared and excited feeling welled up in her chest and she had to sit down, her legs were shaking so. She felt breathless, shivery. "Why? Why would you do such a thing?"

"All I've ever wanted is to make sure this land is cared for the way Elmo and I cared for it. Maybe Andy's right — that we've been sitting on a treasure chest. Maybe Elmo was doing the right thing, though I wish that man would've told me half the things that he was up to. I just know that I want to make decisions with someone who loves this hill like I do. And I believe that person is you. There's just one thing I want you to do in return." She squeezed Katrina's hand. "I want you to forgive John. I know he hurt you deeply, even more deeply when you discovered he was two-timing you. Let him go, Katrina. Let go of the hate and anger and sadness."

Tears filled Katrina's eyes. "If I stop hating him, what will fill that space? I don't want to go back to feeling sad and depressed."

"Love will fill that space. Love for your baby, love for this land, love for the God who gave you this life. Maybe, someday, prayerfully, love for another man. But love can't find a way when hate has a hold on your heart."

Katrina rose and walked over to the window. Bitterness toward John felt like a warm and comforting blanket. She wasn't sure she wanted to let go of it because doing so seemed like letting John off the hook. And yet. And yet, if God was the Creator of all things, if he held everything in his hands, then surely she could trust in his justice. What John did was between him and God. It was time for her to get out of the middle.

Thelma walked over to Katrina and rubbed her back in small circles. "You have to forgive yourself too. You made a mistake, and there is a consequence, but God does his best work with our mistakes, if we only give it to him. It'll take time, it doesn't happen overnight, but if you ask the Lord to help you forgive him, it will happen."

Thelma turned Katrina around to face her. "I've got an appointment with my lawyer tomorrow morning. I'm going to change my will to deed the hill to you and your baby. This hill will be yours. That is, if you'll accept my gift."

Overwhelmed, Katrina didn't know what to say. Then she felt a funny little fluttering in her stomach, as delicate as a butterfly. The baby! For the very first time, she thought she felt the baby move. She put her hands on her tummy and laughed. "Thelma, if you're really sure about this, then I think . . . we accept!"

18

Sunday afternoon was a beautiful autumn day. The leaves had already fallen off most every tree and the air was crisp, but not cold. Birdy was raking leaves off Thelma's front walkway when David drove up the hill in his buggy. She met him as he crested the hill. "Katrina's gone over to your house. Surely you must've passed her."

"I know. We had it all arranged." He hopped out of the buggy. "I realize this is short notice, Birdy, but I was hoping you might come on a picnic with me to Blue Lake Pond."

She looked at him and laughed. He didn't join her. In fact, he seemed nervous.

Wait. Was he serious? "Pardon me?" she whispered, but she wasn't even sure she'd be able to hear him, her heart was pounding so loud.

"It's such a beautiful day, and since it's an off-Sunday, I thought, why not grab the time while I had it."

She couldn't get the words out of her mouth.

As the silence continued, he started to look very uncomfortable. "Perhaps you're busy." Then two patches of color burned on his cheekbones. "Maybe this was a bad idea. I'm sorry, Birdy. I thought —"

"It's a wonderful idea!" She ran inside, told Thelma she'd be gone for a while, grabbed her shawl, and bounded outside. "Let's go!" She jumped into the buggy.

David laughed and climbed in the other side.

When they got to Blue Lake Pond, they walked to a sunny area and sat down to eat the picnic he'd made. She was touched by the care he put into the meal: turkey sandwiches on freshly made bread, apple slices cored and dipped in orange juice to keep from turning brown, thick and chewy Molasses Crinkle cookies. "Molly made those by herself," he pointed out. "That baking lesson you gave her is reaping benefits for the entire family."

"Anytime," Birdy said.

"I haven't seen any sign of Freeman or Levi this week. Not once."

"Nor have I."

"Oh," David said sadly, brushing a fallen

leaf off the picnic blanket. "I've been wondering how this chapter will end." He leaned back on one elbow.

"Pride and stubbornness, in that order," Birdy said.

"I'm sorry for that. Sorry for everyone. I hope we can work this through but I do wonder what the future holds for our church. I sense . . . difficult days ahead."

Birdy looked out at the pond, so still it almost seemed like a mirror reflecting the sky. "Did you know that trees do most of their growth in winter? Their roots push down to find deepwater sources. So what's seen in spring is the proud display of winter labor, but it's the empty times when the most growth has occurred." She turned to him and smiled. "I think we'll see the same in our church."

For a long moment, David stared at her. He stared at her so long that she wondered if she had said something wrong. Or did she have something on her face?

She saw him swallow hard.

"Birdy," he said, his voice cracking with emotion, "I'd like to court you."

Birdy held her breath, every muscle tight, stunned speechless. One minute, she was overcome by David asking her to share a picnic. The next, he was asking to court her.

It was like finding herself in the middle of a dream, and she was afraid that if she said anything, if she even moved, she might wake up and *poof!* It would all be gone.

But David was waiting for her answer. "Birdy? Did you hear me? I asked if you would consider letting me court you."

She thought her heart might have stopped. When it started up again, it beat in fits and starts, unsteady lurches. She had been waiting her entire life for this moment, and now that it was here she didn't know what to do with it. "Yes, yes, I heard you, but . . . why?"

He smiled, a look of relief flittering through his eyes. He placed his hand on Birdy's arm, squeezing a little. "I've prayed for a partner, Birdy, and you're the answer to that prayer. I have no doubt. You're a gift beyond my wildest imagination."

A gift? *David Stoltzfus thinks of me as a gift?* But she saw by his expression that he meant it. The thought sent a thrill of pleasure through her, and she gazed at him in wonder.

"You honestly don't know, do you?" he said.

"Don't know what?"

"That you're beautiful."

"I am not." She looked away, sure she was blushing like a foolish schoolgirl.

374

He sat up and took her face in his hand to turn it toward him again. His fingers felt rough as he caressed her cheek.

"Beauty is more than perfect features, Birdy. There's something about you that draws everyone to you, the way flowers turn toward the sun. You walk into a room and the place comes alive. You are beautiful, Birdy. All the more so because you don't even realize it."

They were such sweet words to be hearing now, such tender words. And yet she felt her smile falter. "The thing is," she began and then stopped, leaving the sentence unfinished.

"The thing is . . . ?"

She risked a look up at him.

The thing was . . . it was the greatest fear she had if this moment, somehow, in some miraculous way, were ever to come true. She had to swallow twice before she could speak. She continued to look at her hands, but she made her voice sound light. "The thing is . . . ," she said, fumbling for the words for a moment longer. And then she found them. "I can never live up to your wife."

"No," he said. "No one could. No one should have to."

She looked up at him through eyes blurred

by real tears. She figured she probably wore an expression of pain on her face, but she couldn't have held it back any more than she could have held back her next breath. "Your Anna sounds . . . nearly perfect."

He stood and reached down to help her up. "Let's walk a little." They went to the edge of the shore and watched the sun slip behind the trees. Then he turned to Birdy and took her hands in his. "The worst day of Anna's life was when I drew the lot to become a minister. She never wanted it for me — she felt it would take me away from the family and there was truth in that." He paused for a long moment, as if gathering the right words. "For me, that was the best day of my life. I think I knew, even as a boy, that God had a calling on my life." He took her hands and lifted them to his chest, pressing her palms into his breast. He tipped his forehead against her and she closed her eyes, afraid suddenly that she might weep. "Birdy, will you let me court you? You haven't answered."

She wanted to say yes, but she couldn't speak. She was laughing and crying at the same time as David kissed her forehead and brushed away her tears with his thumbs. She looked at him at last, feeling happy and shy. "Yes," she said, surprised at how her voice sounded, so strong and sure and confident. "Yes, yes, of course!"

His face softened, and a tenderness came into his eyes. He leaned into her, tilting his head, and his mouth came down onto hers. His lips were warm, his beard gently tickling. He kissed her with such sweetness it was almost unbearable. She closed her eyes and trembled.

Then he pulled her to him and held her against his chest. It was an awkward embrace, for they weren't used to it, but still she felt it was her he held, not his Anna.

Evidently, Luke Schrock did not have a conscience. Jesse saw him huffing and puffing after Yardstick Yoder again, two days in a row, shouting out threats between gasping breaths, that he planned to pummel him if he ever caught him.

It was time to do something. The next day, Jesse waited a block away from the schoolhouse at three o'clock sharp. The very second school was dismissed, Yardstick burst out of the door and bounded away like a jackrabbit. Jesse watched in admiration. A few seconds later, Luke and his cronies came chugging after him. Jesse planted himself in the road to block them. He pointed to Luke. "You mess with

Yardstick and you mess with me."

Luke strutted up to Jesse, nose to nose, and jutted out his chin. "Who says?"

Jesse cocked a grin at the boy and lifted his fist with the gleaming brass knuckles. Luke jumped like a cricket, then lifted his shoulders in an exaggerated shrug. "What do you have against Yardstick, anyway?"

"Ruthie likes him," Ethan Troyer piped up helpfully, and Luke swung around to give a hard jab to his stomach.

Ah, Jesse thought. Unrequited love. It rears its head again in Stoney Ridge.

"Well, touch him and you have to answer to me. Got it?"

Luke frowned, but he got the message and seemed to have run out of conversation. "Come on, let's get out of here." He released a tiny sigh, turned, and shuffled away.

Ethan remained for a moment, looking at Jesse in wide-eyed wonder, and Jesse felt a bright glow. He wasn't immune to being admired.

"What is that thing, anyway?" Ethan asked.

Jesse held up the hardware for inspection. "We call them brass knuckles. They date back to the eighteenth century and were commonly used during the War Between the

States." Jesse had read up on them. He was nothing if not thorough.

Ethan nodded seriously, as if this bit of knowledge only confirmed his own vast experience, and Jesse hid a smile.

He slipped the brass knuckles back in his coat pocket before his nosy sisters caught sight of them and tattled to their father. Down in the schoolhouse playground, the twins played hopscotch. Molly sat on the porch, swinging her legs as she polished off the twins' lunch leftovers. Ruthie stood guard, like always, one eye on Jesse and one eye on the little sisters.

Jesse had meant to return the brass knuckles to Andy at The Chicken Box on that rainy afternoon, but he and Katrina seemed to be having such a serious talk that he felt it would be an inappropriate intrusion. He could be sensitive like that. Plus, if he did it would mean that Katrina would be tipped off to their existence. He patted his pocket, pleased he had a chance to see the persuasive impact of brass knuckles on young Luke Schrock. Jesse didn't like bullies.

He saw Birdy skim out of the schoolhouse and talk to the girls, blissful as she had been lately. Love looked good on her, Jesse realized. She was over her case of the flutters.

Blunders. Sage hen blunders, Jesse thought of them, the clumsiest of all birds. And then there was his father. These last few days, his dad went around with the musing expression of a person caught up in a fresh rhythm of life.

Love. It's amazing what it could do.

It was the end of the day. David was eager to lock up the store. Birdy said she would give Molly a cooking lesson tonight and he couldn't wait to get home. It amazed him — he was in love!

It was a miracle how the Lord had prepared his heart to love again. Birdy had stolen his heart, an unadorned woman whose simplicity and good-heartedness made anyone else seem artificial and hard. He felt as if he was waking up after a long winter's nap to find that spring had arrived.

As he turned the key in the store door, he spun around to find Andy Miller waiting in the parking lot, his big dog by his side. "Andy, hello."

"I've been waiting here all afternoon to talk to you and haven't had the guts to walk inside. I need . . . to make a confession." Andy pushed his hat back and David saw a tightness around Andy's eyes and a hollowness to his face, a sort of bewildered agony.

All he was thinking, all he was feeling, showed on that troubled face.

"Perhaps," David said, "perhaps we should go inside to talk."

Seated in chairs in David's storeroom, Andy poured out his story. David could see the remorse, hear it in his cracking voice, as Andy admitted what he'd been doing on Moss Hill over the last few months. The need for repentance came from his soul, and that was what David wanted to see, that was what he looked for. True repentance.

Confessions had a pattern, he realized, listening to Andy. And they were quite unremarkable. Not, of course, to the confessor, but to the one to whom the sins were confessed. They were all variations on a theme: deceit, betrayal, denial, and an obtuseness about how one's actions could — and did — hurt others. Eventually, great regret, enough to drive one to confession. And then . . . soulful, soul-filled relief.

"Before I left town," Andy said, brushing away tears as they ran down his cheeks, "I wanted to tell you how sorry I was."

"But you're definitely going to go?"

Andy nodded.

"Years ago, when I first opened my first store, I made a promise to God. Whenever someone walked through the doors of my store, I would pray to ask God to help me see that person as he sees him. Whenever I've prayed for you, Andy, I've sensed that God is at work in your soul, but that you're fighting him. There's a verse that keeps coming to mind whenever I've seen you. 'Surely the Lord is in this place, and I did not know it.' " He put a hand on Andy's shoulder. "Andy, maybe you should stay put and get to know *this* place. Keep yourself in an environment where God can shape your heart. Otherwise, your life is going to keep going along the same path."

Quietly, Andy said, "She wants me to leave."

"Katrina? Well, you might have some work to do to regain her trust. But just because she says that doesn't mean she *means* it. And it doesn't mean you have to." He tilted his head. "Unless you want to leave?"

"I don't."

"Then . . . maybe you should go ask her if you can stay."

Late afternoon, Katrina was checking on a few things in the mossery. She loved the smell of this old greenhouse: damp earth and moss. Overhead, the sky grew heavy with clouds, masking the sun as it headed toward the hill. Snow was forecast tonight, and it felt cold enough for it. The baby swirled and rolled inside her and she rubbed her tummy, grateful for this new life. Grateful for everything. She straightened her legs, stretching out her body, stretching out her mind.

It felt so *good* to be here. To be home. She felt it so deep that it hurt — a sweet, sad seizing of the soul.

She heard a bark, a familiar bark, and in burst Keeper through the open door to the mossery. The big dog made a beeline for Katrina, jumping onto her chest and nearly knocking her down. A moment or two later, Andy followed and filled the doorway. His shrill whistle cut through the air and the dog went slinking back to Andy with his tail tucked deep between his legs. Andy shooed him outside, but first bent and pushed his fingers through the dog's thick pelt.

Everything in Katrina went still, as if every cell was holding its breath. He touched two fingers to the brim of his hat. "Hey, Katrina."

"I thought you'd be long gone for greener pastures."

He took off his hat and held it against his abdomen. "I haven't left because I've had some thinking to do. Can we walk a little?" He gestured toward the door and she nodded. They walked side by side up the familiar path of the hillside, and she was aware of his legs and the swing of his arm so close to hers.

"I went to see your father this morning. I have a lot of respect for him."

"So do I."

"I told him everything. About Elmo, about the oil trap discovery, about deceiving Thelma."

"What did he have to say?"

"He told me there was a Bible verse that kept swirling in his mind whenever he prayed for me." Andy's eyes grew glassy. "Imagine that. Your father prays for me." He scuffed the ground with his shoe. "I don't think anyone has prayed for me since my grandmother died."

The way he stood there, looking so alone, it filled her with tenderness. She hadn't known Andy all that long, and he didn't make himself easily known, only when he had a mind to and that came in fits and starts. But this much she thought she knew about him: his life had left a taint on him, wounds and scars that went deep. Yet there was kindness in him, tenderness, laughter, unexpected wells of gentleness. He had no home, no family, and this more than anything struck her heart with pity for him.

Family, friends, a home — those were what gave life meaning and joy.

He had yet to take his eyes off her. He didn't seem to be breathing. "I want to stay in Stoney Ridge, Katrina." She saw him swallow hard. "I'll find work somewhere else, but I'd like to stay. I've spent the last few years on the move and I don't want to do it anymore. For the first time in my life, I want to stay someplace. I want to make it home."

He glanced over his shoulder toward the house and took a step closer. "I wanted to tell you that meeting you, your father, Thelma, you've all changed my life. You, most of all."

She sucked in a deep breath, feeling almost dizzy, and her hand fluttered up to her throat. "Me? How?"

"A hundred ways," he said, "but mainly by watching you cope with the problems you were facing. You didn't run away. You didn't look for the easy way out. You faced things, head-on, and tried to work through them, not around them. You woke up my world."

In a way, she could say the same thing about Andy. She was a different person than she had been a few months ago. She had found herself here and he had been a part of that. Not entirely, but definitely a part.

She stared up into his face, a face that had somehow become dear to her, and a sharpness of tears pricked her eyelids but she fought them back. She had to swallow twice before she could speak. "You might not have heard that Thelma has deeded the property to me."

A pleased look filled his eyes. "Good for her. Good for you." He tilted his head. "You look well. You seem happy."

"It's still hard for me some days, some moments, but I am happy." And the truth felt good to say, good to acknowledge within herself. She thought about the day she found out she was pregnant, how overwhelmed she'd felt. How differently she felt now.

She'd discovered one thing of great importance during this time. She was only nineteen years old, but already she knew what she wanted for the rest of her life.

She wanted that life to be here, on Moss Hill. She wanted to wake up every morning and look out to the hill propping up the sky. She wanted to grow moss and chickens and a vegetable garden and a family on this land, where she could breathe and feel alive. She wanted to be surrounded by her church, and realized, at that exact moment, that she was finally ready to be baptized. That feeling — waiting for faith enough for it to be real — that's what her father had wanted her to do. And now it was.

So. She had learned two things of great importance during this time.

While they were talking, snowflakes came tumbling down, that kind that were big and fluffy and slow falling. The first snow of the year. She smiled, a true smile. "It just so happens that we are in need of a farmhand."

He went utterly still. For the longest moment, he didn't move, didn't even breathe. Snowflakes kept falling on him and he didn't brush them away. And then his face softened and a tenderness came into his eyes, a look that was familiar to her. "Really? Because I happen to have some experience at moss farming."

"Thelma and I . . . we're considering whether or not to have oil wells dug. We haven't decided yet. We're reading up about the pros and the cons, doing our due diligence." That was a new business term she'd learned the other day and she enjoyed tossing it around.

"I want you to know that I voided the royalty agreement with Elmo. I voided it and tore it up."

"I know. Thelma showed it to me."

"Why would you give me a second chance?"

"Because you're a good man, Andy. Not perfect, mind you," she added, "but good." He wasn't like John. Not at all. John would never face the hurt he caused, not the way Andy was doing. John would never stay and see it through, not like Andy was doing. She grinned. "One more thing, though. We need to be as clear as we can about each other. You shouldn't get the wrong idea and think that . . ." There she faltered.

"And think we have a future together," he finished for her. *Yet.* She heard the word clearly in his head.

"Exactly," she said aloud. "Don't go thinking we have a future together." *Not yet,* she thought.

"Your dad told me something else. He said that everyone's journey begins somewhere."

She smiled. "I've heard him use that phrase thousands of times."

"So maybe . . . this is my beginning." With that, he gave her a grin, *such* a grin, and strode toward the barn to unpack his belongings.

MOLLY AND BIRDY'S MOLASSES CRINKLE GINGER COOKIES

3/4 cup butter, softened
1 cup sugar
1/4 cup molasses
1 egg
2 cups flour
1 teaspoon soda
1/4 teaspoon salt
1 teaspoon cinnamon
1 teaspoon ground cloves
1 teaspoon ground ginger
Birdy's extra mix-in option:
1/2 cup crystallized ginger

Mix butter, sugar, molasses, and egg together, then add dry ingredients. Stir until everything is well blended. Refrigerate dough until it is chilled. (Helps to give it that "crinkled look" when it bakes.) Form into balls and roll in sugar. Place wide apart on slightly greased cookie sheet. Bake at

375 degrees for 8–10 minutes. Makes 3–4 dozen.

Birdy's Hint: For a chewy cookie, bake for the minimum time. For a crispy cookie, bake for the maximum time.

DISCUSSION QUESTIONS

1. A common phrase of David Stoltzfus was, "Everybody begins somewhere." What was the starting point of your spiritual journey?
2. What is it about that phrase that prompts mercy, or a margin of grace, toward another?
3. If there's one overriding theme in this novel, it would be how David Stoltzfus always kept his eye on what was most important, what was truly at stake. What does that kind of discernment look like in your life?
4. David had a belief: "The God who spoke, long ago, still speaks." David, Birdy, Katrina — they all sought and sensed a timely word from God. Have you ever sensed God speaking to you? What was it like? A prompting, a nearly audible word, a gut feeling? Did you listen to that prompting and, if so, what was the result?
5. On the surface, the tension between Da-

vid Stoltzfus and Freeman Glick had to do with how a church adjusted to cultural and financial pressure without losing its core values. Such pressure isn't unique to the Amish. Every church faces issues of holding tight to essentials of faith while making accommodations for a changing culture. What kinds of changes and adjustments have you observed in your own church experience?

6. Did your first impression of any character turn out to be wrong? When have you had a similar experience in real life, when you realized your first impression of someone, good or bad, was not at all accurate?

7. Describe Katrina Stoltzfus in the beginning of the book. How did her past define her? Then describe her at the end of the novel. What created that kind of change in her?

8. In what ways, large and small, did Thelma Beiler have an influence on Katrina? How have you been influenced by an older person?

9. Another common phrase of David's was to let God write the love story. What do you think that means? It might sound like a passive response, but consider the way David knew Birdy was the one to marry. He wasn't at all passive about it! But he

did include God in the conversation. What advice would you give a young person who longed for love?

10. On the surface, David Stoltzfus and Birdy Glick seemed an unlikely romance. He was older than her, widowed with six children, and held the position of minister. She was a young spinster-ish type, lived alone, and was awkward around men — particularly so around David. Added to the mix, she was the sister of Freeman Glick, who was not a fan of David. When did it strike you that they might be well suited for each other?

11. Let's talk about Freeman Glick. Have you ever known someone in ministry who had some of Freeman's misguided behavior? What was the result? Why does hypocrisy turn people cold to faith?

12. "One thing I've learned in life," David Stoltzfus said, "is that we're all just a few choices away from becoming just about any kind of person. Good or bad." Do you agree or disagree with his belief?

13. Do you think Katrina Stoltzfus and Andy Miller eventually got together? Was he a keeper? Why or why not?

14. It might surprise you to learn that "quieting" is an actual means to have a minister or bishop or deacon removed.

After reading this novel, were any other aspects of the Amish life new to you?

15. What did you think was ultimately the book's lesson?

ACKNOWLEDGMENTS

My imagined Stoney Ridge could not have taken shape in these pages without the unflinching help of first readers in the right places, especially because it arrived on their desks during a very busy holiday season. My heartfelt thanks to them all: Meredith Muñoz, Tad Fisher, and Lindsey Ciraulo.

I'm similarly indebted to Kent Moore, a talented man who helped untangle oil exploration for me and gave me clear and manageable guidance. Just the right advice delivered in just the right package. I'm more grateful to you than you can imagine! And to Janet Moore, a thank-you for being the message bearer to Kent.

I always enjoy connecting with readers, and computers make this easier than ever. You can find me on Facebook and Twitter almost every day of the week. (But don't tell my family — I've convinced them that every time I am on the computer, I'm writing. Every single time.) You can also write to me via my website, www.suzannewoods fisher.com.

ABOUT THE AUTHOR

Suzanne Woods Fisher is the author of the bestselling Lancaster County Secrets and Stoney Ridge Seasons series. *The Search* received a 2012 Carol Award, *The Waiting* was a finalist for the 2011 Christy Award, and *The Choice* was a finalist for the 2011 Carol Award. Suzanne's grandfather was raised in the Old Order German Baptist Brethren Church in Franklin County, Pennsylvania. Her interest in living a simple, faith-filled life began with her Dunkard cousins. Suzanne is also the author of the bestselling *Amish Peace: Simple Wisdom for a Complicated World* and *Amish Proverbs: Words of Wisdom from the Simple Life,* both finalists for the ECPA Book of the Year award, and *Amish Values for Your Family: What We Can Learn from the Simple Life.* She has an app, Amish Wisdom, to deliver a proverb a day to your iPhone, iPad,

or Android. Visit her at www.suzannewoods
fisher.com to find out more.

Suzanne lives with her family in the San
Francisco Bay Area.